The Shelter Cities lay deep and soulless
beneath the deserted land. But not deep
enough to escape the earth-boring bombs that
turned them into tombs.

From the radioactive destruction emerged
the Wolf people, the nomads, instinctive
killers.

And after them, the League of Sanity,
struggling slowly, painfully to rebuild a wild
world that had known the
NIGHT OF THE WOLF.

Also available from Sphere Books

THE BEST OF FRITZ LEIBER

The Night of the Wolf

FRITZ LEIBER

SPHERE BOOKS LIMITED
30/32 Gray's Inn Road, London WC1X 8JL

First published in Great Britain by Sphere Books Ltd 1976
Copyright © Fritz Leiber 1966

THE LONE WOLF was first published as 'The Creature from
Cleveland Depths' in *Galaxy*, copyright Galaxy Publishing
Corporation 1962; THE WOLF PAIR was first published as 'The
Night of the Long Knives' in *Amazing*, copyright Ziff-Davis
Publishing Co. 1960; CRAZY WOLF was first published as
'Sanity' in *Astounding*, copyright in USA and Great Britain
Street & Smith Publications Inc. 1944: THE WOLF PACK was
first published as 'Let Freedom Ring' in *Amazing*, copyright
Ziff-Davis Publishing Co. 1950.

Printed in Great Britain by
Hazell Watson & Viney Ltd
Aylesbury, Bucks

Dedicated

with warm love

(and wolf whistles)

to

JUDITH MERRIL

CONTENTS

THE LONE WOLF.............................. 9

THE WOLF PAIR............................. 56

CRAZY WOLF................................. 138

THE WOLF PACK............................. 154

WHEN *the first dawn man dashed at the first fire ape with a big meal in his stomach, a thigh bone in his hand, and murder in his heart, the ape knew the man was crazy.*

It just took the man a long time to catch on.

He hid it from himself by inventing paranoid ideas like God.

He passed the time building pyramids, both of stones and of skulls. He also created cathedrals and catacombs, hospitals and hydrogen bombs, security councils in depth and suburban shelters even deeper. Mars chuckled.

The first man stupid enough to stay upstairs, instead of removing his budding family to a shelter-city, was Gusterson. He was a brilliant curmudgeon, a humanist, and he wrote insanity novels. He also dreamed of the League of Sanity, though he didn't tell anybody about it, except maybe Daisy. We may call him—

THE LONE WOLF

I

"COME on, Gussy," Fay prodded quietly, "quit stalking around like a neurotic bear and suggest something for my invention team to work on. I enjoy visiting you and Daisy, but I can't stay aboveground all night."

"If being outside the shelters makes you nervous, don't come around any more," Gusterson told him, continuing to stalk. "Why doesn't your invention team think of something to invent? Why don't you? Hah!" In the "Hah!" lay triumphant condemnation of a whole way of life.

"We do," Fay responded imperturbably, "but a fresh viewpoint sometimes helps."

"I'll say it does! Fay, you burglar, I'll bet you've got twenty people like myself you milk for free ideas. First you irritate their bark, and then you make the rounds every so often to draw off the latex or the maple gloop."

Fay smiled. "It ought to please you that society still has a use for you outré inner-directed types. It takes something to make a junior executive stay aboveground after dark, when the missiles are on the prowl."

"Society can't have much use for us or it'd pay us something," Gusterson sourly asserted, staring blankly at the tankless TV and kicking it lightly as he passed on. TVs with viewing tanks showed shows in three dimensions.

"No, you're wrong about that, Gussy. Money's not the key goad with you inner-directeds. I got that straight from our Motivations chief."

"Did he tell you what we should use instead to pay the grocer? A deep inner sense of achievement, maybe? Fay, why should I do any free thinking for Micro Systems?"

"I'll tell you why, Gussy. Simply because you get a kick out of insulting us with sardonic ideas. If we take one of them seriously, you think we're degrading ourselves, and that pleases you even more. Like making someone laugh at a lousy pun."

Gusterson held still in his roaming and grinned. "That's the reason, huh? I suppose my suggestions would have to be something in the line of ultra-subminiaturized computers, where one sinister fine-etched molecule does the work of three big bumbling brain cells?"

"Not necessarily. Micro Systems is branching out. Wheel as free as a rogue star. But I'll pass along to Promotion your one molecule–three brain cell sparkler. It's a slight exaggeration, but it's catchy."

"I'll have my kids watch your ads to see if you use it, and then I'll sue the whole underworld." Gusterson frowned as he resumed his stalking. He stared puzzledly at the antique TV. "How about inventing a plutonium termite?" he said suddenly. "It would get rid of those stockpiles that are worrying you moles to death."

Fay grimaced noncommittally and cocked his head.

"Well, then, how about a beauty mask? How about that, hey? I don't mean one to repair a woman's complexion, but one she'd wear all the time that'd make her look like a seventeen-year-old sexpot. That'd end *her* worries."

"Hey, that's for me," Daisy called from the kitchen. "I'll make Gusterson suffer. I'll make him crawl around on his hands and knees begging my immature favors."

"No, you won't," Gusterson called back. "You having a face like that would scare the kids. Better cancel that one, Fay. Half the adult race looking like Vina Vidarsson is too awful a thought."

"Yah, you're just scared of making a million dollars," Daisy jeered.

"I sure am," Gusterson said solemnly, scanning the fuzzy floor from one murky glass wall to the other, hesitating at the TV. "How about something homey now, like a flock of little prickly cylinders that roll around the floor collecting lint and flub? They'd work by electricity, or at a pinch cats could bat 'em around. Every so often they'd be automatically herded together and the lint cleaned off the bristles."

"No good," Fay said. "There's no lint underground and cats are *verboten*. And the aboveground market doesn't amount to more moneywise than the state of Southern Illinois. Keep it grander, Gussy, and more impractical—you can't sell people merely useful ideas." From his hassock in the center of the room he looked uneasily around. "Say, did that violet tone in the glass come from the high Cleveland hydrogen bomb, or is it just age and ultraviolet, like desert glass?"

"No, somebody's grandfather liked it that color," Gusterson informed him with happy bitterness. "I like it too—the glass, I mean, not the tint. People who live in glass houses can see the stars—especially when there's a window-washing streak in their germ-plasm."

"Gussy, why don't you move underground?" Fay asked, his voice taking on a missionary note. "It's a lot easier living in one room, believe me. You don't have to tramp from room to room hunting things."

"I like the exercise," Gusterson said stoutly.

"But I bet Daisy'd prefer it underground. And your kids wouldn't have to explain why their father lives like a Red Indian. Not to mention the safety factor and insurance savings and a crypt church within easy slidewalk distance. Incidentally, we see the stars all the time, better than you do—by repeater."

"Stars by repeater," Gusterson murmured to the ceiling,

pausing for God to comment. Then, "No, Fay, even if I could afford it—and stand it—I'm such a bad-luck Harry that just when I got us all safely stowed at the N minus one sublevel, the Soviets would discover an earthquake bomb that struck from below, and I'd have to follow everybody back to the treetops. *Hey! How about bubble homes in orbit around earth?* Micro Systems could subdivide the world's most spacious suburb, and all you moles could go ellipsing. Space is as safe as there is: no air, no shock waves. Free Fall's the ultimate in restfulness—great health benefits. Commute by rocket—or better yet, stay home and do all your business by TV-telephone, or by waldo if it were that sort of thing. Even pet your girl by remote control—she in her bubble, you in yours, whizzing through vacuum. Oh, damn - damn - *damn* - *damn* - DAMN!"

He was glaring at the blank screen of the TV, his big hands clenching and unclenching.

"Don't let Fay give you apoplexy—he's not worth it," Daisy said, sticking her trim head in from the kitchen, while Fay inquired anxiously, "Gussy, what's the matter?"

"Nothing, you worm!" Gusterson roared. "Except that an hour ago I forgot to tune in on the only TV program I've wanted to hear this year—*Finnegans Wake* scored for English, Gaelic and brogue. Oh, damn-*damn*-DAMN!"

"Too bad," Fay said lightly. "I didn't know they were releasing it on flat TV too."

"Well, they were! Some things are too damn big to keep completely underground. And I had to forget! I'm always doing it—I miss everything! Look here, you rat," he blatted suddenly at Fay, shaking his finger under the latter's chin, "I'll tell you what you can have that ignorant team of yours invent. They can fix me up a mechanical secretary that I can feed orders into and that'll remind me when the exact moment comes to listen to TV or phone somebody or mail in a story or write a letter or pick up a magazine or look at an eclipse or a new orbiting station or fetch the kids from school or buy Daisy a bunch of flowers or whatever it is. It's got to be something that's always with me, not something I have to go and consult or that I can get sick of and put down somewhere. And it's got to remind me forcibly enough so that I take notice and don't just shrug it aside, like I sometimes do even when Daisy reminds me of things. That's what your stupid team can invent for me! If they do a good job, I'll pay 'em as much as fifty dollars!"

"That doesn't sound like anything so very original to me," Fay commented coolly, leaning back from the wagging finger. "I think all senior executives have something of that sort. At least, their secretary keeps some kind of file . . . "

"I'm not looking for something with spiked falsies and nylons up to the neck," interjected Gusterson, whose ideas about secretaries were a trifle lurid. "I just want a mech reminder—that's all!"

"Well, I'll keep the idea in mind," Fay assured him, "along with the bubble homes and beauty masks. If we ever develop anything along those lines, I'll let you know. If it's a beauty mask, I'll bring Daisy a pilot model—to use to scare strange kids." He put his watch to his ear. "Good lord, I'm going to have to cut to make it underground before the main doors close. Just ten minutes to Second Curfew! 'By, Gus. 'By, Daze."

Two minutes later, living room lights out, they watched Fay's foreshortened antlike figure scurrying across the balding ill-lit park toward the nearest escalator.

Gusterson said, "Weird to think of that big bright space-poor glamor basement stretching around everywhere underneath. Did you remind Smitty to put a new bulb in the elevator?"

"The Smiths moved out this morning," Daisy said tonelessly. "They went underneath."

"Like cockroaches," Gusterson said. "Cockroaches leavin' a sinkin' apartment building. Next the ghosts'll be retreatin' to the shelters."

"Anyhow, from now on we're our own janitors," Daisy said.

He nodded. "Just leaves three families besides us loyal to this glass death trap. Not countin' ghosts." He sighed. Then, "You like to move below, Daisy?" he asked softly, putting his arm lightly across her shoulders. "Get a woozy eyeful of the bright lights and all for a change? Be a rat for a while? Maybe we're getting too old to be bats. I could scrounge me a company job and have a thinking closet all to myself and two secretaries with stainless steel breasts. Life'd be easier for you and a lot cleaner. And you'd sleep safer."

"That's true," she answered and paused. She ran her fingertip slowly across the murky glass, its violet tint barely perceptible against a cold dim light across the park. "But somehow," she said, snaking her arm around his waist, "I don't think I'd sleep happier—or one bit excited."

II

THREE weeks later Fay, dropping in again, handed to Daisy the larger of the two rather small packages he was carrying.

"It's a so-called beauty mask," he told her, "complete with wig, eyelashes, and wettable velvet lips. It even breathes—pinholed elastiskin with a static adherence-charge. But Micro Systems had nothing to do with it, thank God. Beauty Trix put it on the market ten days ago and it's already started a teen-age craze. Some boys are wearing them too, and the police are yipping at Trix for encouraging transvestism with psychic repercussions."

"Didn't I hear somewhere that Trix is a secret subsidiary of Micro?" Gusterson demanded, rearing up from his ancient electric typewriter. "No, you're not stopping me writing, Fay—it's the gut of evening. If I do any more I won't have any juice to start with tomorrow. I got another of my insanity thrillers moving. A real id-teaser. In this one not only all the characters are crazy but the robot psychiatrist too."

"The vending machines are jumping with insanity novels," Fay commented. "Odd they're so popular."

Gusterson chortled. "The only way you outer-directed moles will accept individuality any more even in a fictional character, without your superegos getting seasick, is for them to be crazy. Hey, Daisy! Lemme see that beauty mask!"

But his wife, backing out of the room, hugged the package to her bosom and solemnly shook her head.

"A hell of a thing," Gusterson complained, "not even to be able to see what my stolen ideas look like."

"I got a present for you too," Fay said. "Something you might think of as a royalty on all the inventions someone thought of a little ahead of you. Fifty dollars by your own evaluation." He held out the smaller package. "Your tickler."

"My *what?*" Gusterson demanded suspiciously.

"Your tickler. The mech reminder you wanted. It turns out that the file a secretary keeps to remind her boss to do certain things at certain times is called a tickler file. So we named this a tickler. Here."

Gusterson still didn't touch the package. "You mean you actually put your invention team to work on that nonsense?"

"Well, what do you think? Don't be scared of it. Here, I'll show you."

As he unwrapped the package, Fay said, "It hasn't been decided yet whether we'll manufacture it commercially. If we do, I'll put through a voucher for you—for 'development consultation' or something like that. Sorry no royalty's possible. Davidson's squad had started to work up the identical idea three years ago, but it got shelved. I found it on a snoop through the closets. There! Looks Georgian-silver rich, doesn't it?"

On the scarred black tabletop was a dully gleaming object about the size and shape of a cupped hand with fingers merging. A tiny pellet on a short near-invisible wire led off from it. On the back was a punctured area suggesting the face of a microphone; there was also a window with a date and time in hours and minutes showing through, and next to that four little buttons in a row. The concave underside of the silvery "hand" was smooth except for a central area where what looked like two little rollers came through.

"It goes on your shoulder under your shirt," Fay explained, "and you tuck the pellet in your ear. We might work up bone conduction on a commercial model. Inside is an ultra-slow fine-wire recorder holding a spool that runs for a week. The clock lets you go to any place on the seven-day wire and record a message. The buttons give you variable speed in going there, so you don't waste too much time making a setting. There's a knack in fingering them efficiently, but it's easily acquired."

Fay picked up the tickler. "For instance, suppose there's a TV show you want to catch tomorrow night at twenty-two hundred." He touched the buttons. There was the faintest whirring. The clock face blurred briefly three times before showing the setting he'd mentioned. Then Fay spoke into the punctured area: "Turn on TV Channel Two, you big dummy!" He grinned over at Gusterson. "When you've got all your instructions to yourself loaded in, you synchronize with the present moment and let her roll. Fit it on your shoulder and forget it. Oh, yes, and it literally does tickle you every time it delivers an instruction. That's what the little rollers are for. Believe me, you can't ignore it. Come on, Gussy, take off your shirt and try it out. We'll feed in some instructions for the next ten minutes so you get the feel of how it works."

"I don't want to," Gusterson said. "Not right now. I want to sniff around it first. My God, it's small! Besides everything else it does, does it think?"

"Don't pretend to be an idiot, Gussy! You know very well that even with ultra-sub-micro nothing quite this small can possibly have enough elements to do any thinking."

Gusterson shrugged. "I don't know about that. I think bugs think."

Fay groaned faintly. "Bugs operate by instinct, Gussy," he said. "A patterned routine. They do not scan situations and consequences and then make decisions."

"I don't expect bugs to make decisions," Gusterson said. "For that matter, I don't like people who go around alla time making decisions."

"Well, you can take it from me, Gussy, that this tickler is just a miniaturized wire recorder and clock . . . and a tickler. It doesn't do anything else."

"Not yet, maybe," Gusterson said darkly. "Not this model. Fay, I'm serious about bugs thinking. Or if they don't exactly think, they feel. They've got an interior drama. An inner glow. They're conscious. For that matter, Fay, I think all your really complex electronic computers are conscious too."

"Quit kidding, Gussy."

"Who's kidding?"

"You are. Computers simply aren't alive."

"What's alive? A word. I think computers are conscious, at least while they're operating. They've got that inner glow of awareness. They sort of . . . well . . . meditate."

"Gussy, computers haven't got any circuits for meditating. They're not programmed for mystical lucubrations. They've just got circuits for solving the problems they're on."

"Okay, you admit they've got problem-solving circuits—like a man has. I say if they've got the equipment for being conscious, they're conscious. What has wings, flies."

"Including stuffed owls and gilt eagles and dodoes—and wood-burning airplanes?"

"Maybe, under some circumstances. There *was* a wood-burning airplane, Fay," Gusterson continued, wagging his wrists for emphasis, "I really think computers are conscious. They just don't have any way of telling us that they are. Or maybe they don't have any *reason* to tell us, like the little Scotch boy who didn't say a word until he was fifteen and was supposed to be deaf and dumb."

"Why didn't he say a word?"

"Because he'd never had anything to say. Or take those Hindu fakirs, Fay, who sit still and don't say a word for thirty years or until their fingernails grow to the next village. If Hindu fakirs can do that, computers can!"

Looking as if he were masticating a lemon, Fay asked quietly, "Gussy, did you say you're working on an insanity novel?"

Gusterson frowned fiercely.

"Now you're kidding," he accused Fay. "The dirty kind of kidding, too."

"I'm sorry," Fay said with light contrition. "Well, now you've sniffed at it, how about trying on Tickler?" He picked up the gleaming blunted crescent and jogged it temptingly under Gusterson's chin.

"Why should I?" Gusterson asked, stepping back. "Fay, I'm up to my ears writing a book. The last thing I want is something interrupting me to make me listen to a lot of junk and do a lot of useless things. *Finnegans Wake*—who wants to listen to that swollen-ego mishmash?"

"But, dammit, Gussy! It was all your idea in the first place!" Fay blatted. Then, catching himself, he added, "I mean, you were one of the first people to think of this particular sort of instrument."

"Maybe so, but I've done some more thinking since then." Gusterson's voice grew a trifle solemn. "Inner-directed worthwhile thinkin'. Fay, when a man forgets to do something, it's because he really doesn't want to do it or because he's all roiled up down in his unconscious. He ought to take it as a danger signal and investigate the roiling, not hire himself a human or mech reminder."

"Bushwa," Fay retorted. "In that case you shouldn't write memorandums or even take notes."

"Maybe I shouldn't," Gusterson agreed lamely. "I'd have to think that over too."

"Ha!" Fay jeered. "No, I'll tell you what your trouble is, Gussy. You're simply scared of this contraption. You've loaded your skull with horror-story nonsense about machines sprouting minds and taking over the world—until you're even scared of a simple miniaturized and clocked recorder." He thrust it out.

"Maybe I am," Gusterson admitted, controlling a flinch. "Honestly, Fay, that thing's got a gleam in its eye as if it had ideas of its own. Nasty ideas."

"Gussy, you nut, it hasn't *got* an eye."

"Not now, no, but it's got the gleam—the eye may come. It's the Cheshire Cat in reverse. Remember, Fay, how in *Alice in Wonderland* the Cheshire Cat faded until even its teeth were gone and only the smile was left? This thing'll start with a nasty gleam and get an eye and then go on from there. If you'd step over here and look at yourself holding it, you could see what I mean. But I don't think computers *sprout* minds, Fay. I just think they've *got* minds, because they've got the mind elements."

"Ho, ho!" Fay mocked. "Everything that has a material side has a mental side," he chanted. "Everything that's a body is also a spirit. Gussy, that dubious old metaphysical dualism went out centuries ago."

"Maybe so," Gusterson said, "but we still haven't anything but that dubious dualism to explain the human mind, have we? It's a jelly of nerve cells and it's a vision of the cosmos. If that isn't dualism, what is?"

"I give up. Gussy, are you going to try out this tickler?"

"No!"

"But dammit, Gussy, we made it just for you!—practically."

"Sorry, but I'm not coming near the thing."

" 'Zen come near me," a husky voice intoned behind them. "Tonight I vant a man."

Standing in the door was something slim in a short silver sheath. It had golden bangs and the haughtiest snub-nosed face in the world. It slunk toward them.

"My God, Vina Vidarsson!" Gusterson yelled.

"Daisy, that's terrific," Fay applauded, going up to her.

She bumped him aside with a swing of her hips, continuing to advance. "Not you, Ratty," she said throatily. "I vant a real man."

"Fay, I suggested Vina Vidarsson's face for the beauty mask," Gusterson said, walking around his wife and shaking a finger. "Don't tell me Trix just happened to think of that too."

"What else could they think of?" Fay laughed. "This season sex means VV and nobody else—the girl with the spiky voom-voom bazoom." An odd little grin flicked his lips, a tic traveled up his face and his body twitched slightly. "Say, folks, I'm going to have to be leaving. It's exactly fifteen minutes to Second Curfew. Last time I had to run and I got heartburn. When *are* you people going to move downstairs? I'll leave Tickler, Gussy. Play around with it and get used to it. 'By now."

"Hey, Fay," Gusterson called curiously, "have you developed absolute time sense?"

Fay grinned a big grin from the doorway—almost too big a grin for so small a man. "I didn't need to," he said softly, patting his right shoulder. "My tickler told me."

He closed the door behind him.

As side-by-side they watched him strut sedately across the murky chilly-looking park, Gusterson mused, "So the little devil had one of those nonsense-gadgets on all the time and I never noticed. Can you beat that?" Something drew across the violet-tinged stars a short bright line that quickly faded. "What's that?" Gusterson asked gloomily. "Next to last stage of missile-here?"

"Won't you settle for an old-fashioned shooting star?" Daisy asked softly. The (wettable) velvet lips of the mask made even her natural voice sound different. She reached a hand back of her neck to pull the thing off.

"Hey, don't do that," Gusterson protested in a hurt voice. "Not for a while anyway."

"Hokay!" she said harshly, turning on him. "Zen down on your knees, dog!"

III

IT WAS a fortnight and Gusterson was loping down the home stretch on his 40,000-word insanity novel before Fay dropped in again, this time promptly at high noon.

Normally Fay cringed his shoulders a trifle and was inclined to slither, but now he strode aggressively, his legs scissoring in a fast, low goosestep. He whipped off the sunglasses that all moles wore topside by day and began to pound Gusterson on the back while calling boisterously, "How are you, Gussy Old Boy, Old Boy?"

Daisy came in from the kitchen to see why Gusterson was choking. She was instantly grabbed and violently bussed to the accompaniment of, "Hiya, Gorgeous! Yum-yum! How about ad-libbing that some weekend?"

She stared at Fay dazedly, rasping the back of her hand across her mouth, while Gusterson yelled, "Quit that! What's got into you, Fay? Have they transferred you out of R and D to Company Morale? Do they line up all the secretaries at roll call and make you give them an eight-hour energizing kiss?"

"Ha, wouldn't you like to know?" Fay retorted. He grinned, twitched jumpingly, held still a moment, then hustled over to the far wall. "Look out there," he rapped, pointing through the violet glass at a gap between the two nearest old skyscraper apartments. "In thirty seconds you'll see them test the new needle bomb at the other end of Lake Erie. It's educational." He began to count off seconds, vigorously semaphoring his arm. ". . . Two . . . three . . . Gussy, I've put through a voucher for two yards for you. Budgeting squawked, but I pressured 'em."

Daisy squealed, "Yards!—are those dollar thousands?" while Gusterson was asking, "Then you're marketing the tickler?"

"Yes. Yes," Fay replied to them in turn. ". . . Nine . . . ten . . ." Again he grinned and twitched. "Time for noon Comstaff," he announced staccato. "Pardon the hush box." He whipped a pancake phone from under his coat, clapped it over his face and spoke fiercely but inaudibly into it, continuing to semaphore. Suddenly he thrust the phone away. "Twenty-nine . . . thirty . . . Thar she blows!"

An incandescent streak shot up the sky from a little above the far horizon and a doubly dazzling point of light appeared just above the top of it, with the effect of God dotting an "i."

"Ha, that'll skewer espionage satellites like swatting flies!" Fay proclaimed as the portent faded. "Bracing! Gussy, where's your tickler? I've got a new spool for it that'll razzle-dazzle you."

"I'll bet," Gusterson said drily. "Daisy?"

"You gave it to the kids and they got to fooling with it and broke it."

"No matter," Fay told them with a large sidewise sweep of his hand. "Better you wait for the new model. It's a six-way improvement."

"So I gather," Gusterson said, eyeing him speculatively. "Does it automatically inject you with cocaine? A fix every hour on the second?"

"Ha-ha, joke. Gussy, it achieves the same effect without using any dope at all. Listen: a tickler reminds you of your duties and opportunities—your chances for happiness and success! What's the obvious next step?"

"Throw it out the window. By the way, how do you do that when you're underground?"

"We have high-speed garbage boosts. The obvious next step is you give the tickler a heart. It not only tells you, it warmly persuades you. It doesn't just say, 'Turn on the TV Channel Two, Joyce program,' it *brills* at you, 'Kid, Old Kid, race for the TV and flip that Two Switch! There's a great show coming through the pipes this second plus ten—you'll enjoy the hell out of yourself! Grab a ticket to ecstasy!' "

"My God," Gusterson gasped, "are those the kind of jolts it's giving you now?"

"Don't you get it, Gussy? You never load your tickler except when you're feeling buoyantly enthusiastic. You don't just tell yourself what to do hour by hour next week, you sell yourself on it. That way you not only make doubly sure you'll obey instructions but you constantly reinoculate yourself with your own enthusiasm."

"I can't stand myself when I'm that enthusiastic," Gusterson said. "I feel ashamed for hours afterward."

"You're warped—all this lonely sky-life. What's more, Gussy, think how still more persuasive some of those instructions would be if they came to a man in his best girl's most bedroomy voice, or his doctor's or psycher's if it's that sort of thing—or Vina Vidarsson's! By the way, Daze, don't wear that beauty mask outside. It's a grand misdemeanor ever since ten thousand teen-agers rioted through Tunnel-Mart wearing them. And VV's suing Trix."

"No chance of that," Daisy said. "Gusterson got excited and bit off the nose." She pinched her own delicately.

"I'd no more obey my enthusiastic self," Gusterson was brooding, "than I'd obey a Napoleon drunk on his own brandy or a hopped-up St. Francis. Reinoculated with my own enthusiasm? I'd die just like from snake-bite!"

"Warped, I said," Fay dogmatized, stamping around. "Gussy, having the instructions persuasive instead of neutral turned out to be only the opening wedge. The next step wasn't so obvious, but I saw it. Using subliminal verbal stimuli in his tickler, a man can be given constant supportive euphoric therapy 24 hours a day! And it makes use of all that empty wire. We've revived the ideas of a pioneer dynamic psycher named Dr. Coué. For instance, right now my tickler is saying to me—in tones too soft to reach my conscious mind, but do they stab into the unconscious!—'Day by day in every way I'm getting sharper and sharper.' It alternates that with 'gutsier and gutsier' and . . . well, forget that. Coué mostly used 'better and better,' but that seems too general. And every hundredth time it says them out loud—inside my ear—and the tickler gives me a brush—just a faint cootch—to make sure I'm keeping in touch."

"That third word-pair," Daisy wondered, feeling her mouth reminiscently. "Ballsier and ballsier?"

Gusterson's eyes had been growing wider and wider. "Fay," he said, "I could no more use my mind for anything if I knew all that was going on in my inner ear than if I were being brushed down with brooms by three witches. Look here," he said with loud authority, "you got to stop all this—it's crazy. Fay, if Micro'll junk the tickler, I'll think you up something else to invent—something real good."

"Your inventing days are over," Fay brilled gleefully. "I mean, you'll never equal your masterpiece."

"How about," Gusterson bellowed, "an anti-individual guided missile? The physicists have got small-scale antigravity good enough to float and fly something the size of a hand grenade. I can smell that even though it's a back-of-the-safe military secret. Well, how about keying such a missile to a man's fingerprints—or brainwaves, maybe, or his unique smell!—so it can spot and follow him around and target in on him, without harming anyone else? Long-distance assassination—and the stinkingest gets it! Or you could simply load it with some disgusting goo and key it to teen-agers as a group—that'd take care of them. Fay, doesn't it give you a rich warm kick to think of my midget missiles buzzing around in your tunnels, seeking out evildoers, like a swarm of angry wasps or angelic bumblebees?"

"You're not luring me down any side trails," Fay said laughingly. He grinned and twitched, then hurried toward the opposite wall, motioning them to follow. Outside, about a hundred yards beyond the purple glass, rose another ancient glass-walled apartment skyscraper. Beyond, Lake Erie rippled glintingly.

"Another bomb test?" Gusterson asked.

Fay pointed at the building. "Tomorrow," he announced, "a modern factory, devoted solely to the manufacture of ticklers, will be erected on that site."

"You mean one of those windowless phallic eyesores?" Gusterson demanded. "Fay, you people aren't even consistent. You've got all your homes underground. Why not your factories?"

"Sh! Not enough room. It's okay to come topside daytimes. But night missiles are scarier. And then there are the wild animals from the Wastes. No kidding, Gussy, don't you hear wolf-howls at night?"

"Only the groans of the deer dying from hunger and lack of hunters," the latter assured him.

Daisy brought them back to the topic at hand.

"I know that building's been empty for a year," she said uneasily, "but how—?"

"Sh! Watch! *Now!*"

The looming building seemed to blur or fuzz for a moment. Then it was as if the lake's bright ripples had invaded the old glass a hundred yards away. Wavelets chased themselves up and down the gleaming walls, became higher, higher . . . and then suddenly the glass cracked all over to tiny fragments and fell away, to be followed quickly by fragmented concrete and plastic and plastic piping, until all that was left was the nude steel framework, vibrating so rapidly as to be almost invisible against the gleaming lake.

Daisy covered her ears, but there was no explosion, only a long-drawn-out low crash as the fragments hit twenty floors below and dust whooshed out sideways.

"Spectacular!" Fay summed up. "Knew you'd enjoy it. That little trick was first conceived by the great Tesla during his last fruity years. Research discovered it in his biog—we just made the dream come true. A tiny resonance device you could carry in your belt-bag attunes itself to the natural harmonic of a structure and then increases amplitude by tiny pushes exactly in time. Just like soldiers marching in step can break down a bridge, only this is as if it were being done by one marching ant." He pointed at the naked framework appearing out of its own blur and said, "We'll be able to hang the factory on that. If not, we'll whip a mega-current through it and vaporize it. No question the micro-resonator is the neatest sweetest wrecking device going. You can expect a lot more of this sort of efficiency now that mankind has the tickler to enable him to use his full potential. What's the matter, folks?"

Daisy was staring around the violet-walled room with dumb mistrust. Her hands were trembling.

"You don't have to worry," Fay assured her with an understanding laugh. "This building's safe for a month more at least." Suddenly he grimaced and leaped a foot in the air. He raised a clawed hand to scratch his shoulder but managed to check the movement. "Got to beat it, folks," he announced tersely. "My tickler gave me the grand cootch."

"Don't go yet," Gusterson called, rousing himself with a shudder which he immediately explained: "I just had the illusion that if I shook myself all my flesh and guts would fall off my shimmying skeleton. Brr! Fay, before you and Micro go off half-cocked, I want you to know there's one insuperable objection to the tickler as a mass-market item. The average man or woman won't go to the considerable time and trouble it must take to load a tickler. He simply hasn't got the compulsive orderliness and willingness to plan that it requires."

"We thought of that weeks ago," Fay rapped, his hand on the door. "Every tickler spool that goes to market is patterned like wallpaper with one of five designs of suitable subliminal supportive euphoric material. 'Ittier and ittier,' 'viriler and viriler'—you know. The buyer is robot-interviewed for an hour, his personalized daily routine laid out and thereafter templated on his weekly spool. He's strongly urged next to take his tickler to his doctor and psycher for further instruction-imposition. We've been working with the medical profession from the start. They love the tickler because it'll remind people to take their medicine on the dot . . . and rest and eat and go to sleep just when and how doc says. This is a big operation, Gussy—a biiiiiiig operation! 'By!"

Daisy hurried to the wall to watch him cross the park. Deep down she was a wee bit worried that he might linger to attach a micro-resonator to *this* building and she wanted to time him. But Gusterson settled down to his typewriter and began to bat away.

"I want to have another novel started," he explained to her, "before the ant marches across this building in about four and a half weeks . . . or a million sharp little gutsy, ballsy guys come swarming out of the ground and heave it into Lake Erie."

IV

EARLY NEXT morning windowless walls began to crawl up the stripped skyscraper between them and the lake. Daisy pulled the black-out curtains on that side. For a day or two longer their thoughts and conversations were haunted by Gusterson's vague sardonic visions of a horde of tickler-energized moles pouring up out of the tunnels to tear down the remaining trees, tank the atmosphere, and perhaps somehow dismantle the stars—at least on this side of the world—but then they both settled back into their customary easygoing routines. Gusterson typed. Daisy made her daily shopping trip to a little topside daytime store and started painting a mural on the floor of the empty apartment next theirs but one.

"We ought to lasso some neighbors," she suggested once. "I need somebody to hold my brushes and admire. How about you making a trip below at the cocktail hours, Gusterson, and picking up a couple of girls for a starter? Flash the old viriler charm, cootch them up a bit, emphasize the delights of high living, but make sure they're compatible roommates. You could pick up that two-yard check from Micro at the same time."

"You're an immoral money-ravenous wench," Gusterson said absently, trying to dream of an insanity beyond insanity that would make his next novel a real id-rousing best-vender.

"If that's your vision of me, you shouldn't have chewed up the VV mask."

"I'd really prefer you with green stripes," he told her. "But stripes, spots, or sunbathing, you're better than those cocktail moles."

Actually both of them acutely disliked going below. They much preferred to perch in their eyrie and watch the people of Cleveland Depths, as they privately called the local sub-suburb, rush up out of the shelters at dawn to work in the concrete fields and windowless factories, make their daytime jet trips and freeway jaunts, do their noon-hour and coffee-break guerrilla practice, and then go scurrying back at twilight to the atomic-proof, brightly lit, vastly exciting, claustrophobic caves.

Fay and his projects began once more to seem dreamlike, though Gusterson did run across a cryptic advertisement for ticklers in *The Manchester Guardian*, which he got daily by facsimile. Their three children reported similar ads, of no interest to young fry, on the TV, and one afternoon they came home with the startling news that the monitors at their subsurface school had been issued ticklers. On sharp interrogation by Gusterson, however, it appeared that these last were not ticklers but merely two-way radios linked to the school police station.

"Which is bad enough," Gusterson commented later to Daisy. "But it'd be even dirtier to think of those clock-watching superegos being strapped to kids' shoulders. Can you imagine Huck Finn with a tickler, tellin' him when to tie up the raft to a towhead and when to take a swim?"

"I bet Fay could," Daisy countered. "When's he going to bring you that check, anyhow? Iago wants a jetcycle and I promised Imogene a Vina Kit, and then Claudius'll have to have something."

Gusterson scowled thoughtfully. "You know, Daze," he said, "I got a feeling Fay's in the hospital, all narcotized up and being fed intravenously. The way he was jumping around last time, that tickler was going to cootch him to pieces in a week."

As if to refute this intuition, Fay turned up that very evening. The lights were dim. Something had gone wrong with the building's old transformer and, pending repairs, the two remaining occupied apartments were making do with batteries, which turned bright globes to mysterious amber candles and made Gusterson's ancient typewriter operate sluggishly.

Fay's manner was subdued or at least closely controlled, and for a moment Gusterson thought he'd shed his tickler. Then the little man came out of the shadows and Gusterson saw the large bulge on his right shoulder.

"Yes, we had to up it a bit sizewise," Fay explained in clipped tones. "Additional superfeatures. While brilliantly successful on the whole, the subliminal euphorics were a shade too effective. Several hundred users went hoppity manic. We gentled the cootch and qualified the subliminals— you know, 'Day by day in every way I'm getting sharper *and more serene*'—but a stabilizing influence was still needed, so after a top-level conference we decided to combine Tickler with Moodmaster."

"My God," Gusterson interjected, "do they have a machine now that does that?"

"Of course. They've been using them on ex-mental patients for years."

"I just don't keep up with progress," Gusterson said, shaking his head bleakly. "I'm falling behind on all fronts."

"You ought to have your tickler remind you to read Science Service releases," Fay told him. "Or simply instruct it to scan the releases and—no, that's still in research." He looked at Gusterson's shoulder and his eyes widened. "You're not wearing the new-model tickler I sent you," he said accusingly.

"I never got it," Gusterson assured him. "Postmen deliver topside mail and parcels by throwing them on the high-speed garbage boosts and hoping a tornado will blow them to the right addresses." Then he added helpfully, "Maybe the Russians stole it while it was riding the whirlwinds."

"That's not a suitable topic for jesting," Fay frowned. "We're hoping that Tickler will mobilize the full potential of the Free World for the first time in history. Gusterson, you are going to have to wear a ticky-tick. It's becoming impossible for a man to get through modern life without one."

"Maybe I will," Gusterson said appeasingly, "but right now tell me about Moodmaster. I want to put it in my new insanity novel."

Fay shook his head. "Your readers will just think you're behind the times. If you use it, underplay it. But anyhow, Moodmaster is a simple physiotherapy engine that monitors bloodstream chemicals and body electricity. It ties directly into the bloodstream, keeping blood sugar, et cetera, at optimum levels and injecting euphrin or depressin as necessary —and occasionally a touch of extra adrenaline, as during work emergencies."

"Is it painful?" Daisy called from the bedroom.

"Excruciating," Gusterson called back, "Excuse it, please," he grinned at Fay. "Hey, didn't I suggest cocaine injections last time I saw you?"

"So you did," Fay agreed flatly. "Oh, by the way, Gussy, here's that check for a yard I promised you. Micro doesn't muzzle the ox."

"Hooray!" Daisy cheered faintly.

"I thought you said it was going to be for two," Gusterson complained.

"Budgeting always forces a last-minute compromise," Fay shrugged. "You have to learn to accept those things."

"I love accepting money and I'm glad any time for three feet," Daisy called agreeably. "Six feet might make me wonder if I weren't an insect, but getting a yard just makes me feel like a gangster's moll."

"Want to come out and gloat over the yard paper, Toots, and stuff it in your diamond-embroidered net stocking top?" Gusterson called back.

"No, I'm doing something to that portion of me just now. But hang onto the yard, Gusterson."

"Aye-aye, Cap'n," he assured her. Then, turning back to Fay, "So you've taken the Dr. Coué repeating out of the tickler?"

"Oh, no. Just balanced it off with depressin. The subliminals are still a prime sales-point. All the tickler features are cumulative, Gussy. You're still underestimating the scope of the device."

"I guess I am. What's this 'work-emergencies' business? If you're using the tickler to inject drugs into workers to keep them going, that's really just my cocaine suggestion modernized and I'm putting in for another thou. Hundreds of years ago the South American Indians chewed coca leaves to kill fatigue sensations."

"That so? Interesting—and it proves priority for the Indians, doesn't it? I'll make a try for you, Gussy, but don't expect anything." He cleared his throat, his eyes grew distant and, turning his head a little to the right, he enunciated sharply, "Pooh-Bah. Time: Inst oh five. One oh five seven. Oh oh.

Record: Gussy coca thou budget. Cut." He explained, "We got a voice-cued setter now on the deluxe models. You can record a memo to yourself without taking off your shirt. Incidentally, I use the ends of the hours for trifle-memos. I've already used up the fifty-nines and eights for tomorrow and started on the fifty-sevens."

"I understood most of your memo," Gusterson told him gruffly. "The last 'Oh oh' was for seconds, wasn't it? Now I call that crude—why not microseconds too? But how do you remember where you've made a memo so you don't rerecord over it? After all, you're rerecording over the wallpaper all the time."

"Tickler beeps and then hunts for the nearest information-free space."

"I see. And what's the 'Pooh-Bah' for?"

Fay smiled. "Cut. My password for activating the setter, so it won't respond to chance numerals it overhears."

"But why 'Pooh-Bah'?"

Fay grinned. "Cut. And you a writer. It's a literary reference, Gussy. Pooh-Bah (cut!) was Lord High Everything Else in *The Mikado*. He had a little list, and nothing on it would ever be missed."

"Oh, yeah," Gusterson remembered, glowering. "As I recall it, all that went on that list were the names of people who were slated to have their heads chopped off by Ko-Ko. Better watch your step, Shorty. It may be a backhanded omen. Maybe all those workers you're puttin' ticklers on to pump them full of adrenaline so they'll overwork without noticin' it will revolt and come out someday choppin' for your head."

"Spare me the Marxist mythology," Fay protested. "Gussy, you've got a completely wrong slant on Tickler. It's true that most of our mass sales so far, bar government and army, have been to large companies purchasing for their employees—"

"Ah-ha!"

"—but that's because there's nothing like a tickler for teaching a new man his job. It tells him from instant to instant what he must do—while he's already on the job and without disturbing other workers. Magnetizing a wire with a job pattern is the easiest thing going. And you'd be astonished what the subliminals do for employee morale. It's this way, Gussy: most people are too improvident and unimaginative to see in advance the advantages of ticklers. They buy one because the company strongly suggests it and payment is on easy installments withheld from salary. They find a tickler makes the workday go easier. The little fellow perched on your shoulder is a friend exuding comfort and good advice. The first thing he's set to say is 'Take it easy, pal.'

"Within a week they're wearing their tickler 24 hours a day—and buying a tickler for the wife, so she'll remember to comb her hair and smile real pretty and cook favorite dishes."

"I get it, Fay," Gusterson cut in. "The tickler is the newest fad for increasing worker efficiency. Once, I read somewheres, it was salt tablets. They had salt-tablet dispensers everywhere, even in air-conditioned offices where there wasn't a moist armpit twice a year and the gals sweat only champagne. A decade later people wondered what all those dusty white pills were for. Sometimes they were mistook for tranquilizers. It'll be the same way with ticklers. Somebody'll open a musty closet and see jumbled heaps of these gripping-hand silvery gadgets gathering dust curls and—"

"They will not!" Fay protested vehemently. "Ticklers are not a fad—they're history-changers, they're Free-World revolutionary! Why, before Micro Systems put a single one on the market, we'd made it a rule that every Micro employee had to wear one! If that's not having supreme confidence in a product—"

"Every employee except the top executives, of course," Gusterson interrupted jeeringly. "And that's not demoting you, Fay. As the R and D chief most closely involved, you'd naturally have to show special enthusiasm."

"But you're wrong there, Gussy," Fay crowed. "Man for man, our top executives have been more enthusiastic about their personal ticklers than any other class of worker in the whole outfit."

Gusterson slumped and shook his head. "If that's the case," he said darkly, "maybe mankind deserves the tickler."

"I'll say it does!" Fay agreed loudly without thinking. Then, "Oh, can the carping, Gussy. Tickler's a great invention. Don't deprecate it just because you had something to do with its genesis. You're going to have to get in the swim and wear one."

"Maybe I'd rather drown horribly."

"Can the gloom-talk too! Gussy, I said it before and I say it again, you're just scared of this new thing. Why, you've even got the drapes pulled so you won't have to look at the tickler factory."

"Yes, I am scared," Gusterson said. "Really sca . . . AWP!"

Fay whirled around. Daisy was standing in the bedroom doorway, wearing the short silver sheath. This time there was no mask, but her bobbed hair was glitteringly silvered, while her legs, arms, hands, neck, face—every bit of her exposed skin—was painted with beautifully even vertical green stripes.

"I did it as a surprise for Gusterson," she explained to Fay. "He says he likes me this way. The green glop's supposed to be smudgeproof."

Gusterson said, "It better be." Then his face got a rapt expression. "I'll tell you why your tickler's so popular, Fay," he said softly. "It's not because it backstops the memory or because it boosts the ego with subliminals. It's because it takes the hook out of a guy, it takes over the job of withstanding the pressure of living. See, Fay, here are all these little guys in this subterranean rat race with atomic-death squares and chromium-plated reward squares and enough money if you pass Go almost to get to Go again—and a million million rules of the game to keep in mind. Well, here's this one little guy and every morning he wakes up there's all these things he's got to keep in mind to do or he'll lose his turn three times in a row and maybe a terrible black rook in iron armor'll loom up and bang him off the chessboard. But now, look, now he's got his tickler, and he tells his sweet silver tickler all these things and the tickler's got to remember them. Of course he'll have to do them eventually, but meanwhile the pressure's off him, the hook's out of his short hairs. He's shifted the responsibility . . ."

"Well, what's so bad about that?" Fay broke in loudly. "What's wrong with taking the pressure off little guys? Why shouldn't Tickler be a superego surrogate? Micro's Motivations chief noticed that positive feature straight off and scored it three pluses. Besides, it's nothing but a gaudy way of saying that Tickler backstops the memory. Seriously, Gussy, what's so bad about it?"

"I don't know," Gusterson said slowly, his eyes still far away. "I just know it feels bad to me." He crinkled his big forehead. "Well for one thing," he said, "it means that a man's taking orders from something else. He's got a kind of master. He's sinking back into a slave psychology."

"He's only taking orders from himself," Fay countered disgustedly. "Tickler's just a mech reminder, a notebook, in essence no more than the back of an old envelope. It's no master."

"Are you absolutely sure of that?" Gusterson asked quietly.

"Why, Gussy, you big oaf—" Fay began heatedly. Suddenly his features quirked and he twitched. " 'Scuse me, folks," he said rapidly, heading for the door, "but my tickler told me I gotta go."

"Hey Fay, don't you mean you told your tickler to tell you when it was time to go?" Gusterson called after him.

Fay looked back in the doorway. He wet his lips, his eyes moved from side to side. "I'm not quite sure," he said in an odd strained voice and darted out.

Gusterson stared for some seconds at the pattern of emptiness Fay had left. Then he shivered. Then he shrugged. "I must be slipping," he muttered. "I never even suggested something for him to invent." Then he looked around at Daisy, who was still standing poker-faced in her doorway.

"Hey, you look like something out of the Arabian Nights," he told her. "Are you supposed to be anything special? How far do those stripes go, anyway?"

"You could probably find out," she told him coolly. "All you have to do is kill me a dragon or two first."

He studied her. "My God," he said reverently, "I really have all the fun in life. What do I do to deserve this?"

"You've got a big gun," she told him, "and you go out in the world with it and hold up big companies and take yards and yards of money away from them in rolls like ribbon and bring it all home to me."

"Don't say that about the gun again," he said. "Don't whisper it, don't even think it. I've got one, dammit—thirty-eight caliber, yet—and I don't want some psionic monitor with two-way clairaudience they haven't told me about catching the whisper and coming to take the gun away from us. It's one of the few individuality symbols we've got left."

Suddenly Daisy whirled away from the door, spun three times so that her silvered hair stood out like a metal coolie hat, and sank to a curtsey in the middle of the room.

"I've just thought of what I am," she announced, fluttering her eyelashes at him. "I'm a sweet silver tickler with green stripes."

V

NEXT day Daisy cashed the Micro check for ten hundred aluminum-bronze pseudo-silver smackers, which she hid in a broken radionic coffee urn. Gusterson sold his insanity novel and started a new one about a mad medic with a hiccupy hysterical chuckle, who gimmicked Moodmasters to turn mental patients into nymphomaniacs, mass murderers and compulsive saints. But this time he couldn't get Fay out of his mind, or the last chilling words the nervous little man had spoken.

For that matter, he couldn't blank the underground out of his mind as effectively as usually. He had the feeling that a new kind of mole was loose in the burrows and that the ground at the foot of their skyscraper might start humping up any minute.

Toward the end of one afternoon he tucked a half-dozen newly typed sheets in his pocket, shrouded his typer, went to the hatrack and took down his prize: a miner's hard-top cap with electric headlamp.

"Goin' below, Cap'n," he shouted toward the kitchen.

"Be back for second dog watch," Daisy replied. "Remember what I told you about lassoing me some art-conscious girl neighbors."

"Only if I meet a piebald one with a taste for Scotch—or maybe a pearl-gray biped jaguar with violet spots," Gusterson told her, clapping on the cap with a We-Who-Are-About-To-Die gesture.

Halfway across the park to the escalator bunker Gusterson's heart began to tick. He resolutely switched on his headlamp.

As he'd known it would, the hatch robot whirred an extra and higher-pitched ten seconds when it came to his topside address, but it ultimately dilated the hatch for him, first handing him a claim check for his ID card.

Gusterson's heart was ticking like a sledgehammer by now. He hopped clumsily onto the escalator, clutched the moving guard rail to either side, then shut his eyes as the steps went over the edge and became what felt like vertical. An instant later he forced his eyes open, he unclipped a hand from the rail and touched the second switch beside his headlamp, which instantly began to blink white, as if he were a civilian plane flying into a nest of military jobs.

With a further effort, he kept his eyes open and flinchingly surveyed the scene around him. After zigging through a bombproof furlong of roof, he was dropping into a large twilit cave. The blue-black ceiling twinkled with stars. The walls were pierced at floor level by a dozen archways with busy niche stores and glowing advertisements crowded between them. From the archways some three dozen slidewalks curved out, tangenting off each other in a bewildering multiple cloverleaf. The slidewalks were packed with people, traveling motionless, like purposeful statues, or pivoting with practiced grace, from one slidewalk to another, like a thousand toreros doing veronicas.

The slidewalks were moving faster than he recalled from his last venture underground, and at the same time the whole pedestrian concourse was quieter than he remembered. It was as if the five thousand or so moles in view were all listening—for what? But there was something else that had changed about them—a change that he couldn't for a moment define, or unconsciously didn't want to. Clothing style? No . . . My God, they weren't all wearing identical monster masks? No . . . Hair color? . . . Well . . .

He was studying them so intently that he forgot his escalator was landing. He came off it with a heel-jarring stumble and bumped into a knot of four men on the tiny triangular hold-still. These four at least sported a new style-wrinkle: ribbed gray shoulder-capes that made them look as if their heads were poking up out of the center of bulgy umbrellas or giant mushrooms.

One of them grabbed hold of Gusterson and saved him from staggering onto a slidewalk that might have carried him to Toledo.

"Gussy, you dog, you must have esped I wanted to see you," Fay cried, patting him on the elbows. "Meet Davidson and Kester and Hazen, colleagues of mine. We're all Micro-men." Fay's companions were staring strangely at Gusterson's blinking headlamp. Fay explained rapidly, "Mr. Gusterson is an insanity novelist. You know, I-D."

"Inner-directed spells *id*," Gusterson said absently, still staring at the interweaving crowd beyond them, trying to figure out what made them different from last trip. "Creativity fuel. Cranky. Explodes through the parietal fissure if you look at it cross-eyed. Been known to kill knot-heads, open minds, and other people with holes in their heads."

"Ha-ha," Fay laughed. "Well, boys, I've found my man. How's the new novel perking, Gussy?"

"Got my climax, I think," Gusterson mumbled, still peering puzzledly around Fay at the slidestanders. "Moodmaster's going to come alive. Ever occur to you that 'mood' is 'doom' spelled backward? And then . . ." He let his voice trail off as he realized that Kester and Davidson and Hazen had made their farewells and were sliding into the distance. He reminded himself wryly that nobody ever wants to hear an author talk—he's much too good a listener to be wasted that way. Let's see, was it that everybody in the crowd had the same facial expression . . . ? Or showed symptoms of the same disease . . . ?

"I was coming to visit you, but now you can pay me a call," Fay was saying. "There are two matters I want to—"

Gusterson stiffened. *"My God, they're all hunchbacked!"* he yelled.

"Shh! Of course they are," Fay whispered reprovingly. "They're all wearing their ticklers. But you don't need to be insulting about it."

"I'm gettin' out o' here." Gusterson turned to flee as if from five thousand Richard the Thirds.

"Oh no you're not," Fay amended, drawing him back with one hand. Somehow, underground, the little man seemed to carry more weight. "You're having cocktails in my thinking box. Besides, climbing a down escaladder will give you a heart attack."

In his home habitat Gusterson was about as easy to handle as a rogue rhinoceros, but away from it—and especially if underground—he became more like a pliable elephant. All his bones dropped out through his feet, as he described it to Daisy. So now he submitted miserably as Fay surveyed him up and down, switched off his blinking headlamp ("That coalminer caper is corny, Gussy.")

and then, surprisingly, rapidly stuffed his belt-bag under the right shoulder of Gusterson's coat and buttoned the latter to hold it in place.

"So you won't stand out," he explained. Another swift survey. "You'll do. Come on, Gussy. I got lots to brief you on." Three rapid paces and then Gusterson's feet would have gone out from under him except that Fay gave him a mighty shove. The small man sprang onto the slidewalk after him and then they were skimming effortlessly side by side. "Think of it as underground surfing," Fay said. "It's exhilarating . . . if you view it the right way," he trailed off wanly.

Gusterson felt frightened and twice as hunchbacked as the slidestanders around him—morally as well as physically.

Nevertheless he countered bravely, "I got things to brief *you* on. I got six pages of cautions on ti—"

"Shh!" Fay stopped him. "Let's use my hushbox."

He drew out his pancake phone and stretched it so that it covered both their lower faces, like a double yashmak. Gusterson, his neck pushing into the ribbed bulge of the shoulder cape so he could be cheek to cheek with Fay, felt horribly conspicuous, but then he noticed that none of the slidestanders were paying them the least attention. The reason for their abstraction occurred to him. They were listening to their ticklers! He shuddered.

"I got six pages of caution on ticklers," he repeated into the hot, moist quiet of the pancake phone. "I typed 'em so I wouldn't forget 'em in the heat of polemicking. I want you to read every word. Fay, I've had it on my mind ever since I started wondering whether it was you or your tickler made you duck out of our place last time you were there. I want you to—"

"Ha-ha! All in good time." In the pancake phone Fay's laugh was brassy. "But I'm glad you've decided to lend a hand, Gussy. This thing is moving faaaasst. Nationwise, adult underground ticklerization is ninety per cent complete."

"I don't believe that," Gusterson protested while glaring at the hunchbacks around them. The slidewalk was gliding down a low glow-ceiling tunnel lined with doors and advertisements. Rapt-eyed people were pirouetting on and off. "A thing just can't develop that fast, Fay. It's against nature."

"Ha, but we're not in nature, we're in culture. The progress of an industrial scientific culture is geometric. It goes n-times as many jumps as it takes. More then geometric— exponential. Confidentially, Micro's Math chief tells me we're currently on a fourth-power progress curve trending into a fifth."

"You mean we're goin' so fast we got to watch out we don't bump ourselves in the rear when we come around again?" Gusterson asked, scanning the tunnel ahead for curves. "Or just shoot straight up to infinity?"

"Exactly! Of course most of the last power and a half is due to Tickler itself. Gussy, the tickler's already eliminated absenteeism, alcoholism, and aboulia in numerous urban areas —and that's just one letter of the alphabet! If Tickler doesn't turn us into a nation of photo-memory constant-creative-flow geniuses in six months, I'll come live topside."

"You mean because a lot of people are standing around glassy-eyed listening to something mumbling in their ear that it's a good thing?"

"Gussy, you don't know progress when you see it. Tickler is the greatest invention since language. Bar none, it's the greatest instrument ever devised for integrating a man into all phases of his environment. Under the present routine a newly purchased tickler first goes to government and civilian defense for primary patterning, then to the purchaser's employer, then to his doctor-psycher, then to his local bunker captain, then to *him. Everything* that's needful for a man's welfare gets on the spools. Efficiency cubed! Incidentally, Russia's got the tickler now. Our dip-satellites have photographed it. It's like ours except the Commies wear it on the left shoulder . . . but they're two weeks behind us developmentwise and they'll never close the gap!"

Gusterson reared up out of the pancake phone to take a deep breath. A sulky-lipped sylph-figured girl two feet from him twitched—medium cootch, he judged—then fumbled in her belt-bag for a pill and popped it in her mouth.

"Hell, the tickler's not even efficient yet about little things," Gusterson blatted, diving back into the privacy-yash-mak he was sharing with Fay. "Whyn't that girl's doctor have the Moodmaster component of her tickler inject her with medicine?"

"Her doctor probably wants her to have the discipline of pill-taking—or the exercise," Fay answered glibly. "Look sharp now. Here's where we fork. I'm taking you through Micro's postern."

A ribbon of slidewalk split itself from the main band and angled off into a short alley. Gusterson hardly felt the constant-speed juncture as they crossed it. Then the secondary ribbon speeded up, carrying them at about thirty feet a second toward the blank concrete wall in which the alley ended. Gusterson prepared to jump, but Fay grabbed him with one hand and with the other held up toward the wall a badge and a button. When they were about ten feet away the wall whipped aside, then whipped shut behind them so fast that Gusterson wondered momentarily if he still had his heels and the seat of his pants.

Fay, tucking away his badge and pancake phone, dropped the button in Gusterson's vest pocket. "Use it when you leave," he said casually. "That is, if you leave."

Gusterson, who was trying to read the Do and Don't posters papering the walls they were passing, started to probe that last sinister supposition, but just then the ribbon slowed, a swinging door opened and closed behind them, and they found themselves in a luxuriously furnished thinking box measuring at least eight feet by five.

"Hey, this is something," Gusterson said appreciatively to show he wasn't an utter yokel. Then, drawing on research he'd done for period novels, "Why, it's as big as a Pullman car compartment, or a first mate's cabin in the War of 1812. You really must rate."

Fay nodded, smiled wanly and sat down with a sigh on a compact overstuffed swivel chair. He let his arms dangle and his head sink into his puffed shoulder cape. Gusterson stared at him. It was the first time he could ever recall the little man showing fatigue.

"Tickler currently does have one serious drawback," Fay volunteered. "It weighs twenty-eight pounds. You feel it when you've been on your feet a couple of hours. No question we're going to give the next model that antigravity feature you mentioned for pursuit grenades. We'd have had it in this model except there were so many other things to be incorporated." He sighed again. "Why, the scanning and decision-making elements alone tripled the mass."

"Hey," Gusterson protested, thinking especially of the sulky-lipped girl, "do you mean to tell me all those other people were toting two stone?"

Fay shook his head heavily. "They were all wearing Mark

Three or Four. I'm wearing Mark Six," he said, as one might say, "I'm carrying the genuine Cross, not one of the balsa ones."

But then his face brightened a little and he went on. "Of course the new improved features make it more than worth it . . . and you hardly feel it at all at night when you're lying down . . . and if you remember to talcum under it twice a day, no sores develop . . . at least not very big ones . . ."

Backing away involuntarily, Gusterson felt something prod his right shoulderblade. Ripping open his coat, he convulsively plunged his hand under it and tore out Fay's belt-bag . . . and then set it down very gently on the top of a shallow cabinet and relaxed with the sigh of one who has escaped a great, if symbolic, danger. Then he remembered something Fay had mentioned. He straightened again.

"Hey, you said it's got scanning and decision-making elements. That means your tickler thinks, even by your fancy standards. And if it thinks, it's conscious—except maybe at robotic gut-level."

"Gussy," Fay said wearily, frowning, "all sorts of things nowadays have S and DM elements. Mail sorters, missiles, robot medics, high-style mannequins, just to name some of the Ms. They 'think,' to use that archaic word, but it's neither here nor there. And they're certainly not conscious."

"Your tickler thinks," Gusterson repeated stubbornly, "just like I warned you it would. It sits on your shoulder, ridin' you like you was a pony or a starved St. Bernard, and now it thinks."

"Suppose it does?" Fay yawned. "What of it?" He gave a rapid sinuous one-sided shrug that made it look for a moment as if his left arm had three elbows. It stuck in Gusterson's mind, for he had never seen Fay use such a gesture and he wondered where he'd picked it up. Maybe imitating a double-jointed Micro Finance chief? Fay yawned again and said, "Please, Gussy, don't disturb me for a minute or so." His eyes half closed.

Gusterson studied Fay's sunken-cheeked face and the great puff of his shoulder cape.

"Say, Fay," he asked in a soft voice after about five minutes, "are you meditating?"

"Why, no," Fay responded, starting up and then stifling another yawn. "Just resting a bit. I seem to get more tired these days, somehow. You'll have to excuse me, Gussy. But what made you think of meditation?"

"Oh, I just got to wonderin' in that direction," Gusterson said. "You see, when you first started to develop Tickler, it occurred to me that there was one thing about it that might be real good even if you did give it S and DM elements. It's this: having a mech secretary to take charge of his obligations and routine in the real world might allow a man to slide into the other world, the world of thoughts and feelings and intuitions, and sort of ooze around in there and accomplish things. Know any of the people using Tickler that way, hey?"

"Of course not," Fay denied with a bright incredulous laugh. "Who'd want to loaf around in an imaginary world and take a chance of *missing out on what his tickler's doing?*—I mean, on what his tickler has in store for him—what he's *told* his tickler to have in store for him."

Ignoring Gusterson's shiver, Fay straightened up and seemed to brisken himself. "Ha, that little slump did me good. A tickler *makes* you rest, you know—it's one of the great things about it. Pooh-Bah's kinder to me than I ever was to myself." He buttoned open a tiny refrigerator and took out two waxed cardboard cubes and handed one to Gusterson. "Martini? Hope you don't mind drinking from the carton. Cheers. Now, Gussy old pal, there are two matters I want to take up with you—"

"Hold it," Gusterson said with something of his old authority. "There's something I got to get off my mind first." He pulled the typed pages out of his inside pocket and straightened them. "I told you about these," he said. "I want you to read them before you do anything else. Here."

Fay looked toward the pages and nodded, but did not take them yet. He lifted his hands to his throat and unhooked the clasp of his cape, then hesitated.

"You wear that thing 'to hide the hump your tickler makes?" Gusterson filled in. "You got better taste than those other moles."

"Not to hide it, exactly," Fay protested, "but just so the others won't be jealous. I wouldn't feel comfortable parading a free-scanning decision-capable Mark Six tickler in front of people who can't buy it—until it goes on open sale at twenty-two fifteen tonight. Lot of shelterfolk won't be sleeping tonight. They'll be queued up to trade in their old tickler for a Mark Six almost as good as Pooh-Bah."

He started to jerk his hands apart, hesitated again with an oddly apprehensive look at the big man, then whirled off the cape.

VI

GUSTERSON sucked in such a big gasp that he hiccuped. The right shoulder of Fay's jacket and shirt had been cut away. Thrusting up through the neatly hemmed hole was a silvery gray hump with a one-eyed turret atop it and two multijointed metal arms ending in little claws.

It looked like the top half of a pseudo-science robot—a squat evil child robot, Gusterson told himself, which had lost its legs in a railway accident—and it seemed to him that a red fleck was moving around in the huge single eye.

"I'll take that memo now," Fay said coolly, reaching out his hand. He caught the rustling sheets as they slipped from Gusterson's fingers, evened them up very precisely by tapping them on his knee . . . and then handed them over his shoulder to his tickler, which clicked its claws around either margin and then began rather swiftly to lift the top sheet past its single eye at a distance of about six inches.

"The first matter I want to take up with you, Gussy," Fay began, paying no attention whatsoever to the little scene on his shoulder, "—or warn you about, rather—is the imminent ticklerization of schoolchildren, geriatrics, convicts, and topsiders. At three zero zero tomorrow, ticklers become mandatory for all adult shelterfolk. The mop-up operations won't be long in coming—in fact, these days we find that the square root of the estimated time of a new development is generally the best time estimate. Gussy, I strongly advise you to start wearing a tickler now. And Daisy and your moppets. If you heed my advice, your kids will have the jump on their class. Transition and conditioning are easy, since Tickler itself sees to it."

Pooh-Bah leafed the first page to the back of the packet

and begun lifting the second past his eye—a little more swiftly than the first.

"I've got a Mark Six tickler all warmed up for you," Fay pressed, "*and* a shoulder cape. You won't feel one bit conspicuous." He noticed the direction of Gusterson's gaze and remarked, "Fascinating mechanism, isn't it? Of course twenty-eight pounds are a bit oppressive, but then you have to remember it's only a way-station to free-floating Mark Seven or Eight."

Pooh-Bah finished page two and began to race through page three.

"But I wanted *you* to read it," Gusterson said bemusedly, staring.

"Pooh-Bah will do a better job than I could," Fay assured him. "Get the gist without losing the chaff."

"But dammit, it's all about *him*," Gusterson said a little more strongly. "He won't be objective about it."

"A better job," Fay reiterated, "*and* more fully objective. Pooh-Bah's set for full précis. Stop worrying about it. He's a dispassionate machine, not a fallible, emotionally disturbed human misled by the will-o'-the-wisp of consciousness. Second matter: Micro Systems is impressed by your contributions to Tickler and will recruit you as a senior consultant with a salary and thinking box as big as my own, family quarters to match. It's an unheard-of high start. Gussy, I think you'd be a fool—"

He broke off, held up a hand for silence, and his eyes got a listening look. Pooh-Bah had finished page six and was holding the packet motionless. After about ten seconds Fay's face broke into a big fake smile. He stood up, suppressing a wince, and held out his hand. "Gussy," he said loudly, "I am happy to inform you that all your fears about Tickler are so much thistledown. My word on it. There's nothing to them at all. Pooh-Bah's précis, which he's just given to me, proves it."

"Look," Gusterson said solemnly, "there's one thing I want you to do. Purely to humor an old friend. But I want you to do it. *Read that memo yourself.*"

"Certainly I will, Gussy," Fay continued in the same ebullient tones. "I'll read it—" he twitched and his smile disappeared, "a little later."

"Sure," Gusterson said dully, holding his hand to his stomach. "And now if you don't mind, Fay, I'm goin' home.

I feel just a bit sick. Maybe the ozone and the other additives in your shelter air are too heady for me. It's been years since I tramped through a pine forest."

"But, Gussy! You've hardly got here. You haven't even sat down. Have another martini. Have a seltzer pill. Have a whiff of oxy. Have a—"

"No, Fay, I'm going home right away. I'll think about the job offer. *Remember to read that memo.*"

"I will, Gussy, I certainly will. You know your way? The button takes you through the wall. 'By, now."

He sat down abruptly and looked away. Gusterson pushed through the swinging door. He tensed himself for the step onto the slowly moving reverse ribbon. Then on an impulse he pushed ajar the swinging door and looked back inside.

Fay was sitting as he'd left him, apparently lost in listless brooding. On his shoulder Pooh-Bah was rapidly crossing and uncrossing its little metal arms, tearing the memo to smaller and smaller shreds. It let the scraps drift slowly toward the floor and oddly writhed its three-elbowed left arm . . . and then Gusterson knew from whom, or rather from what, Fay had copied his new shrug.

VII

WHEN Gusterson got home toward the end of the second dog watch, he slipped aside from Daisy's questions and set the children laughing with a graphic enactment of his slidestanding technique and a story about getting his head caught in a thinking box built for a midget physicist. After supper he played with Imogene, Iago, and Claudius until it was their bedtime, and thereafter was unusually attentive to Daisy, admiring her fading green stripes, though he did spend a while in the next apartment, where they stored their outdoor camping equipment.

But the next morning he announced to the children that it was a holiday—the Feast of St. Gusterson—and then took Daisy into the bedroom and told her everything.

When he'd finished she said, "This is something I've got to see for myself."

Gusterson shrugged. "If you think you've got to. I say we should head for the hills right now. One thing I'm standing on: the kids aren't going back to school."

"Agreed," Daisy said. "But, Gusterson, we've lived through a lot of things without leaving home altogether. We lived through the Everybody-Six-Feet-Underground-by-Christmas campaign and the Robot Watchdog craze, when you got your left foot half chewed off. We lived through the Venomous Bats and Indoctrinated Saboteur Rats and the Hypnotized Monkey Paratrooper scares. We lived through the Voice of Safety and Anti-Communist Somno-Instruction and Rightest Pills and Jet-Propelled Vigilantes. We lived through the Cold-Out, when you weren't supposed to turn on a toaster for fear its heat would be a target for prowl missiles and when people with fevers were unpopular. We lived through—"

Gusterson patted her hand. "You go below," he said. "Come back when you've decided this is different. Come back as soon as you can anyway. I'll be worried about you every minute you're down there."

When she was gone—in a green suit and hat to minimize or at least justify the effect of the faded stripes—Gusterson doled out to the children provender and equipment for a camping expedition to the next floor. Iago led them off in stealthy Indian file. Leaving the hall door open Gusterson got out his .38 and cleaned and loaded it, meanwhile concentrating on a chess problem with the idea of confusing a hypothetical psionic monitor. By the time he had hid the revolver again he heard the elevator creaking back up.

Daisy came dragging in without her hat, looking as if she'd been concentrating on a chess problem for hours herself and just now given up. Her stripes seemed to have vanished; then Gusterson decided this was because her whole complexion was a touch green.

She sat down on the edge of the couch and said without looking at him, "Did you tell me, Gusterson, that everybody was quiet and abstracted and orderly down below, especially the ones wearing ticklers, meaning pretty much everybody?"

"I did," he said. "I take it that's no longer the case. What are the new symptoms?"

She gave no indication. After some time she said, "Gusterson, do you remember the Doré illustrations to the *Inferno?* Can you visualize the paintings of Hieronymous Bosch with the hordes of proto-Freudian devils tormenting people all over the farmyard and city square? Did you ever see the Disney animations of Moussorgsky's witches' sabbath music? Back in the foolish days before you married me, did that drug-addict girl friend of yours ever take you to a genuine orgy?"

"As bad as that, hey?"

She nodded emphatically and all of a sudden shivered violently. "Several shades worse," she said. "If they decide to come topside—" She shot up. "Where are the kids?"

"Upstairs campin' in the mysterious wilderness of the twenty-first floor," Gusterson reassured her. "Let's leave 'em there until we're ready to—"

He broke off. They both heard the faint sound of thudding footsteps.

"They're on the stairs," Daisy whispered, starting to move toward the open door. "But are they coming from up or down?"

"It's just one person," judged Gusterson, moving after his wife. "Too heavy for one of the kids."

The footsteps doubled in volume and came rapidly closer. Along with them there was an agonized gasping. Daisy stopped, staring fearfully at the open doorway. Gusterson moved past her. Then he stopped too.

Fay stumbled into view and would have fallen on his face except he clutched both sides of the doorway halfway up. He was stripped to the waist. There was a little blood on his shoulder. His narrow chest was arching convulsively, the ribs standing out starkly, as he sucked in oxygen to replace what he'd burned up running up twenty flights. His eyes were wild.

"They've taken over," he panted. Another gobbling breath. "Gone crazy." Two more gasps. "Gotta stop 'em."

His eyes filmed. He swayed forward. Then Gusterson's big arms were around him and he was carrying him to the couch.

Daisy came running from the kitchen with a damp cool towel. Gusterson took it from her and began to mop Fay off. He sucked in his own breath as he saw that Fay's right ear was raw and torn. He whispered to Daisy, "Look at where the thing savaged him."

The blood on Fay's shoulder came from his ear. Some of it stained a flush-skin gum-pink plastic fitting that had two small valved holes in it, and that puzzled Gusterson until he remembered that Moodmaster tied into the blood-stream. For a second he thought he was going to vomit.

The dazed look slid aside from Fay's eyes. He was gasping less painfully now. He sat up, pushing the towel away, buried his face in his hands for a few seconds, then looked over the fingers at the two of them.

"I've been living in a nightmare for the last week," he said in a taut small voice, "knowing the thing had come alive and trying to pretend to myself that it hadn't. Knowing it was taking charge of me more and more. Having it whisper in my ear, over and over again, in a cracked little rhyme that I could only hear every hundredth time, 'Day by day, in every way, you're learning to listen. . . and *obey*. Day by day—' "

His voice started to go high. He pulled it down and continued harshly, "I ditched it this morning when I showered. It let me break contact to do that. It must have figured it had complete control of me, mounted or dismounted. I think it's telepathic, and then it did some, well, rather unpleasant things to me late last night. But I pulled together my fears and my will and I ran for it. The slidewalks were chaos. The Mark Six ticklers showed some purpose, though I couldn't tell you what, but as far as I could see the Mark Threes and Fours were just cootching their mounts to death—Chinese feather torture. Giggling, gasping, choking . . . gales of mirth. People are dying of laughter . . . ticklers! . . . the irony of it! It was the complete lack of order and sanity that let me get topside. There were things I saw—" Once again his voice went shrill. He clapped his hand to his mouth and rocked back and forth on the couch.

Gusterson gently but firmly laid a hand on his good shoulder. "Steady," he said. "Here, swallow this."

Fay shoved aside the short brown drink. "We've got to stop them," he cried. "Mobilize the topsiders—contact the wilderness patrols and manned satellites—pour ether in the tunnel airpumps—invent and crash-manufacture missiles that will home on ticklers without harming humans—SOS Mars and Venus—dope the shelter water supply—do something! Gussy, you don't realize what people are going through down there every second."

"I think they're experiencing the ultimate in outer-directedness," Gusterson said gruffly.

"Have you no heart?" Fay demanded. His eyes widened, as if he were seeing Gusterson for the first time. Then, accusingly, pointing a shaking finger: *"You invented the tickler, George Gusterson! It's all your fault! You've got to do something about it!"*

Before Gusterson could retort to that, or begin to think of a reply, or even assimilate the full enormity of Fay's statement, he was grabbed from behind and frog-marched away from Fay. Something that felt remarkably like the muzzle of a large-caliber gun was shoved in the small of his back.

Under cover of Fay's outburst a huge crowd of people had entered the room from the hall—eight, to be exact. But the weirdest thing about them to Gusterson was that from the first instant he had the impression that only one mind had entered the room and that it did not reside in any of the eight persons, even though he recognized three of them, but in something that they were carrying.

Several things contributed to this impression. The eight people all had the same blank expression—watchful yet empty-eyed. They all moved in the same slithery crouch. And they had all taken off their shoes. Perhaps, Gusterson thought wildly, they believed he and Daisy ran a Japanese flat.

Gusterson was being held by two burly women, one of them quite pimply. He considered stamping on her toes, but just at that moment the gun dug in his back with a corkscrew movement.

The man holding the gun on him was Fay's colleague Davidson. Some yards beyond Fay's couch, Kester was holding a gun on Daisy, without digging it into her, while the single strange man holding Daisy herself was doing so quite decorously—a circumstance which afforded Gusterson minor relief, since it made him feel less guilty about not going berserk.

Two more strange men, one of them in purple lounging pajamas, the other in the gray uniform of a slidewalk inspector, had grabbed Fay's skinny upper arms, one on either side, and were lifting him to his feet, while Fay was struggling with such desperate futility and gibbering so pitifully that Gusterson momentarily had second thoughts about the moral imperative to go berserk when menaced by hostile force, or seeing a friend so menaced. But again the gun dug into him with a twist.

Approaching Fay face-on was the third Micro-man Gusterson had met yesterday—Hazen. It was Hazen who was carrying—quite reverently or solemnly—or at any rate very carefully the object that seemed to Gusterson to be the mind of the little storm troop presently desecrating the sanctity of his own individual home.

All of them were wearing ticklers, of course—the three Micro-men the heavy emergent Mark 6s with their clawed and jointed arms and monocular cephalic turrets, the rest lower-numbered Marks of the sort that merely made Richard-the-Third humps under clothing.

The object that Hazen was carrying was the Mark 6 tickler Gusterson had seen Fay wearing yesterday. Gusterson was sure it was Pooh-Bah because of its air of command, and because he would have sworn on a mountain of Bibles that he recognized the red fleck lurking in the back of its single eye. And Pooh-Bah alone had the aura of full conscious thought. Pooh-Bah alone had mana.

It is not good to see an evil legless child robot with dangling straps bossing—apparently by telepathic power—not only three objects of its own kind and five close primitive relatives, but also eight human beings . . . and in addition throwing into a state of twitching terror one miserable, thin-chested, half-crazy research-and-development director.

Pooh-Bah pointed a claw at Fay. Fay's handlers dragged him forward, still resisting but more feebly now, as if half-hypnotized or at least cowed.

Gusterson grunted an outraged, "Hey!" and automatically struggled a bit, but once more the gun dug in. Daisy shut her eyes, then firmed her mouth and opened them again to look.

Seating the tickler on Fay's shoulder took a little time, because two blunt spikes in its bottom had to be fitted into the valved holes in the flush-skin plastic disk. When at last they plunged home, Gusterson felt very sick indeed—and then even more so, as the tickler itself poked a tiny pellet on a fine wire into Fay's ear.

The next moment Fay had straightened up and motioned

his handlers aside. He tightened the straps of his tickler around his chest and under his armpits. He held out a hand and someone gave him a shoulderless shirt and coat. He slipped into them smoothly, Pooh-Bah dexterously using its little claws to help put its turret and body through the neatly hemmed holes. The small storm troop looked at Fay with deferential expectation. He held still for a moment, as if thinking, and then walked over to Gusterson and looked him in the face and again held still.

Fay's expression was jaunty on the surface, agonized underneath. Gusterson knew that he wasn't thinking at all, but only listening for instructions from something that was whispering on the very threshold of his inner ear.

"Gussy, old boy," Fay said, twitching a depthless grin, "I'd be very much obliged if you'd answer a few simple questions." His voice was hoarse at first, but he swallowed twice and corrected that. "What exactly did you have in mind when you invented ticklers? What exactly are they supposed to be?"

"Why, you miserable—" Gusterson began in a kind of confused horror, then got hold of himself and said curtly, "They were supposed to be mech reminders. They were supposed to record memoranda and—"

Fay held up a palm and shook his head and again listened for a space. Then, "That's how ticklers were supposed to be of use to humans," he said. "I don't mean that at all. I mean how ticklers were supposed to be of use to themselves. Surely you had some notion." Fay wet his lips. "If it's any help," he added, "keep in mind that it's not Fay who's asking this question, but Pooh-Bah."

Gusterson hesitated. He had the feeling that every one of the eight dual beings in the room was hanging on his answer and that something was boring into his mind and turning over his next thoughts and peering at and under them before he had a chance to scan them himself. Pooh-Bah's eye was like a red searchlight.

"Go on," Fay prompted. "What were ticklers supposed to be—for themselves?"

"Nothin'," Gusterson said softly. "Nothin' at all."

He could feel the disappointment well up in the room—and with it a touch of something like panic.

This time Fay listened for quite a long while. "I hope you don't mean that, Gussy," he said at last very earnestly. "I mean, I hope you hunt deep and find some ideas you forgot, or maybe never realized you had at the time. Let me put it to you differently. What's the place of ticklers in the natural scheme of things? What's their aim in life? Their special reason? Their genius? Their final cause? What gods should ticklers worship?"

But Gusterson was already shaking his head. He said, "I don't know anything about that at all."

Fay sighed and gave simultaneously with Pooh-Bah the now-familiar triple-jointed shrug. Then the man briskened himself. "I guess that's as far as we can get right now," he said. "Keep thinking, Gussy. Try to remember something. You won't be able to leave your apartment—I'm setting guards. If you want to see me, tell them. Or just think. In due course you'll be questioned further in any case. Perhaps by special methods. Perhaps you'll be ticklerized. That's all. Come on, everybody, let's get going."

The pimply woman and her pal let go of Gusterson, Daisy's man loosed his decorous hold, Davidson and Kester sidled away with an eye behind them, and the little storm troop trudged out.

Fay looked back in the doorway. "I'm sorry, Gussy," he said, and for a moment his old self looked out of his eyes. "I wish I could—" A claw reached for his ear, a spasm of pain crossed his face, he stiffened and marched off. The door shut.

Gusterson took two deep breaths that were close to angry sobs. Then, still breathing stentorously, he stamped into the bedroom.

"What—?" Daisy asked, looking after him.

He came back carrying his .38 and headed for the door.

"What are you up to?" she demanded, knowing very well.

"I'm going to blast that iron monkey off Fay's back if it's the last thing I do!"

She threw her arms around him.

"Now lemme go," Gusterson growled. "I gotta be a man one time anyway."

As they struggled for the gun, the door opened noiselessly, Davidson slipped in and deftly snatched the weapon out of their hands before they realized he was there. He said nothing, only smiled at them and shook his head in sad reproof as he went out.

Gusterson slumped. "I *knew* they were all psionic," he said softly. "I just got out of control now—that last look Fay gave us." He touched Daisy's arm. "Thanks, kid."

He walked to the glass wall and looked out desultorily. After a while he turned and said, "Maybe you better be with the kids, hey? I imagine the guards'll let you through."

Daisy shook her head. "The kids never come home until supper. For the next few hours they'll be safer without me."

Gusterson nodded vaguely, sat down on the couch and propped his chin on the base of his palm. After a while his brow smoothed and Daisy knew that the wheels had started to turn inside and the electrons to jump around—except that she reminded herself to permanently cross out those particular figures of speech from her vocabulary.

After about half an hour Gusterson said softly, "I think the ticklers are so psionic that it's as if they just had one mind. If I were with them very long I'd start to be part of that mind. Say something to one of them and you say it to all."

Fifteen minutes later: "They're not crazy, they're just newborn. The ones that were creating a cootching chaos downstairs were like babies kickin' their legs and wavin' their arms, tryin' to see what their bodies could do. Too bad their bodies are us."

Ten minutes more: "I gotta do something about it. Fay's right. It's all my fault. He's just the apprentice; I'm the old sorcerer himself."

Five minutes more, gloomily: "Maybe it's man's destiny to build live machines and then bow out of the cosmic picture. Except the ticklers need us, dammit, just like nomads need horses."

Another five minutes: "Maybe somebody could dream up a purpose in life for ticklers. Even a religion—the First Church of Pooh-Bah Tickler. But I hate selling other people spiritual ideas, and that'd still leave ticklers parasitic on humans . . ."

As he murmured those last words Gusterson's eyes got wide as a maniac's and a big smile reached for his ears. He stood up and faced himself toward the door.

"What are you intending to do now?" Daisy asked flatly.

"I'm merely goin' out an' save the world," he told her. "I may be back for supper and I may not."

VIII

DAVIDSON pushed out from the wall against which he'd been resting himself and his two-stone tickler and moved to block the hall. But Gusterson simply walked up to him. He shook his hand warmly and looked his tickler full in the eye and said in a ringing voice, "Ticklers should have bodies of their own!" He paused and then added casually, "Come on, let's visit your boss."

Davidson listened for instructions and then nodded. But he watched Gusterson warily as they walked down the hall.

In the elevator Gusterson repeated his message to the second guard, who turned out to be the pimply woman, now wearing shoes. This time he added, "Ticklers shouldn't be tied to the frail bodies of humans, which need a lot of thoughtful supervision and drug-injecting and can't even fly."

Crossing the park, Gusterson stopped a hump-backed soldier and informed him, "Ticklers gotta cut the apron string and snap the silver cord and go out in the universe and find their own purposes." Davidson and the pimply woman didn't interfere. They merely waited and watched and then led Gusterson on.

On the escaladder he told someone, "It's cruel to tie ticklers to slow-witted snaily humans when ticklers can think and live . . . ten thousand times as fast," he finished, plucking the figure from the murk of his unconscious.

By the time they got to the bottom, the message had become, "Ticklers should have a planet of their own!"

They never did catch up with Fay, although they spent two hours skimming around on slidewalks under the subterranean stars, pursuing rumors of his presence. Clearly the boss tickler (which was how they thought of Pooh-Bah) led an energetic life. Gusterson continued to deliver his message to all and sundry at thirty-second intervals. Toward the end he found himself doing it in a dreamy and forgetful way. His mind, he decided, was becoming assimilated to the communal telepathic mind of the ticklers. It did not seem to matter at the time.

After two hours Gusterson realized that he and his guides were becoming part of a general movement of people, a flow as mindless as that of blood corpuscles through the veins, yet at the same time dimly purposeful—at least there was the feeling that it was at the behest of a mind far above.

The flow was topside. All the slidewalks seemed to lead to the concourses and the escaladders. Gusterson found himself part of a human stream moving into the tickler factory adjacent to his apartment—or another factory very much like it.

Thereafter Gusterson's awarenesses were dimmed. It was as if a bigger mind were doing the remembering for him and it were permissible and even mandatory for him to dream his way along. He knew vaguely that days were passing. He knew he had work of a sort: at one time he was bringing food to gaunt-eyed tickler-mounted humans working feverishly in a production line—human hands and tickler claws working together in a blur of rapidity on silvery mechanisms that moved along jumpily on a great belt; at another he was sweeping piles of metal scraps and garbage down a gray corridor.

Two scenes stood out a little more vividly.

A windowless wall had been knocked out for twenty feet. There was blue sky outside, its light almost hurtful, and a drop of many stories. A file of humans were being processed. When one of them got to the head of the file his (or her) tickler was ceremoniously unstrapped from his shoulder and welded onto a silvery cask with smoothly pointed ends. The welding sparks were red stars. The result was something that looked—at least in the case of the Mark 6 ticklers—like a stubby silver submarine, child size. It would hum gently, lift off the floor and then fly slowly out through the big blue gap. Then the next tickler-ridden human would step forward for processing.

The second scene was in a park, the sky again blue, but big and high with an argosy of white clouds. Gusterson was lined up in a crowd of humans that stretched as far as he could see, row on irregular row. Martial music was playing. Overhead hovered a flock of littler silver submarines, lined up rather more orderly in the air than the humans were on the ground. The music rose to a heart-quickening climax. The tickler nearest above Gusterson gave (as if to say, "And now—who knows?") a triple-jointed shrug that stung his memory. Then the ticklers took off straight up on their new and shining bodies. They became a flight of silver geese . . . of silver midges . . . and the humans around Gusterson lifted a ragged cheer . . .

That scene marked the beginning of the return of Gusterson's mind and memory. He shuffled around for a bit, spoke vaguely to three or four people he recalled from the dream days, and then headed for home and supper—three weeks late, and as disoriented and emaciated as a bear coming out of hibernation.

IX

SIX MONTHS later Fay was having dinner with Daisy and Gusterson. The cocktails had been poured and the children were playing in the next apartment. The transparent violet walls brightened, then gloomed, as the sun dipped below the horizon.

Gusterson said, "I see where a spaceship out beyond the orbit of Mars was holed by a tickler. I wonder where the little guys are headed now?"

Fay started to give a writhing left-armed shrug, but stopped himself with a grimace.

"Maybe out of the solar system altogether," suggested Daisy, who'd recently dyed her hair fire-engine red and was wearing red leotards.

"They got a weary trip ahead of them," Gusterson said, "unless they work out a hyper-Einsteinian drive on the way."

Fay grimaced again. He was still looking rather peaked. He said plaintively, "Haven't we heard enough about ticklers for a while?"

"I guess so," Gusterson agreed, "but I get to wondering about the little guys. They were so serious and intense about everything. I never did solve their problem, you know. I just shifted it onto other shoulders than ours. No joke intended," he hurried to add.

Fay forbore to comment. "By the way, Gussy," he said, "have you heard anything from the Red Cross about that world-saving medal I nominated you for? I know you think the whole concept of world-saving medals is ridiculous, especially when they started giving them to all heads of state who didn't start atomic wars while in office, but—"

"Nary a peep," Gusterson told him. "I'm not proud, Fay. I could use a few world-savin' medals. I'd start a flurry in the old-gold market. But I don't worry about those things. I don't have time to. I'm busy these days thinkin' up a bunch of new inventions."

"Gussy!" Fay said sharply, his face tightening in alarm, "Have you forgotten your promise?"

" 'Course not, Fay. My new inventions aren't for Micro or any other firm. They're just a legitimate part of my literary endeavors. Happens my next insanity novel is goin' to be about a mad inventor."

*Despite tactical victories like Gussy's, Greed and
Fear kept marching hand in hand. Eventually they
used their two free hands to push a few buttons.*

*The result was spectacular, especially in the
U.S.A. Massive coveys of deep-driving hydrogen
bombs turned the shelter cities to death traps.
Mars howled with mirth.*

*For a few hundred men and women, in fewer
towns than it takes the fingers of one hand to
number, the League of Sanity became a serious
concern.*

*But in the endless Deathlands between the
towns were two wanderers, a man and a girl,
anything but humanists, whom we may call—*

THE WOLF PAIR

I

*Any man who saw you, or even heard your footsteps must
be ambushed, stalked and killed, whether needed for food
or not. Otherwise, so long as his strength held out, he
would be on your trail.*

—The Twenty-Fifth Hour

By Herbert Best

I was one hundred miles from Nowhere—and I mean that
literally—when I spotted this girl out of the corner of my
eye. I'd been keeping an extra lookout because I still expected
the other undead bugger left over from the murder party
at Nowhere to be stalking me.

I'd been following a line of high-voltage towers all

canted over at the same gentlemanly tipsy angle by an old blast from the Last War. I judged the girl was going in the same general direction and was being edged over toward my course by a drift of dust that even at my distance showed dangerous metallic gleams and dark humps that might be dead men or cattle.

She looked slim, dark topped, and on guard. Small like me and like me wearing a scarf loosely around the lower half of her face in the style of the old buckaroos.

We didn't wave or turn our heads or give the slightest indication we'd seen each other as our paths slowly converged. But we were intensely, minutely watchful—I knew I was and she had better be.

Overhead the sky was a low dust haze, as always. I don't remember what a high sky looks like. Three years ago I think I saw Venus. Or it may have been Sirius or Jupiter.

The hot smoky light was turning from the amber of midday to the bloody bronze of evening.

The line of towers I was following showed the faintest spread in the direction of their canting—they must have been only a few miles from blast center. As I passed each one I could see where the metal on the blast side had been eroded—vaporized by the original blast, mostly smoothly, but with welts and pustules where the metal had merely melted and run. I supposed the lines the towers carried had all been vaporized too, but with the haze I couldn't be sure, though I did see three dark blobs up there that might be vultures perching.

From the drift around the foot of the nearest tower a human skull peered whitely. That is rather unusual. Years later now you still see more dead bodies with the meat on them than skeletons. Intense radiation has killed their bacteria and preserved them indefinitely from decay, just like the packaged meat in the last advertisements, or the hopes of the Egyptian Pharaohs. In fact such bodies are one of the signs of a really hot drift—you avoid them. The vultures pass up such poisonously hot carrion too—they've learned their lesson.

Ahead some big gas tanks began to loom up, like deformed battleships and flat-tops in a smoke screen, their prows being the juncture of the natural curve of the off-blast side with the massive concavity of the on-blast side.

None of the three other buggers and me had had too clear an idea of where Nowhere had been—hence, in part, the name—but I knew in a general way that I was somewhere in the Deathlands between Porter County and Ouachita Parish, probably much nearer the former.

It's a real mixed-up America we've got these days, you know, with just the faintest trickle of a sense of identity left, like a guy in the paddedest cell in the most locked up ward in the whole loony bin. If a time traveler from mid twentieth century hopped forward to it across the few intervening decades and looked at a map of it, if anybody has a map of it, he'd think that the map had run—that it had got some sort of disease that had swollen a few tiny parts beyond all bounds, paper tumors, while most of the other parts, the parts he remembered carrying names in such big print and showing such bold colors, had shrunk to nothingness.

He'd never have guessed we'd got to Mars and Venus—and to the moons of Jupiter even—before the button-punching disease took hold . . . and spread to the colonies.

To the east he'd see Atlantic Highlands and Savannah Fortress. To the west, Walla Walla Territory, Pacific Palisades, and Los Alamos—and there he'd see an actual change in the coastline, I'm told, where three of the biggest stockpiles of fusionables let go and opened Death Valley to the sea—so that Los Alamos is closer to being a port. Centrally he'd find Porter County and Manteno Asylum surprisingly close together near the Great Lakes, which are tilted and spilled out a bit toward the southwest with the big quake.

Funny that an insane asylum should be one of the locales to survive nuclear bomb-out. But then they used to put those places as far as possible from everything else, I'm told. They were flagged for safety, if anybody had thought.

South-centrally: Ouachita Parish inching up the Mississippi from old Louisiana under the cruel urging of the Fischer Sheriffs.

Those he'd find and a few, a very few other places, including a couple I suppose I haven't heard of. Practically all of them would surprise him—no one can predict what scraps of a blasted nation are going to hang onto a shred of organization and ruthlessly maintain it and very slowly and very jealously extend it.

But biggest of all, occupying practically all the map, reducing all those swollen localities I've mentioned back to tiny blobs, bounding most of America and thrusting its jetty pseudopods everywhere, he'd see the great inkblot of the Deathlands. I don't know how else than by an area of solid, absolutely unrelieved black you'd represent the Deathlands with its multicolored radioactive dusts and its skimpy freightage of lonely Deathlanders, each bound on his murderous, utterly pointless, but utterly absorbing business —an area where names like Nowhere, It, Anywhere, and the Place are the most natural thing in the world when a few of us decide to try to pad down together for a few nervous months or weeks.

As I say, I was somewhere in the Deathlands near Manteno Asylum.

The girl and me were getting closer now, well within pistol or dart range, though beyond any but the most expert or lucky knife throw. She wore boots and a weathered long-sleeved shirt and jeans. The black topping was hair, piled high in an elaborate coiffure that was held in place by twisted shavings of bright metal. A fine bug-trap, I told myself.

In her left hand, which was closest to me, she carried a dart gun, pointed away from me, across her body. It was the kind of potent tiny crossbow you can't easily tell whether the spring is loaded. Back around on her left hip a small leather satchel was strapped to her belt. Also on the same side were two sheathed knives, one of which was an oddity—it had no handle, just the bare tang. For nothing but throwing, I guessed.

I let my own left hand drift a little closer to my Banker's Special in its open holster—Ray Banker's great psychological weapon, though (who knows?) the two .38 cartridges it contained might actually fire. The one I'd put to the test at Nowhere had, and very lucky for me.

She seemed to be hiding her right arm from me. Then I spotted the weapon it held, one you don't often see, a stevedore's hook. She *was* hiding her right hand, all right, she had the long sleeve pulled down over it so just the hook stuck out. I asked myself if the hand were perhaps covered with radiation scars or sores or otherwise disfigured. We Deathlanders have our vanities. I'm sensitive about my baldness.

Then she let her right arm swing more freely and I

saw how short it was. She had no right hand. The hook was attached to the wrist stump.

I judged she was about ten years younger than me. I'm pushing forty, I think, though some people have judged I'm younger. No way of my knowing for sure. In this life you forget trifles like chronology.

Anyway, the age difference meant she would have quicker reflexes. I'd have to keep that in mind.

The greenishly glinting dust drift that I'd judged she was avoiding swung closer ahead. The girl's left elbow gave a little kick to the satchel on her hip and there was a sudden burst of irregular ticks that almost made me start. I steadied myself and concentrated on thinking whether I should attach any special significance to her carrying a Geiger counter. Naturally it wasn't the sort of thinking that interfered in any way with my watchfulness—you quickly lose the habit of that kind of thinking in the Deathlands or you lose something else.

It could mean she was some sort of greenhorn. Most of us old-timers can visually judge the heat of a dust drift or crater or rayed area more reliably than any instrument. Some buggers claim they just feel it, though I've never known any of the latter too eager to navigate in unfamiliar country at night—which you'd think they'd be willing to do if they could feel nuclear heat blind.

But she didn't look one bit like a tenderfoot—like for instance some citizeness newly banished from Manteno. Or like some Porter burgher's unfaithful wife or troublesome girlfriend whom he'd personally carted out beyond the ridges of cleaned-out hot dust that help guard such places, and then abandoned in revenge or from boredom—and they call themselves civilized, those cultural queers!

No, she looked like she *belonged* in the Deathlands. But then why the counter?

Her eyes might be bad, real bad. I didn't think so. She raised her boot an extra inch to step over a little jagged fragment of concrete. No.

Maybe she was just a born double-checker, using science to back up knowledge based on experience as rich as my own or richer. I've met the supercareful type before. They mostly get along pretty well, but they tend to be a shade slow in the clutches.

Maybe she was *testing* the counter, planning to use it some other way or trade it for something.

Maybe she made a practice of traveling by *night!* Then the counter made good sense. But then why use it by day? Why reveal it to me in any case?

Was she trying to convince me that she was a greenhorn? Or had she hoped that the sudden noise would throw me off guard? But who would go to the trouble of carrying a Geiger counter for such devious purposes? And wouldn't she have waited until we got closer before trying the noise gambit?

Think-shmink—it gets you nowhere!

She kicked off the counter with another bump of her elbow and started to edge in toward me faster. I turned the thinking all off and gave my whole mind to watchfulness.

Soon we were barely more than eight feet apart, almost within lunging range without even the preliminary one-two step, and still we hadn't spoken or looked straight at each other, though being that close we'd had to cant our heads around a bit to keep each other in peripheral vision. Our eyes would be on each other steadily for five or six seconds, then dart forward an instant to check for rocks and holes in the trail we were following in parallel. A cultural queer from one of the "civilized" places would have found it funny, I suppose, if he'd been able to watch us perform in an arena or from behind armor glass for his exclusive pleasure.

The girl had eyebrows as black as her hair, which in its piled-up and metal-knotted savagery called to mind African queens despite her pale complexion—very little ultraviolet gets through the dust. From the inside corner of her right eye socket a narrow radiation scar ran up between her eyebrows and across her forehead at a rakish angle until it disappeared under a sweep of hair at the upper left corner of her forehead.

I'd been smelling her, of course, for some time.

I could even tell the color of her eyes now. They were blue. It's a color you never see. Almost no dusts have a bluish cast, there are few blue objects except certain dark steels, the sky never gets very far away from the orange range, though it is green from time to time, and water reflects the sky.

Yes, she had blue eyes, blue eyes and that jaunty scar, blue eyes and that jaunty scar and a dart gun and a steel hook for a right hand, and we were walking side by side, eight feet apart, not an inch closer, still not looking straight at each other, still not saying a word, and I realized that the initial period of unadulterated watchfulness was over, that I'd had adequate opportunity to inspect this girl and size her up, and that night was coming on fast, and that here I was, once again, back with *the problem of the two urges*.

I could try either to kill her or go to bed with her.

I know that at this point the cultural queers (and certainly our imaginary time traveler from mid twentieth century) would make a great noise about not understanding and not believing in the genuineness of the simple urge to murder that governs the lives of us Deathlanders. Like detective-story pundits, they would say that a man or woman murders for gain, or concealment of crime, or from thwarted sexual desire or outraged sexual possessiveness—and maybe they would list a few other "rational" motives—but not, they would say, just for the simple sake of murder, for the sure release and relief it gives, for the sake of wiping out one recognizable bit more (the closest bit we can, since those of us with the courage or lazy rationality to wipe out ourselves have long since done so)—wiping out one recognizable bit more of the whole miserable, unutterably disgusting human mess. Unless, they would say, a person is completely insane, which is actually how all outsiders view us Deathlanders. They can think of us in no other way.

I guess cultural queers and time travelers simply *don't* understand, though to be so blind it seems to me that they have to overlook much of the history of the Last War—and of all wars, for that matter—and of the subsequent years, especially the mushrooming of crackpot cults with a murder tinge: the werewolf gangs, the Berserkers and Amuckers, the revival of Siva worship and the Black Mass, the machine wreckers, the kill-the-killers movements, the new witchcraft, the Unholy Creepers, the Unconsciousers, the radioactive blue gods and rocket devils of the Atomites, and a dozen other groupings clearly prefiguring Deathlander psychology. Those cults had all been as unpredictable as Thugee or the Dancing Madness of the Middle Ages or the Children's Crusade, yet they had happened just the same.

But cultural queers are good at overlooking things. They

have to be, I suppose. They think they're humanity growing again. Yes, despite their laughable warpedness and hysterical crippledness, they actually believe—each howlingly different community of them—that they're the new Adams and Eves. They're all excited about themselves and whether or not they wear fig leaves. They don't carry with them, twenty-four hours a day, like us Deathlanders do, the burden of all that was forever lost.

Since I've gone this far I'll go a bit further and make the paradoxical admission that even we Deathlanders don't really understand our urge to murder. Oh, we have our rationalizations of it, just like everyone has of his ruling passion—we call ourselves junkmen, scavengers, gangrene surgeons; we sometimes believe we're doing the person we kill the ultimate kindness, yes and get slobbery tearful about it afterward; we sometimes tell ourselves we've finally found and are rubbing out the one man or woman who was responsible for everything; we talk, mostly to ourselves, about the aesthetics of homicide; we occasionally admit, but only each to himself alone, that we're just plain nuts.

But we don't really understand our urge to murder, we only *feel* it.

At the hateful sight of another human being, we feel it begin to grow in us until it becomes an overpowering impulse that jerks us, like a puppet is jerked by its strings, into the act itself or its attempted commission.

Like I was feeling it grow in me now as we did this parallel deathmarch through the reddening haze, me and this girl and our problem. This girl with the blue eyes and the jaunty scar.

The problem of the *two* urges, I said. The other urge, the sexual, is one that I know all cultural queers (and certainly our time traveler) would claim to know all about. Maybe they do. But I wonder if they understand how intense it can be with us Deathlanders when it's the only release (except maybe liquor and drugs, which we seldom can get and even more rarely dare use)—the only complete release, even though a brief one, from the overpowering loneliness and from the tyranny of the urge to kill.

To embrace, to possess, to glut lust on, yes even briefly to love, briefly to shelter in—that was good, that was a relief and release to be treasured.

But it couldn't last. You could draw it out, prop it

up perhaps for a few days, for a month even (though sometimes not for a single night)—you might even start to talk to each other a little, after a while—but it could never last. The glands always tire, if nothing else.

Murder was the only *final* solution, the only *permanent* release. Only we Deathlanders know how good it feels. But then after the kill the loneliness would come back, redoubled, and after a while I'd meet another hateful human . . .

Our problem of the two urges. As I watched this girl slogging along parallel to me, as I kept constant watch on her of course, I wondered how *she* was feeling the two urges. Was she attracted to the ridgy scars on my cheeks half-revealed by my scarf?—to me they have a pleasing symmetry. Was she wondering how my head and face looked without the black felt skullcap low-visored over my eyes? Or was she thinking mostly of that hook swinging into my throat under the chin and dragging me down?

I couldn't tell. She looked as poker-faced as I was trying to.

For that matter, I asked myself, how was *I* feeling the two urges?—how was I feeling them as I watched this girl with the blue eyes and the jaunty scar and the arrogantly thinned lips that asked to be smashed, and the slender throat? —and I realized that there was no way to describe that, not even to myself. I could only feel the two urges grow in me, side by side, like monstrous twins, until they would simply be too big for my taut body and one of them would have to be born fast.

I don't know which one of us started to slow down first, it happened so gradually, but the dust puffs that rise from the ground of the Deathlands under even the lightest treading became smaller and smaller around our steps and finally vanished altogether, and we were standing still. Only then did I notice the obvious physical trigger for our stopping. An old freeway ran at right angles across our path. The shoulder by which we'd approached it was sharply eroded, so that the pavement, which even had a shallow cave eroded under it, was a good three feet above the level of our path, forming a low wall. From where I'd stopped I could almost reach out and touch the rough-edged smooth-topped concrete. So could she.

We were right in the midst of the gas tanks now, six

or seven of them towered around us, squeezed like beer cans by the decade-old blast but their metal looking sound enough until you became aware of the red light showing through in odd patterns of dots and dashes where vaporization or later erosion had been complete. Almost but not quite lacework. Just ahead of us, right across the freeway, was the six-story skeletal structure of an old cracking plant, sagged like the power towers away from the blast and the lower stories drifted with piles and ridges and smooth gobbets of dust.

The light was getting redder and smokier every minute.

With the cessation of the physical movement of walking, which is always some sort of release for emotions, I could feel the twin urges growing faster in me. But that was all right, I told myself—this was the crisis, as she must realize too, and that should key us up to bear the urges a little longer without explosion.

I was the first to start to turn my head. For the first time I looked straight into her eyes and she into mine. And as always happens at such times, a third urge appeared abruptly, an urge momentarily as strong as the other two—the urge to speak, to tell and ask all about it. But even as I started to phrase the first crazily happy greeting, my throat lumped, as I'd known it would, with the awful melancholy of all that was forever lost, with the uselessness of any communication, with the impossibility of recreating the past, our individual pasts, any pasts. And as it always does, the third urge died.

I could tell she was feeling that ultimate pain just like me. I could see her eyelids squeeze down on her eyes and her face lift and her shoulders go back as she swallowed hard.

She was the first to start to lay aside a weapon. She took two sidewise steps toward the freeway and reached her whole left arm further across her body and laid the dart gun on the concrete and drew back her hand from it about six inches. At the same time looking at me hard— fiercely angrily, you'd say—across her left shoulder. She had the experienced duelist's trick of seeming to look into my eyes but actually focusing on my mouth. I was using the same gimmick myself—it's tiring to look straight into another person's eyes, and it can put you off guard.

My left side was nearest the wall so I didn't for the

moment have the problem of reaching across my body. I took the same sidewise steps she had, and using just two fingers, very gingerly—*disarmingly*, I hoped—I lifted my antique firearm from its holster and laid it on the concrete and drew back my hand from it all the way. Now it was up to her again, or should be. Her hook was going to be quite a problem, I realized, but we needn't come to it right away.

She temporized by successively unsheathing the two knives at her left side and laying them beside the dart gun. Then she stopped and her look told me plainly that it was up to me.

Now I am a bugger who believes in carrying *one perfect knife*—otherwise, I know for a fact, you'll go knife-happy and end up by weighing yourself down with dozens, literally. So I am naturally very reluctant to get out of touch in any way with Mother, who is a little rusty along the sides but made of the toughest and most sharpenable alloy steel I've ever run across.

Still, I was most curious to find out what she'd do about that hook, so I finally laid Mother on the concrete beside the .38 and rested my hands lightly on my hips, all ready to enjoy myself—at least I hoped I gave that impression.

She smiled, it was almost a nice smile—by now we'd let our scarves drop since we weren't raising any more dust—and then she took hold of the hook with her left hand and started to unscrew it from the leather-and-metal base fitting over her stump.

Of course, I told myself. And her second knife, the one without a grip, must be that way so she could screw its tang into the base when she wanted a knife on her right hand instead of a hook. I ought to have guessed.

I grinned my admiration of her mechanical ingenuity and immediately unhitched my knapsack and laid it beside my weapons. Then a thought occurred to me. I opened the knapsack, and moving my hand slowly and very openly so she'd have no reason to suspect a ruse, I drew out a blanket and, trying to show her both sides of it in the process, as if I were performing some damned conjuring trick, dropped it gently on the ground between us.

She unsnapped the straps on her satchel that fastened it to her belt and laid it aside and then she took off her belt too, slowly drawing it through the wide loops of weathered denim. Then she looked meaningfully at my belt.

I had to agree with her. Belts, especially heavy-buckled ones like ours, can be nasty weapons. I removed mine. Simultaneously each belt joined its corresponding pile of weapons and other belongings.

She shook her head, not in any sort of negation, and ran her fingers into the black hair at several points, to show me it hid no weapon, then looked at me questioningly. I nodded that I was satisfied—I hadn't seen anything run out of it, by the way. Then she looked up at my black skullcap and she raised her eyebrows and smiled again, this time with a spice of mocking anticipation.

In some ways I hate to part with that headpiece more than I do with Mother. Not really because of its sandwiched lead-mesh inner lining—if the rays haven't baked my brain yet they never will, and I'm sure that the patches of lead mesh sewed into my pants over my loins give a lot more practical protection. But I was getting real attracted to this girl by now, and there are times when a person must make a sacrifice of his vanity. I whipped off my stylish black felt and tossed it on my pile and dared her to laugh at my shiny egg top.

Strangely she didn't even smile. She parted her lips and ran her tongue along the upper one. I gave an eager grin in reply, an incautiously wide one, and she saw my plates flash.

My plates are something rather special, though they are by no means unique. Back toward the end of the Last War, when it was obvious to any realist how bad things were going to be, though not how strangely terrible, a number of people, like myself, had all their teeth jerked and replaced with durable plates. I went some of them one better. My plates were stainless steel biting and chewing ridges, smooth continuous ones that didn't attempt to copy individual teeth. A person who looks closely at a slab of chewing tobacco, say, I offer him will be puzzled by the smoothly curved incision, made as if by a razor blade mounted on the arm of a compass. Magnetic powder buried in my gums makes for a real nice fit.

This sacrifice was worse than my hat and Mother combined, but I could see the girl expected me to make it and would take no substitutes, and in this attitude I had to admit that she showed very sound judgment, because I keep the incisor parts of those plates filed to razor sharpness. I have to be careful about my tongue and lips but I figure it's worth it. With my dental scimitars I can in a wink bite out a chunk of throat and windpipe or jugular, though I've never had occasion to do so yet.

For the first minute it made me feel like an old man, a real dodderer, but by now the attraction this girl had for me was getting irrational. I carefully laid the two plates on top of my knapsack.

In return, as a sort of reward you might say, she opened her mouth wide and showed me what was left of her own teeth—about two-thirds of them, a patchwork of tartar and gold.

We took off our boots, pants and shirts, she watching very suspiciously—I knew she'd been skeptical of my carrying only one knife.

Oddly perhaps, considering how touchy I am about my baldness, I felt no sensitivity about revealing the lack of hair on my chest and in fact a sort of pride in displaying the slanting radiation scars that have replaced it, though they are crawling keloids of the ugliest, bumpiest sort. I guess to me such scars are tribal insignia—one-man and one-woman tribes of course. No question but that the scar on the girl's forehead had been the first focus of my desire for her and it still added to my interest.

By now we weren't staying as perfectly on guard or watching each other's clothing for concealed weapons as carefully as we should—I know I wasn't. It was getting dark fast, there wasn't much time left, and the other interest was simply becoming too great.

We were still automatically careful about how we did things. For instance the way we took off our pants was like ballet, simultaneously crouching a little on the left foot and whipping the right leg out of its sheath in one movement, all ready to jump without tripping ourselves if the other person did anything funny, and then skinning down the left pants-leg with a movement almost as swift.

But as I say, it was getting too late for perfect watchfulness, in fact for any kind of effective watchfulness at all. The complexion of the whole situation was changing in a rush. The possibilities of dealing or receiving death—along with the chance of the minor indignity of cannibalism, which some of us practice—were suddenly gone, all gone. It was going to be all right this time, I was telling myself. This was the time it would be different, this was the time love would last, this was the time lust would be the firm foundation for understanding and trust, this time there would be really safe sleeping. This girl's body would be home for me, a beautiful tender inexhaustibly exciting home, and mine for her, for always.

As she threw off her shirt, the last darkly red light showed me another smooth slantwise scar, this one around her hips, like a narrow girdle that has slipped down a little on one side.

II

Murder most foul, as in the best it is;
But this most foul, strange and unnatural.

—Hamlet

BY WILLIAM SHAKESPEARE

WHEN I woke the light was almost full amber and I could feel no flesh against mine, only the blanket under me. I very slowly rolled over and there she was, sitting on the corner of the blanket not two feet from me, combing her long black hair with a big, wide-toothed comb she'd screwed into the leather-and-metal cap over her wrist stump.

She'd put on her pants and shirt, but the former were rolled up to her knees and the latter, though tucked in, wasn't buttoned.

She was looking at me, contemplating me you might say, quite dreamily but with a faint, easy smile.

I smiled back at her.

It was lovely.

Too lovely. There had to be something wrong with it.

There was. Oh, nothing big. Just a solitary trifle—nothing worth noticing really.

But the tiniest solitary things can sometimes be the most irritating, like *one* mosquito.

When I'd first rolled over she'd been combing her hair straight back, revealing a wedge of baldness following the continuation of her forehead scar deep back across her scalp. Now with a movement that was swift though not hurried-looking she swept the mass of her hair forward and to the left, so that it covered the bald area. Also her lips straightened out.

I was hurt. She shouldn't have hidden her bit of baldness, it was something we had in common, something that brought us closer. And she shouldn't have stopped smiling at just that moment. Didn't she realize I loved that blaze on her scalp just as much as any other part of her, that she no longer had any need to practice vanity in front of me?

Didn't she realize that as soon as she stopped smiling, her contemplative stare became an insult to me? What right had she to stare, critically I felt sure, at my bald head? What right had she to know about the nearly healed ulcer on my left shin?—that was a piece of information worth a man's life in a fight. What right had she to cover up, anyways, while I was still naked? She ought to have waked me up so that we could have got dressed as we'd undressed, together. There were lots of things wrong with her manners.

Oh, I know that if I'd been able to think calmly, maybe if I'd just had some breakfast or a little coffee inside me, or even if there'd been some hot breakfast to eat at that moment, I'd have recognized my irritation for the irrational, one-mosquito surge of negative feeling that it was.

Even without breakfast, if I'd just had the knowledge that there was a reasonably secure day ahead of me in which there'd be an opportunity for me to straighten out my feelings, I wouldn't have been irked, or at least being irked wouldn't have bothered me terribly.

But a sense of security is an even rarer commodity in the Deathlands than a hot breakfast.

Given just the ghost of a sense of security and/or some hot breakfast, I'd have told myself that she was merely being amusingly coquettish about her bald streak and her hair, that it was natural for a woman to try to preserve some mystery about herself in front of the man she beds with.

But you get leery of any kind of mystery in the Deathlands. It makes you frightened and angry, like it does an animal. Mystery is for cultural queers, strictly. The only way for two people to get along together in the Deathlands, even for a while, is never to hide anything and never to make a move that doesn't have an immediate clear explanation. You can't talk, you see, certainly not at first, and so you can't explain anything (most explanations are just lies and dreams, anyway), so you have to be doubly careful and explicit about everything you do.

This girl wasn't being either. Right now, on top of her other gaucheries, she was unscrewing the comb from her wrist—an unfriendly if not quite a hostile act, as anyone must admit.

Understand, please, I wasn't *showing* any of these negative reactions of mine any more than she was showing hers, except for her stopping smiling. In fact *I hadn't* stopped smiling. I was playing the game to the hilt.

But inside me everything was stewed up and the other urge had come back and presently it would begin to grow again.

That's the trouble, you know, with sex as a solution to the problem of the two urges. It's fine while it lasts, but it wears itself out and then you're back with Urge Number One and you have nothing left to balance it with.

Oh, I wouldn't kill this girl today, I probably wouldn't seriously think of killing her for a month or more, but old Urge Number One would be there and growing, mostly undercover, all the time. Of course there were things I could do to slow its growth, lots of little gimmicks, in fact—I was pretty experienced at this business.

For instance, I could take a shot at talking to her pretty soon. For a catchy starter, I could tell her about Nowhere, how these five other buggers and me found ourselves independently skulking along after this scavenging expedition from Porter, how we naturally joined forces in that situation, how we set a pitfall for Porter's alky-powered jeep and wrecked it and them, how when our haul turned out to be unexpectedly big the four of us left from the kill chummied up and padded down together and amused each other for a while and played games, you might say. Why, at one point we even had an old crank phonograph going and read some books. And, of course, how when the loot gave out and the fun wore off, we had our murder party and I survived along with, I think, a bugger named Jerry—at any rate, he was gone when the blood stopped spurting, and I'd had no stomach for tracking him, though I probably should have.

And in return she could tell me how she had killed off her last set of girlfriends, or boyfriends, or friend, or whatever it was.

After that, we could have a go at exchanging news, rumors and speculations about local, national and world events. Was it true that Atlantic Highlands had planes of some sort or were they from Europe? Were they actually crucifying the Deathlanders around Walla Walla or only nailing up their dead bodies as dire warnings to others such? Had Manteno made Christianity compulsory yet, or were they still tolerating Zen Buddhists? Was it true that Los Alamos had been completely wiped out by plague, but the area was taboo to Deathlanders because of the robot guards they'd left behind—metal guards eight feet tall who tramped across the white sands, wailing? Did they still have free love in Pacific Palisades? Did she know there'd been a pitched battle fought by expeditionary forces from Ouachita and Savannah Fortress? Over the loot of Birmingham, apparently, after yellow fever had finished off that principality. Had she rooted out any "observers" lately?—some of the "civilized" communities, the more "scientific" ones, try to maintain a few weather stations and the like in the Deathlands, camouflaging them elaborately and manning them with one or two impudent characters to whom we give a hard time if we uncover them. Had she heard the tale that was going around that South America and the French Riviera had survived the Last War absolutely untouched?—and the obviously ridiculous rider that they had blue skies there and saw stars every third night? Did she think that subsequent conditions were showing that the Earth actually had plunged into an interstellar dust cloud coincidentally with the start of the Last War (the dust cloud used as a cover for the first attacks, some said), or did she still hold with the majority that the dust was solely of atomic origin with a little help from volcanoes and dry spells? How many green sunsets had she seen in the last year?

After we'd chewed over those racy topics and some more like them, and incidentally got bored with guessing and fabricating, we might, if we felt especially daring and conversation were going particularly well, even take a chance on talking a little about our childhoods, about how things were before the Last War (though she was almost too young for that)—about the *little* things we remembered—the big things were much too dangerous topics to venture on, and sometimes even the little memories could suddenly twist you up as if you'd swallowed lye.

But after that there wouldn't be anything left to talk about. Anything you'd risk talking about, that is. For instance, no matter how long we talked, it was very unlikely that we'd either of us tell the other anything complete or very accurate about how we lived from day to day, about our techniques of surviving and staying sane or at least functional —that would be too imprudent, it would go too much against the grain of any player of the murder game. Would I tell her, or anyone, about how I worked the ruses of playing dead and disguising myself as a woman, about my trick of picking a path just before dark and then circling back to it by a presurveyed route, about the chess games I played with myself, about the bottle of green, terribly hot-looking powder I carried to sprinkle behind me to bluff off pursuers? A fat chance of my revealing things like that!

And when all the talk was over, what would it have gained us? Our minds would be filled with a lot of painful stuff better kept buried—meaningless hopes, scraps of vicarious living in "cultured" communities, memories that were nothing but melancholy given concrete form. The melancholy is easiest to bear when it's the diffused background for everything; and all garbage is best kept in the can. Oh yes, our talking would have gained us a few more days of infatuation, of phantom security, but those we could have—almost as many of them, at any rate—without talking.

For instance, things were smoothing over already between her and me again and I no longer felt quite so irked. She'd replaced the comb with an inoffensive-looking pair of light pliers and was doing up her hair with the metal shavings. And I was acting as if content to watch her, as in a way I was. I'd still made no move to get dressed.

She looked real sweet, you know, primping herself that way. Her face was a little flat, but it was young, and the scar gave it just the fillip it needed.

But what was going on behind that forehead right now, I asked myself? I felt real psychic this morning, my mind as clear as a bottle of White Rock you find miraculously unbroken in a blasted tavern, and the answers to the question I'd asked myself came effortlessly.

She was telling herself she'd got herself a man again, a man who was adequate in the primal clutch (I gave myself that pat on the back), and that she wouldn't have to be plagued and have her safety endangered by *that* kind of mind-dulling restlessness and yearning for a while.

She was lightly playing around with ideas about how she'd found a home and a protector, knowing she was kidding herself, that it was the most gimcracky feminine make-believe, but enjoying it just the same.

She was sizing me up, deciding in detail just what I went for in a woman, what whetted my interest, so she could keep that roused as long as seemed desirable or prudent to her to continue our relation.

She was kicking herself, only lightly to begin with, because she hadn't taken any precautions—because we who've escaped hot death against all reasonable expectations by virtue of some incalculable resistance to the ills of radioactivity, quite often find we've escaped sterility too. I'd felt her cervix with my glans last night and I was pretty damn sure. If she should become pregnant, she was telling herself, then she had a real sticky business ahead of her where no man could be trusted for a second.

And because she was thinking of this and because she was obviously a realistic Deathlander, she was reminding herself that a woman is basically less impulsive and daring and resourceful than a man and so had always better be sure she gets in the first blow. She would be thinking that I was a realist myself and a smart man, one able to understand her predicament quite clearly—and because of that a much sooner danger to her. She was feeling old Number One Urge starting to grow in her again and wondering whether it mightn't be wisest to give it the hothouse treatment.

That is the trouble with a clear mind. For a little while you see things as they really are and you can accurately predict how they're going to shape the future . . . and then suddenly you realize you've predicted yourself a week or a month into the future and you can't live the intervening time any more because you've already imagined it in detail. People who live in communities, even the cultural queers of our maimed era, aren't much bothered by it—there must be some sort of blinkers they hand you out along with the key to the city—but in the Deathlands it's a fairly common phenomenon and there's no hiding from it.

Me and my clear mind!—once again it had done me out of days of fun, changed a thoroughly explored love affair into a one-night stand. Oh, there was no question about it, this girl and I were finished, right this minute, as of now, because she was just as psychic as I was this morning and had sensed every last thing that I'd been thinking.

With a movement smooth enough not to look rushed I swung into a crouch. She was on her knees faster than that, her left hand hovering over the little set of tools for her stump, which like any good mechanic she'd lined up neatly on the edge of the blanket—the hook, the comb, a long telescoping fork, a couple of other items, and the knife. I'd grabbed a handful of blanket, ready to jerk it from under her. She'd seen that I'd grabbed it. Our gazes dueled.

There was a high-pitched whine over our heads! Quite loud from the start, though it sounded as if it were very deep up in the haze. It swiftly dropped in pitch and volume.

The top of the skeletal cracking plant across the freeway glowed with St. Elmo's fire! Three times it glowed that way, so bright we could see the violet-blue flames of it reaching up despite the full amber daylight.

The whine died away, but in the last moment, paradoxically, it seemed to be coming closer!

This shared threat—for any unexpected event is a threat in the Deathlands and a mysterious event doubly so—put a stop to our murder game. The girl and I were buddies again, buddies to be relied on in a pinch, for the duration of the threat at least. No need to say so or to reassure each other of the fact in any way, it was taken for granted. Besides, there was no time. We had to use every second allowed us in getting ready for whatever was coming.

First I grabbed up Mother. Then I relieved myself—fear made it easy. Then I skinned into my pants and boots, slapped in my teeth, thrust the blanket and knapsack into the shallow cave under the edge of the freeway, looking around me all the time so as not to be surprised from any quarter.

Meanwhile the girl had put on her boots, located her

dart gun, unscrewed the pliers from her stump, put the knife in, and was arranging her scarf so it made a sling for the maimed arm—I wondered why but had no time to waste guessing, even if I'd wanted to, for at that moment a small dull silver plane, beetle-shaped more than anything else, loomed out of the haze beyond the cracking plant and came silently drifting down toward us.

The girl thrust her satchel into the cave and along with it her dart gun. I caught her idea and tucked Mother into my pants behind my back.

I'd thought from the first glimpse of it that the plane was disabled—I guess it was its silence that gave me the idea. This theory was confirmed when one of its very stubby wings or vanes touched a corner pillar of the cracking plant. The plane was moving in too slow a glide to be wrecked, in fact it was moving in a slower glide than I would have believed possible—but then it's many years since I have seen a plane in flight.

It wasn't wrecked but the little collision spun it around twice in a lazy circle and it landed on the freeway with a scuffing noise not fifty feet from us. You couldn't exactly say it had crashed in, but it stayed at an odd tilt. It looked crippled all right.

An oval door in the plane opened, and a man dropped lightly out on the concrete. And what a man! He was nearer seven feet tall than six, close-cropped blond hair, face and hands richly tanned, the rest of him covered by trim garments of a gleaming gray. He must have weighed as much as the two of us together, but he was beautifully built, muscular yet supple-seeming. His face looked brightly intelligent and even-tempered and kind.

Yes, kind!—damn him! It wasn't enough that his body should fairly glow with a health and vitality that was an insult to our seared skins and stringy muscles and ulcers and half-rotted stomachs and half-arrested cancers, he had to look kind too—the sort of man who would put you to bed and take care of you, as if you were some sort of interesting sick fox, and maybe even say a little prayer for you, and all manner of other abominations.

I don't think I could have endured my fury standing still. Fortunately there was no need to. As if we'd rehearsed the whole thing for hours, the girl and I scrambled up onto the freeway and scurried toward the man from the plane, cunningly swinging away from each other so that it would be harder for him to watch the two of us at once, but not enough to make it obvious that we intended an attack from two quarters.

We didn't run though we covered the ground as fast as we dared—running would have been too much of a giveaway too, and the Pilot, which was how I named him to myself, had a strange-looking small gun in his right hand. In fact the way we moved was part of our act—I dragged one leg as if it were crippled, and the girl faked another sort of limp, one that made her approach a series of half curtsies. Her arm in the sling was all twisted, but at the same time she was accidently showing her breasts—I remember thinking *you won't distract this breed bull that way, sister, he probably has a harem of six-foot heifers*. I had my head thrown back and my hands stretched out supplicatingly. Meanwhile the both of us were babbling a blue streak. I was rapidly croacking something like, "Mister for God's sake save my pal he's hurt a lot worse'n I am not a hundred yards away he's dyin' mister he's dyin' o' thirst his tongue's black'n all swole up oh save him mister save my pal he's not a hundred yards away he's dyin' mister dyin'—" and she was singsonging an even worse rigamarole about how "they" were after us from Portêr and going to crucify us because we believed in science and how they'd already impaled her mother and her ten-year-old sister and a lot more of the same.

It didn't matter that our stories didn't fit or make sense, the babble had a convincing tone and was getting us closer to this guy, which was all that counted. He pointed his gun at me and then I could see him hesitate, and I thought exultingly *it's a lot of healthy meat you got there, mister, but it's tame meat, mister, tame!*

He compromised by taking a step back and sort of hooting at us and waving us off with his left hand, as if we were a couple of stray dogs.

It was greatly to our advantage that we'd acted without hesitation, and I don't think we'd have been able to do that except that we'd been all set to kill each other when he dropped in. Our muscles and nerves and minds were keyed for instant ruthless attack. And some "civilized" people still say the urge to murder doesn't contribute to self-preservation!

We were almost close enough now and he was steeling himself to shoot, and I remember wondering for a split second what his damn gun did to you, and then me and the girl had started the alternation routine. I'd stop dead, as if completely cowed by the threat of his weapon, and as he took note of it she'd go in a little further, and as his gaze shifted to her she'd stop dead, and I'd go in another foot and then try to make my halt even more convincing as his gaze darted back to me. We worked it perfectly, our rhythm was beautiful, as if we were old dancing partners, though the whole thing was absolutely impromptu.

Still, I honestly don't think we'd ever have got to him if it hadn't been for the distraction that came just then to help us. I could tell, you see, that he'd finally steeled himself and we still weren't quite close enough. He wasn't as tame as I'd hoped. I reached behind me for Mother, determined to do a last-minute rush and leap anyway, when there came this sick scream.

I don't know how else to describe it briefly. It was a scream, feminine for choice, it came from some distance and the direction of the old cracking plant; it had a note of anguish and warning, yet at the same time it was weak and almost faltering, you might say, and squeaky at the end, as if it came from a person half-dead and a throat choked with phlegm. It had all those qualities or a wonderful mimicking of them.

And it had quite an effect on our boy in gray, for in the act of shooting me down he started to turn and look over his shoulder.

Oh, it didn't altogether stop him from shooting me. He got me partly covered again as I was in the middle of my lunge. I found out what his gun did to you. My right arm, which was the part he'd covered, just went dead, and I finished my lunge slamming up against his iron knees, like a high school kid trying to block out a pro footballer, with the knife slipping uselessly away from my fingers.

But in the blessed meanwhile the girl had lunged too, not with a slow slash, thank God, but with a high, slicing thrust aimed arrow-straight for a point just under his ear.

She connected and a fan of blood sprayed her full in the face.

I grabbed my knife with my left hand as it fell, scrambled

to my feet, and drove the knife at his throat in a round-house swing that happened to come handiest at the time. The point went through his flesh like nothing and jarred against his spine with a violence that I hoped would shock into nervous insensibility the stoutest medulla oblongata and prevent any dying reprisals on his part.

I got my wish, in large part. He swayed, straightened, dropped his gun, and fell flat on his back, giving his skull a murderous crack on the concrete for good measure. He lay there and after a half-dozen gushes the bright blood quit pumping strongly out of his neck.

Then came the part that was like a dying reprisal, though obviously not being directed by him as of now. And come to think of it, it may have had its good points.

The girl, who was clearly a most cool-headed cuss, snatched for his gun where he'd dropped it, to make sure she got it ahead of me. She snatched, yes—and then jerked back, letting off a sizable squeal of pain, anger, and surprise.

Where we'd seen his gun hit the concrete there was now a tiny incandescent puddle. A rill of blood snaked out from the pool around his head and touched the whitely glowing puddle and a jet of steam sizzled up.

Somehow the gun had managed to melt itself in the moment of its owner dying. Well, at any rate that showed it hadn't contained any gunpowder or ordinary chemical explosives, though I already knew it operated on other principles from the way it had been used to paralyze me. More to the point, it showed that the gun's owner was the member of a culture that believed in taking very complete precautions against its gadgets falling into the hands of strangers.

But the gun fusing wasn't quite all. As the girl and me shifted our gaze from the puddle, which was cooling fast and now glowed red like the blood—as we shifted our gaze back from the puddle to the dead man, we saw that at three points (points over where you'd expect pockets to be) his gray clothing had charred in small irregularly shaped patches from which threads of black smoke were twisting upward.

Just at that moment, so close as to make me jump in spite of years of learning to absorb shocks stoically—right at my elbow it seemed (the girl jumped too, I may say)—a voice said, "Done a murder, hey?"

Advancing briskly around the skewily grounded plane from the direction of the cracking plant was an old geezer, a seasoned, hard-baked Deathlander if I ever saw one. He had a shock of bone-white hair, the rest of him that showed from his weathered gray clothing looked fried by the sun's rays and others to a stringy crisp, and strapped to his boots and weighing down his belt were a good dozen knives.

Not satisfied with the unnerving noise he'd made already, he went on brightly, "Neat job too, I give you credit for that, but why the hell did you have to set the guy afire?"

III

We are always, thanks to our human nature, potential criminals. None of us stands outside humanity's black collective shadow.

—The Undiscovered Self

BY CARL JUNG

ORDINARILY scroungers who hide around on the outskirts until the killing's done and then come in to share the loot get what they deserve—wordless orders, well backed up, to be on their way at once. Sometimes they even catch an after-clap of the murder urge, if it hasn't all been expended on the first victim or victims. Yet they *will* do it, trusting I suppose to the irresistible glamor of their personalities. There were several reasons why we didn't at once give Pop this treatment.

In the first place we didn't either of us have our distance weapons. My revolver and her dart gun were both tucked in the cave back at the edge of the freeway. And there's one bad thing about a bugger so knife-happy he lugs them around by the carload—he's generally good at tossing them. With his dozen or so knives Pop definitely outgunned us.

Second, we were both of us without the use of an arm. That's right, the both of us. My right arm still dangled like a string of sausages and I couldn't yet feel any signs of it coming undead. While she'd burned her fingers badly grabbing at the gun—I could see their red-splotched tips now as she pulled them out of her mouth for a second to wipe the Pilot's blood out of her eyes. All she had was her stump with the knife screwed to it. Me, I can throw a knife left-handed if I have to, but you bet I wasn't going to risk Mother that way.

Then I'd no sooner heard Pop's voice, breathy and a little high like an old man's will get, than it occurred to me that he must have been the one who had given the funny scream that had distracted the Pilot's attention and let us get him. Which incidentally made Pop a quick thinker and imaginative to boot, and meant that he'd helped on the killing.

Besides all that, Pop did not come in fawning and full of extravagant praise, as most scroungers will. He just assumed equality with us right from the start, and he talked in an absolutely matter-of-fact way, neither praising nor criticizing one bit—too damn matter-of-fact and open, for that matter, to suit my taste, but then I have heard other buggers say that some old men are apt to get talkative, though I had never worked with or run into one myself. Old people are very rare in the Deathlands, as you might imagine.

So the girl and me just scowled at him but did nothing to stop him as he came along. Near us, his extra knives would be no advantage to him.

"Hum," he said, "looks a lot like a guy I murdered five years back down Los Alamos way. Same silver monkey suit and almost as tall. Nice chap too—was trying to give me something for a fever I'd faked. That his gun melted? My man didn't smoke after I gave him his quietus, but then it turned out he didn't have any metal on him. I wonder if this chap—" He started to kneel down by the body.

"Hands off, Pop!" I gritted at him. That was how we started calling him Pop.

"Why sure, sure," he said, staying there on one knee. "I won't lay a finger on him. It's just that I've heard the Alamosers have it rigged so that any metal they're carrying melts when they die, and I was wondering about this boy. But he's all yours, friend. By the way, what's your name, friend?"

"Ray," I snarled. "Ray Baker." I think the main reason I told him was that I didn't want him calling me "friend" again. "You talk too much, Pop."

"I suppose I do, Ray," he agreed. "What's your name, lady?"

The girl just sort of hissed at him, and he grinned at me as if to say, "Oh, women!" Then he said, "Why don't you go through his pockets, Ray? I'm real curious."

"Shut up," I said, but I felt that he'd put me on the spot just the same. I was curious about the guy's pockets myself, of course, but I was also wondering if Pop was alone or if he had somebody with him, and whether there was anybody else in the plane or not—things like that, too many things. At the same time I didn't want to let on to Pop how useless my right arm was—if I'd just get a twinge of feeling in that arm, I knew I'd feel a lot more confident fast. I knelt down across the body from him, started to lay Mother aside and then hesitated.

The girl gave me an encouraging look, as if to say, "I'll take care of the old geezer." On the strength of her look I put down Mother and started to pry open the Pilot's left hand, which was clenched in a fist that looked a mite too big to have nothing inside it.

The girl started to edge behind Pop, but he caught the movement right away and looked at her with a grin that was so knowing and yet so friendly, and yet so pitying at the same time—with the pity of the old pro for even the seasoned amateur—that in her place I think I'd have blushed myself, as she did now . . . through the streaks of the Pilot's blood.

"You don't have to worry none about me, lady," he said, running a hand through his white hair and incidentally touching the pommel of one of the two knives strapped high on the back of his jacket so he could reach one over either shoulder. "I quit murdering some years back. It got to be too much of a strain on my nerves."

"Oh yeah?" I couldn't help saying as I pried up the Pilot's index finger and started on the next. "Then why the stab-factory, Pop?"

"Oh you mean those," he said, glancing down at his knives. "Well, the fact is, Ray, I carry them to impress buggers dumber than you and the lady here. Anybody wants to think I'm still a practicing murderer I got no objections.

Matter of sentiment, too, I just hate to part with them—they bring back important memories. And then—you won't believe this, Ray, but I'm going to tell you just the same—guys just up and give me their knives, and I doubly hate to part with a gift."

I wasn't going to say "Oh yeah?" again or "Shut up!" either, though I certainly wished I could turn off Pop's spigot, or thought I did. Then I felt a painful tingling shoot down my right arm. I smiled at Pop and said, "Any other reasons?"

"Yep," he said. "Got to shave and I might as well do it in style. A new blade every day in the fortnight is twice as good as the old ads. You know, it makes you keep a knife in fine shape if you shave with it. What you got there, Ray?"

"You were wrong, Pop," I said. "He did have some metal on him that didn't melt."

I held up for them to see the object I'd extracted from his left fist: a bright steel cube measuring about an inch across each side, but it felt lighter than if it were solid metal. Five of the faces looked absolutely bare. The sixth had a round button recessed in it.

From the way they looked at it neither Pop nor the girl had the faintest idea of what it was. I certainly hadn't.

"Had he pushed the button?" the girl asked. Her voice was throaty but unexpectedly refined, as if she'd done no talking at all, not even to herself, since coming to the Deathlands, and so retained the cultured intonations she'd had earlier, whenever and wherever that had been. It gave me a funny feeling, of course, because they were the first words I'd heard her speak.

"Not from the way he was holding it," I told her. "The button was pointed up toward his thumb but the thumb was on the outside of his fingers." I felt an unexpected satisfaction at having expressed myself so clearly, and I told myself not to get childish.

The girl slitted her eyes. "Don't you push it, Ray," she said.

"Think I'm nuts?" I told her, meanwhile sliding the cube into the smaller pocket of my pants, where it fit tight and wouldn't turn sideways and the button maybe get pressed by accident. The tingling in my right arm was almost unbearable now, but I was getting control over the muscles again.

"Pushing that button," I added, "might melt what's left of the plane, or blow us all up." It never hurts to emphasize that you may have another weapon in your possession, even it it's just a suicide bomb.

"There was a man pushed another button once," Pop said softly and reflectively. His gaze went far out over the Deathlands and took in a good half of the horizon and he slowly shook his head. Then his face brightened. "Did you know, Ray," he said, "that I actually met that man? Long afterward. You don't believe me, I know, but I actually did. Tell you about it some other time."

I almost said, "Thanks, Pop, for sparing me at least for a while," but I was afraid that would set him off again. Besides, it wouldn't have been quite true. I've heard other buggers tell the yarn of how they met (and invariably rubbed out) the actual guy who pushed the button or buttons that set the fusion missiles blasting toward their targets, but I felt a sudden curiosity as to what Pop's version of the yarn would be. Oh well, I could ask him some other time, if we both lived that long. I started to check the Pilot's pockets. My right hand could help a little now.

"Those look like mean burns you got there, lady," I heard Pop tell the girl. He was right. There were blisters easy to see on three of the fingertips. "I've got some salve that's pretty good," he went on, "and some clean cloth. I could put on a bandage for you if you wanted. If your hand started to feel poisoned from my salve you could always tell Ray here to slip a knife in me."

Pop was a cute gasser, you had to admit. I reminded myself that it was Pop's business to play up to the both of us, charm being the secret weapon of all scroungers.

The girl gave a harsh little laugh. "Very well," she said, "but we will use my salve. I know it works for me." And she started to lead Pop to where we'd hidden our things.

"I'll go with you," I told them, standing up.

It didn't look like we were going to have any more murders today—Pop had got through the preliminary ingratiations pretty well, and the girl and me had had our catharsis—but that would be no excuse for any such stupidity as letting the two of them get near my .38.

Strolling to the cave and back I eased the situation a

bit more by saying, "That scream you let off, Pop, really helped. I don't know what gave you the idea, but thanks."

"Oh that," he said. "Forget about it."

"I won't," I told him. "You may say you've quit killing, but you helped on a do-in today."

"Ray," he said a little solemnly, "if it'll make you feel any happier, I'll take a bit of the responsibility for every murder that's been done since the beginning of time."

I looked at him for a while. Then, "Pop, you're not by any chance the religious type?" I asked suddenly.

"Lord, no," he told us.

That struck me as a satisfactory answer. God preserve me from the religious type! We have quite a few of those in the Deathlands. It generally means that they try to convert you to something before they kill you. Or sometimes afterward.

We completed our errands. I felt a lot more secure with Old Financier's Friend strapped to my middle. Mother is wonderful but she is not enough.

I dawdled over inspecting the Pilot's pockets, partly to give my right hand time to come back all the way. And to tell the truth I didn't much enjoy the job—a corpse, especially such a handsome cadaver as this, just didn't go with Pop's brand of light patter.

Pop did up the girl's hand in high style, bandaging each finger separately and then persuading her to put on a big left-hand work glove he took out of his small pack.

"Lost the right," he explained, "which was the only one I ever used anyway. Never knew until now why I kept this. How does it feel, Alice?"

I might have known he'd worm her name out of her. It occurred to me that Pop's ideas of scrounging might extend to Alice's favors. The urge doesn't die out when you get old, they tell me. Not completely.

He'd also helped her replace the knife on her stump with the hook.

By that time I'd poked into all the pilot's pockets I could get at without stripping him and found nothing but three irregularly shaped blobs of metal, still hot to the touch. Under the charred spots, of course.

I didn't want the job of stripping him. Somebody else could do a little work, I told myself. I've been bothered by bodies before (as who hasn't, I suppose?), but this one was really beginning to make me sick. Maybe I was cracking up, it occurred to me. Murder is a very wearing business, as all Deathlanders know, and although some crack earlier than others, all crack in the end.

I must have been showing how I was feeling because, "Cheer up, Ray," Pop said. "You and Alice have done a big murder—I'd say the subject was six foot ten—so you ought to be happy. You've drawn a blank on his pockets but there's still the plane."

"Yeah, that's right," I said, brightening a little. "There's still the stuff in the plane." I knew there were some items I couldn't hope for, like .38 shells, but there'd be food and other things.

"Nuh-uh," Pop corrected me. "I said *the plane*. You may have thought it's wrecked, but I don't. Have you taken a real gander at it? It's worth doing, believe me."

I jumped up. My heart was suddenly pounding. I was glad of an excuse to get away from the body, but there was a lot more in my feelings than that. I was filled with an excitement to which I didn't want to give a name because it would make the letdown too great.

One of the wide stubby wings of the plane, raking downward so that its tip almost touched the concrete, had hidden the undercarriage of the fuselage from our view. Now, coming around the wing. I saw that *there was no undercarriage*.

I had to drop to my hands and knees and scan around with my cheek next to the concrete before I'd believe it. *The "wrecked" plane was at all points at least six inches off the ground.*

I got to my feet again. I was shaking. I wanted to talk but I couldn't. I grabbed the leading edge of the wing to stop from falling. The whole body of the plane gave a fraction of an inch and then resisted my leaning weight with lazy power, just like a gyróscope.

"Antigravity," I croaked, though you couldn't have heard me two feet. Then my voice came back. "Pop, Alice! They got antigravity! Antigravity—and it's working!"

Alice had just come around the wing and was facing me. She was shaking too, and her face was white like I knew mine was. Pop was politely standing off a little to one side, watching us curiously. "Told you you'd won a real prize," he said in his matter-of-fact way.

Alice wet her lips. "Ray," she said, "we can get away."

Just those four words, but they did it. Something in me unlocked—no, exploded describes it better.

"We can go places!" I almost shouted.

"Beyond the dust," she said. "Mexico City. South America!" She was forgetting the Deathlander's cynical article of belief that the dust never ends, but then so was I. It makes a difference whether or not you've got a means of doing something.

"Rio!" I topped her with. "The Indies. Hong Kong. Bombay. Egypt. Bermuda. The French Riviera!"

"Bullfights and clean beds," she burst out with. "Restaurants. Swimming pools. Bathrooms!"

"Skindiving," I took it up with, as hysterical as she was. "Road races and roulette tables."

"Bentleys and Porsches!"

"Aircoups and DC4s and Comets!"

"Martinis and hashish and ice cream sodas!"

"Hot food! Fresh coffee! Gambling, smoking, dancing, music, drinks!" I was going to add *women,* but then I thought of how hard-bitten little Alice would look beside the dream creatures I had in mind. I tactfully suppressed the word but I filed the idea away.

I don't think either of us knew exactly what we were saying. Alice in particular I don't believe was old enough to have experienced almost any of the things the words referred to. They were mysterious symbols of long-interdicted delights spewing out of us.

"Ray," Alice said, hurrying to me, "let's get aboard."

"Yes," I said eagerly and then I saw a little problem. The door to the plane was a couple of feet above our heads. Whoever hoisted himself up first—or got hoisted up, as would have to be the case with Alice on account of her hand—would be momentarily at the other's mercy. I guess it occurred to Alice too because she stopped and looked at me. It was a little like the old teaser about the fox, the goose, and the corn.

Maybe, too, we were both a little scared the plane was boobytrapped.

Pop solved the problem in the direct way I might have expected of him by stepping quietly between us, giving a light leap, catching hold of the curving sill, chinning himself on it, and scrambling up into the plane so quickly that we'd hardly have had time to do anything about it if we'd wanted to. Pop couldn't be much more than a bantamweight, even with all his knives. The plane sagged an inch and then swung up again.

As Pop disappeared from view I backed off, reaching for my .38, but a moment later he stuck out his head and grinned down at us, resting his elbows on the sill.

"Come on up," he said. "It's quite a place. I promise not to push any buttons 'til you get here, though there's whole regiments of them."

I grinned back at Pop and gave Alice a boost up. She didn't like it, but she could see it had to be her next. She hooked onto the sill and Pop caught hold of her left wrist below the big glove and heaved.

Then it was my turn. I didn't like it. I didn't like the idea of those two buggers poised above me while my hands were helpless on the sill. But I thought *Pop's a nut. You can trust a nut, at least a little ways, though you can't trust nobody else.* I heaved myself up. It was strange to feel the plane giving and then bracing itself like something alive. It seemed to have no trouble accepting our combined weight, which after all was hardly more than half again the Pilot's.

Inside the cabin was pretty small but as Pop had implied, oh my! Everything looked soft and smoothly curved, like you imagine your insides being, and almost everything was a restfully dull silver. The general shape of it was something like the inside of an egg. Forward, which was the larger end, were a couple of screens and a wide viewport and some small dials and the button brigades Pop had mentioned, lined up like blank typewriter keys but enough for writing Chinese.

Just aft of the instrument panel were two very comfortable-looking strange low seats. They seemed to be facing backward until I realized they were meant to be knelt into. The occupant, I could see, would sort of sprawl forward, his hands free for button-pushing and such. There were spongy chinrests.

Aft was a tiny instrument panel and a kind of sideways

seat, not nearly so fancy. The door by which we'd entered was to the side, a little aft.

I didn't see any indications of cabinets or fixed storage spaces of any kind, but somehow stuck to the walls here and there were quite a few smooth blobby packages, mostly dull silver too, some large, some small—valises and handbags, you might say.

All in all, it was a lovely cabin and, more than that, it seemed lived in. It looked as if it had been shaped for, and maybe by, one man. It had a personality you could feel, a strong but warm personality of its own.

Then I realized whose personality it was. I almost got sick—so close to it I started telling myself it must be something antigravity did to your stomach.

But it was all too interesting to let you get sick right away. Pop was poking into two of the large mound-shaped cases that were sitting loose and open on the right-hand seat, as if ready for emergency use. One had a folded something with straps on it that was probably a parachute. The second had, I judged, a thousand or more of the inch cubes such as I'd pried out of the Pilot's hand, all neatly stacked in a cubical box inside the soft outer bag. You could see the one-cube gap where he'd taken the one.

I decided to take the rest of the bags off the walls and open them, if I could figure out how. The others had the same idea, but Alice had to take off her hook and put on her pliers before she could make progress. Pop helped her. There was room enough for us to do these things without crowding each other too closely.

By the time Alice was set to go I'd discovered the trick of getting the bags off. You couldn't pull them away from the wall no matter what force you used, at least I couldn't, and you couldn't even slide them straight along the walls, but if you just gave them a gentle counterclockwise twist they came off like nothing. Twisting them clockwise glued them back on. It was very strange, but I told myself that if these boys could generate antigravity fields they could create screwy fields of other sorts.

It also occurred to me to wonder if "these boys" came from Earth. The Pilot had looked human enough, but these accomplishments didn't—not by my standards for human achievement in the Age of the Deaders. At any rate I had to admit to myself that my pet term "cultural queer" did not describe to my own satisfaction members of a culture which could create things like this cabin. Not that I liked making the admission. It's hard to admit an exception to a pet gripe against things.

The excitement of getting down and opening the Christmas packages saved me from speculating too much along these or any other lines.

I hit a minor jackpot right away. In the same bag were a compass, a catalytic pocket lighter, a knife with a saw-tooth back edge that made my affection for Mother waver, a dust mask, what looked like a compact water-filtration unit, and several other items adding up to a deluxe Death-lands Survival Kit.

There were some goggles in the kit I didn't savvy until I put them on and surveyed the landscape out the viewport. A nearby dust drift I knew to be hot glowed green as death in the slightly smoky lenses. Wow! Those specs had Geiger counters beat a mile, and I privately bet myself they worked at night. I stuck them in my pocket quick.

We found bunches of tiny electronics parts—I think they were; spools of magnetic tape, but nothing to play it on; reels of very narrow film with frames much too small to see anything at all unmagnified; about three thousand cigarettes in unlabeled transparent packs of twenty—we lit up quick, using my new lighter; a picture book that didn't make much sense because the views might have been of tissue sections or starfields, we couldn't quite decide, and there were no captions to help; a thin book with ricepaper pages covered with Chinese characters—*that* was a puzzler; a thick book with nothing but columns of figures, all zeros and ones and nothing else; some tiny chisels; and a mouth organ. Pop, who'd made a point of just helping in the hunt, appropriated that last item—I might have known he would, I told myself. Now we could expect "Turkey in the Straw" at odd moments.

Alice found a whole bag of what were women's things judging from the frilliness of the garments included. She set aside some squeeze-packs and little gadgets and elastic items right away, but she didn't take any of the clothes. I caught her measuring some kind of transparent chemise against herself when she thought we weren't looking; it was for a girl maybe six sizes bigger.

And we found food. Cans of food that was heated up

inside by the time you got the top rolled off, though the outside could still be cool to the touch. Cans of boneless steak, boneless chops, cream soup, peas, carrots, and fried potatoes—they weren't labeled at all, but you could generally guess the contents from the shape of the can. Eggs that heated when you touched them and were soft-boiled evenly and barely firm by the time you had the shell broke. And small plastic bottles of strong coffee that heated up hospitably too—in this case the tops did a five-second hesitation in the middle of your unscrewing them.

At that point, as you can imagine, we let the rest of the packages go and had ourselves a feast. The food ate even better than it smelled. It was real hard for me not to gorge.

Then as I was slurping down my second bottle of coffee I happened to look out the viewport and see the Pilot's body and the darkening puddle around it, and the coffee began to taste, well, not bad, but sickening. I don't think it was guilty conscience. Deathlanders outgrow that if they ever have it to start with; loners don't keep consciences—it takes cultures to give you those and make them work. Artistic inappropriateness is the closest I can come to describing what bothered me. Whatever it was, it made me feel lousy for a minute.

About the same time Alice did an odd thing with the last of *her* coffee. She slopped it on a rag and used it to wash her face. I guess she'd caught a reflection of herself with the blood smears. She didn't eat any more after that either. Pop kept on chomping away, a slow feeder and appreciative.

To be doing something, I started to inspect the instrument panel, and right away I was all excited again. The two screens were what got me. They showed shadowy maps, one of North America, the other of the world. The first one was a whole lot like the map I'd been imagining earlier— faint colors marked the small "civilized" areas including one in Eastern Canada and another in Upper Michigan that must be "countries" I didn't know about, and the Deathlands were real dark, just as I'd always maintained they should be!

South of Lake Michigan was a brightly luminous green point that must be where we were, I decided. And for some reason the colored areas representing Los Alamos and Atlantic Highlands were glowing brighter than the others—they had an active luminosity. Los Alamos was blue, Atla-Hi violet. Los Alamos was shown having more territory than I expected. Savannah Fortress, for that matter, was a whole *lot* bigger than I'd have made it, pushing out pseudopods west and northeast along the coast, though its red didn't have the extra glow. But its growth-pattern reeked of imperialism.

The world screen showed dim color patches too, but for the moment I was more interested in the other.

The button armies marched right up to the lower edge of the screens, and right away I got the crazy hunch that they were connected with spots on the map. Push the button for a certain spot and the plane would go there! Why, one button even seemed to have a faint violet nimbus around it (or else my eyes were going bad) as if to say, "Push me and we go to Atlantic Highlands."

A crazy notion, as I say, and no sensible way to handle a plane's navigation according to any standards I could imagine, but then as I've also said this plane didn't seem to be designed according to any standards but rather in line with one man's ideas, including his whims.

At any rate that was my hunch about the buttons and the screens. It tantalized rather than helped, for the only button that seemed to be marked in any way was the one (guessing by color) for Atlantic Highlands, and I certainly didn't want to go there. Like Alamos, Atla-Hi has the reputation for being a mysteriously dangerous place. Not openly mean and death-on-Deathlanders like Walla Walla or Porter, but buggers who swing too close to Atla-Hi have a way of never turning up again. You never expect to see again two out of three buggers who pass in the night, but for three out of three to keep disappearing is against statistics.

Alice was beside me now, scanning things over too, and from the way she frowned and what not I gathered she had caught my hunch and also shared my puzzlement.

Now was the time, all right, when we needed an instruction manual, and not one in Chinese neither!

Pop swallowed a mouthful and said, "Yep, now'd be a good time to have him back for a minute, to explain things a bit. Oh, don't take offense, Ray; I know how it was for you and for you too, Alice. I know the both of you *had to* murder him; it wasn't a matter of free choice, it's the way us Deathlanders are built. Just the same, it'd be nice to have a way of killing 'em and keeping them on hand at the same time. I remember feeling that way after murdering the Alamoser I told you about. You see, I come down with the very fever I'd faked and almost died of it, while the man who could have cured me easy wouldn't do nothing but perfume the landscape with the help of a gang of anaerobic bacteria. Stubborn single-minded cuss!"

The first part of that oration started up my sickness again and irked me not a little. Dammit, what right had Pop to talk about how all us Deathlanders *had to* kill (which was true enough and by itself would have made me cotton to him) if, as he'd claimed earlier, *he'd* been able to quit killing? Pop was an old hypocrite, I told myself—he'd helped murder the Pilot, he'd admitted as much—and Alice and me'd be better off, if we bedded the both of them down together. But then the second part of what Pop said so made me want to feel pleasantly sorry for myself and laugh at the same time that I forgave the old geezer. Practically everything Pop said had that reassuring touch of insanity about it.

So it was Alice who said, "Shut up, Pop"—and rather casually at that—and she and me went on to speculate and then to argue about which buttons we ought to push, if any, and in what order.

"Why not just start anywhere and keep pushing 'em one after another?—you're going to have to eventually, may as well start now," was Pop's lighthearted contribution to the discussion. "Got to take some chances in this life." He was sitting in the back seat and still nibbling away like a white-topped mangy old squirrel.

Of course Alice and me knew more than that. We kept making guesses as to how the buttons worked and then backing up our guesses with hot language. It was a little like two savages trying to decide how to play chess by looking at the pieces. And then the old escape-to-paradise theme took hold of us again and we studied the colored blobs on the world screen, trying to decide which would have the fanciest accommodations for blasé ex-murderers. On the North America screen, too, there was an intriguing pink patch in southern Mexico that seemed to take in old Mexico City and Acapulco too.

"Quit talking and start pushing," Pop prodded us. "This way you're getting nowhere fast. I can't stand hesitation; it riles my nerves."

Alice thought you ought to push ten buttons at once, using both hands, and she was working out patterns for me to try. But I was off on a kick about how we should darken the plane to see if any of the other buttons glowed beside the one with the Atla-Hi violet.

"Look here, you killed a big man to get this plane," Pop broke in, coming up behind me. "Are you going to use it for discussion groups or are you going to fly it?"

"Quiet," I told him. I'd got a new hunch and was using the dark glasses to scan the instrument panel. They didn't show anything.

"Dammit, I can't stand this any more," Pop said and reached a hand and arm between us and brought it down on about fifty buttons, I'd judge.

The other buttons just went down and up, but the Atla-Hi button went down and stayed down.

The violet blob of Atla-Hi on the screen got even brighter in the next few moments.

The door closed with a tiny thud.

We took off.

IV

Any man who deals in murder, must have very incorrect ways of thinking, and truly inaccurate principles.

—Murder Considered as One of the Fine Arts

BY THOMAS DE QUINCEY

FOR that matter we took off *fast* with the plane swinging to beat hell. Alice and me was in the two kneeling seats and we hugged them tight, but Pop was loose and sort of rattled around the cabin for a while—and serve him right!

On one of the swings I caught a glimpse of the seven dented gas tanks, looking like dull crescents from this angle through the orange haze and getting rapidly smaller as they hazed out.

After a while the plane leveled off and quit swinging, and a while after that my image of the cabin quit swinging too. Once again I just managed to stave off the vomits, this time the vomits from natural causes. Alice looked very pale around the gills and kept her face buried in the chin-rest of her chair.

Pop ended up right in our faces, sort of spread-eagled against the instrument panel. In getting himself off it he must have braced his hands against half the buttons at one time or another and I noticed that none of them went down a fraction. They were *locked*. It had probably happened automatically when the Atla-Hi button got pushed.

I'd have stopped him messing around in that apish way, but with the ultra-queasy state of my stomach I lacked all ambition and was happy just not to be smelling him so close.

I still wasn't taking too great an interest in things as I idly watched the old geezer rummaging around the cabin for something that got misplaced in the shake-up. Eventually he found it—a small almond-shaped can. He opened it. Sure enough it turned out to have almonds in it. He fitted himself in the back seat and munched them one at a time. Ish!

"Nothing like a few nuts to top off with," he said cheerfully.

I could have cut his throat even more cheerfully, but the damage had been done and you think twice before you kill a person in close quarters when you aren't absolutely sure you'll be able to dispose of the body. How did I know I'd be able to open the door? I remember philosophizing that Pop ought at least to have broke an arm so he'd be as badly off as Alice and me (though for that matter my right arm was fully recovered now), but he was all in one piece. There's no justice in events, that's for sure.

The plane ploughed along silently through the orange soup, though there was really no way to tell it was moving now—until a skewy spindle shape loomed up ahead and shot back over the viewport. I think it was a vulture. I don't know how vultures manage to operate in the haze, which ought to cancel their keen eyesight, but they do. It shot past *fast*.

Alice lifted her face out of the sponge stuff and began to study the buttons again. I heaved myself up and around a little and said, "Pop, Alice and me are going to try to work out how this plane navigates. This time we don't want no interference." I didn't say a word more about what he'd done. It never does to hash over stupidities.

"That's perfectly fine, go right ahead," he told me. "I feel calm as a kitten now we're going somewheres. That's all that ever matters with me." He chuckled a bit and added, "You got to admit I gave you and Alice something to work with," but then he had the sense to shut up tight.

We weren't so chary of pushing buttons this time, but ten minutes or so convinced us that you couldn't push any of the buttons any more, they *were* all locked down—all locked except for maybe one, which we didn't try at first for a special reason.

We looked for other controls—sticks, levers, pedals, finger-holes and the like. There weren't any. Alice went back and tried the buttons on Pop's minor console. They were locked too. Pop looked interested but didn't say a word.

We realized in a general way what had happened, of course. Pushing the Atla-Hi button had set us on some kind of irreversible automatic. I couldn't imagine the why of gim-micking a plane's controls like that, unless maybe to keep loose children or prisoners from being able to mess things up while the pilot took a snooze, but there were a lot of whys to this plane that didn't seem to have any standard answers.

The business of taking off on irreversible automatic had happened so neatly that I naturally wondered whether Pop might not know more about navigating this plane than he let on, a whole lot more in fact, and the seemingly idiotic petulance of his pushing all the buttons have been a shrewd cover for pushing the Atla-Hi button. But if Pop had been acting, he'd been acting beautifully, with a serene disregard for the chances of breaking his own neck. I decided this was a possibility I could think about later and maybe act on then, after Alice and me had worked through the more obvious stuff.

The reason we hadn't tried the one button yet was that

it showed a green nimbus, just like the Atla-Hi button had had a violet nimbus. Now there was no green on either of the screens except for the tiny green star that I had figured stood for the plane, and it didn't make sense to go where we already were. And if it meant some other place, some place not shown on the screens, you bet we weren't going to be too quick about deciding to go there. It might not be on Earth.

Alice expressed it by saying, "My namesake was always a little too quick at responding to those DRINK ME cues."

I suppose she thought she was being cryptic, but I fooled her. *"Alice in Wonderland?"* I asked. She nodded and gave me a little smile, not at all like one of the EAT ME smiles she'd given me last evening.

It is funny how crazily happy a little touch of the intellectual past like that can make you feel—and how horribly uncomfortable a moment later.

We both started to study the North America screen again and almost at once we realized that it had changed in one small particular. The green star had twinned. Where there had been one point of green light there were now two, very close together like the double star in the handle of the Dipper. We watched it for a while. The distance between the two stars grew perceptibly greater. We watched it for a while longer, considerably longer. It became clear that the position of the more westerly star on the screen was fixed, while the more easterly star was moving east toward Atla-Hi with about the speed of the tip of the minute hand on a wristwatch (two inches an hour, say). The pattern began to make sense.

I figured it this way: the moving star must stand for the plane, the other green dot must stand for where the plane had just been. For some reason the spot on the freeway by the old cracking plant was recognized as a marked locality by the screen. Why, I don't know. It reminded me of the old "X Marks the Spot" of newspaper murders, but that would be getting very fancy. Anyway the spot we'd just taken off from was so marked, and in that case the button with green nimbus . . .

"Hold tight, everybody," I said to Alice, grudgingly including Pop in my warning. "I got to try it."

I gripped my seat with my knees and one arm and pushed the green button. It pushed.

The plane swung around in a level loop, not too tight to disturb the stomach much, and steadied out again.

I couldn't judge how far we'd swung but Alice and me watched the green stars and after about a minute she said, "They're getting closer," and a little while later I said, "Yeah, for sure."

I scanned the board. The green button—the cracking-plant button, to call it that—was locked down of course. The Atla-Hi button was up, glowing violet. All the other buttons were still up and *locked* up—I tried them all again.

It was clear as day used to be. We could either go to Atla-Hi or we could go back where we'd started from. There was no third possibility.

It was a little hard to take. You think of a plane as freedom, as something that will carry you anywhere in the world you choose to go, especially any paradise, and then you find yourself worse limited than if you'd stayed on the ground—at least that was the way it was happening to us.

But Alice and me were realists. We knew it wouldn't help to wail. We were up against another of those "two" problems, the problem of two destinations, and we had to choose ours.

If we go back, I thought, *we can trek on somewhere—anywhere—richer by the loot from the plane, especially that Survival Kit. Trek on with some loot we'll mostly never understand and with the knowledge that we are leaving a plane that can fly, that we are shrinking back from an unknown adventure.*

Also, if we go back, there's something else we'll have to face, something we'll have to live with for a little while at least that won't be nice to live with after this cozily personal cabin, something that shouldn't bother me at all but, dammit, it does.

Alice made the decision for us and at the same time showed she was thinking about the same thing as me.

"I don't want to have to smell him, Ray," she said. "I am not going back to keep company with that filthy corpse. I'd rather anything than that." And she pushed the Atla-Hi button again, and as the plane started to swing she looked at me defiantly as if to say I'd reverse the course again over her dead body.

"Don't tense up," I told her. "I want a new shake of the dice myself."

"You know, Alice," Pop said reflectively, "it was the smell of my Alamoser got to me too. I just couldn't bear it. I couldn't get away from it because my fever had me pinned down, so there was nothing left for me to do but go crazy. No Atla-Hi for me, just Bug-land. My mind died, though not my memory. By the time I'd got my strength back I'd started to be a new bugger. I didn't know no more about living than a newborn babe, except I knew I couldn't go back—go back to murdering and all that. My new mind knew that much, though otherwise it was just a blank. It was all very funny."

"And then I suppose," Alice cut in, her voice corrosive with sarcasm, "you hunted up a wandering preacher, or perhaps a kindly old hermit who lived on hot manna, and he showed you the blue sky!"

"Why no, Alice," Pop said. "I told you I don't go for religion. As it happens, I hunted me up a couple of murderers, guys who were worse cases than myself but who'd wanted to quit because it wasn't getting them nowhere and who'd found, I'd heard, a way of quitting, and the three of us had a long talk together."

"And they told you the great secret of how to live in the Deathlands without killing," Alice continued acidly. "Drop the nonsense, Pop. It can't be done."

"It's hard, I'll grant you," Pop said. "You have to go crazy or something almost as bad—in fact, maybe going crazy is the easiest way. But it can be done and, in the long run, murder is even harder."

I decided to interrupt this idle chatter. Since we were now definitely headed for Atla-Hi and there was nothing to do until we got there, unless one of us got a brainstorm about the controls, it was time to start on the less obvious stuff I'd tabled in my mind.

"Why are you on this plane, Pop?" I asked sharply. "What do you figure on getting out of Alice and me?—and I don't mean the free meals."

He grinned. His teeth were white and even—plates, of course. "Why, Ray," he said, "I was just giving Alice the reason. I like to talk to murderers, practicing murderers preferred. I need to—*have* to talk to 'em, to keep myself straight. Otherwise I might start killing again and I'm not up to that any more."

"Oh, so you get your kicks at second hand, you old peeper," Alice put in, but, "Quit lying, Pop," I said. "About having quit killing, for one thing. In my books, which happen to be the old books in this case, the accomplice is every bit as guilty as the man with the slicer. You helped us kill the Pilot by giving that funny scream, and you know it."

"Who says I did?" Pop countered, rearing up a little. "I never said so. I just said, 'Forget it.'" He hesitated a moment, studying me. Then he said, "I wasn't the one gave that scream. In fact, I'd have stopped it if I'd been able."

"Who did then?"

Again he studied me as he hesitated. "I'm not telling," he said, settling back.

"Pop!" I said, sharp again. "Buggers who pad together tell everything."

"Oh yeah," he agreed, smiling. "I remember saying that to quite a few guys in my day. It's a very restful comradely sentiment. I killed every last one of 'em, too."

"You may have, Pop," I granted, "but we're two to one."

"So you are," he agreed softly, looking the both of us over. I knew what he was thinking—that Alice still had just her pliers on and that in these close quarters his knives were as good as my gun.

"Give me your right hand, Alice," I said. Without taking my eyes off Pop I reached the knife without a handle out of her belt and then I started to unscrew the pliers out of her stump.

"Pop," I said as I did so, "you may have quit killing for all I know. I mean you may have quit killing clean decent Deathland style. But I don't believe one bit of that guff about having to talk to murderers to keep your mind sweet. Furthermore—"

"It's true though," he interrupted. "I got to keep myself reminded of how lousy it feels to be a murderer."

"So?" I said. "Well, here's one person who believes you've got a more practical reason for being on this plane. Pop, what's the bounty Atla-Hi gives you for every Deathlander you bring in? What would it be for two live Deathlanders?

And what sort of reward would they pay for a lost plane brought in? Seems to me they might very well make you a citizen for that."

"Yes, even give you your own church," Alice added with a sort of wicked gaiety. I squeezed her stump gently to tell her let me handle it.

"Why, I guess you can believe that if you want to," Pop said and let out a soft breath. "Seems to me you need a lot of coincidences and happenstances to make that theory hold water, but you sure can believe it if you want to. I got no way, Ray, to prove to you I'm telling the truth except to say I am."

"Right," I said and then I threw the next one at him real fast. "What's more, Pop, weren't you traveling in this plane to begin with? That cuts a happenstance. Didn't you hop out while we were too busy with the Pilot to notice and just *pretend* to be coming from the cracking plant? Weren't the buttons locked because you were the Pilot's prisoner?"

Pop creased his brow thoughtfully. "It could have been that way," he said at last. "Could have been—according to the evidence as you saw it. It's quite a bright idea, Ray. I can almost see myself skulking in this cabin, while you and Alice—"

"You were skulking somewhere," I said. I finished screwing in the knife and gave Alice back her hand. "I'll repeat it, Pop," I said. "We're two to one. You'd better talk."

"Yes," Alice added, disregarding my previous hint. "You may have given up fighting, Pop, but I haven't. Not fighting, nor killing, nor anything in between those two. Any least thing." My girl was being her most pantherish.

"Now who says I've given up *fighting?*" Pop demanded, rearing a little again. "You people assume too much; it's a dangerous habit. Before we have any trouble and somebody squawks about me cheating, let's get one thing straight. If anybody jumps me I'll try to disable them, I'll try to hurt them in any way short of killing, and that means hamstringing and rabbit-punching and everything else. Every least thing, Alice. And if they happen to die while I'm honestly just trying to hurt them in a way short of killing, then I won't grieve too much. My conscience will be reasonably clear. Is that understood?"

I had to admit that it was. Pop might be lying about

a lot of things, but I just didn't believe he was lying about this. And I already knew Pop was quick for his age and strong enough. If Alice and me jumped him now there'd be blood let six different ways. You can't jump a man who has a dozen knives easy to hand and not expect that to happen, two to one or not. We'd get him in the end, but it would be gory.

"And now," Pop said quietly, "I *will* talk a little if you don't mind. Look here, Ray . . . Alice, . . . the two of you are confirmed murderers, I know you wouldn't tell me nothing different, and being such you both know that there's nothing in murder in the long run. It satisfies a hunger and maybe gets you a little loot and it lets you get on to the next killing. But that's all, absolutely all. Yet you got to do it because it's the way you're built. The urge is there, it's an overpowering urge, and you got nothing to oppose it with. You feel the Big Grief and the Big Resentment, the dust is eating at your bones, you can't stand the city squares—the Porterites and Mantenors and such—because you know they're whistling in the dark and it's a dirty tune, so you go on killing. But if there were a decent practical way to quit, you'd take it. At least I think you would. When you still thought this plane could take you to Rio or Europe you felt that way, didn't you? You weren't planning to go there as murderers, were you? You were going to leave your trade behind."

It was pretty quiet in the cabin for a couple of seconds. Then Alice's thin laugh sliced the silence. "We were dreaming then," she said. "We were out of our heads. But now you're talking about practical things, as you say. What do you expect us to do if we quit our trade, as you call it—go into Walla Walla or Ouachita and give ourselves up? I might lose more than my right hand at Ouachita this time—that was just on suspicion."

"Or Atla-Hi," I added meaningfully. "Are you expecting us to admit we're murderers when we get to Atla-Hi, Pop?"

The old geezer smiled and thinned his eyes. "Now that wouldn't accomplish much, would it? Most places they'd just string you up, maybe after tickling your pain nerves a bit, or if it was Manteno they might put you in a cage and feed you slops and pray over you, and would that help you or anybody else? If a man or woman quits killing there's a lot of things he's got to straighten out—first his own mind and feelings, next he's got to do what he can to make up for the murders he's done—help the next of kin if any and so on—then he's got to carry the news to other killers who haven't heard it yet. He's got no time to waste being hanged. Believe me, he's got work lined up for him, work that's got to be done mostly in the Deathlands, and it's the sort of work the city squares can't help him with one bit, because they just don't understand us murderers and what makes us tick. We have to do it ourselves."

"Hey, Pop," I cut in, getting a little interested in the argument (there wasn't anything else to get interested in until we got to Atla-Hi or Pop let down his guard), "I dig you on the city squares (I call 'em cultural queers) and what sort of screwed-up fatheads they are; but just the same, for a man to quit killing he's got to quit lone-wolfing it. He's got to belong to a community, he's got to have a culture of some sort, no matter how disgusting or nutsy."

"Well," Pop said, "don't us Deathlanders have a culture? With customs and folkways and all the rest? A very tight little culture, in fact. Nutsy as all get out, of course, but that's one of the beauties of it."

"Oh sure," I granted him, "but it's a culture based on murder and devoted wholly to murder. Murder is our way of life. That gets your argument nowhere, Pop."

"Correction," he said. "Or rather, reinterpretation." And now for a little while his voice got less old-man harsh and yet bigger somehow, as if it were more than just Pop talking. "Every culture," he said, "is a way of growth as well as a way of life, because the first law of life is growth. Our Deathland culture is devoted to growing *through* murder *away from* murder. That's my thought. It's about the toughest way of growth anybody was ever asked to face up to, but it's a way of growth just the same. A lot bigger and fancier cultures never could figure out the answer to the problem of war and killing—*we* know that, all right, we inhabit their grandest failure. Maybe us Deathlanders, working with murder every day, unable to pretend that it isn't part of every one of us, unable to put it out of our minds like the city squares do—maybe us Deathlanders are the ones to do that little job."

"But hell, Pop," I objected, getting excited in spite of myself, "even if we got a culture here in the Deathlands, a culture that can grow, it ain't a culture that can deal with repentant murderers. In a *real* culture a murderer feels guilty and confesses and then he gets hanged or imprisoned a long time and that squares things for him and everybody. You need religion and courts and hangmen and screws and all the rest of it. I don't think it's enough for a man just to say he's sorry and go around gladhanding other killers—*that* isn't going to be enough to wipe out his sense of guilt."

Pop squared his eyes at mine. "Are you so fancy that you have to have a sense of guilt, Ray?" he demanded. "Can't you just see when something's lousy? A sense of guilt's a luxury. Of course it's not enough to say you're sorry—you're going to have to spend a good part of the rest of your life making up for what you've done . . . and what you will do, too! But about hanging and prisons—was it ever proved those were the right things for murderers? As for religion, now—some of us who've quit killing are religious and a lot of us (me included) aren't; and some of the ones that are religious figure (maybe because there's no way for them to get hanged) that they're damned eternally —but that doesn't stop them doing good work. I ask you now, is any little thing like being damned eternally a satisfactory excuse for behaving like a complete rat?"

That did it, somehow. That last statement of Pop's appealed so much to me and was so completely crazy at the same time, that I couldn't help warming up to him. Don't get me wrong, I didn't really fall for his line of chatter at all, but I found it fun to go along with it—so long as the plane was in this shuttle situation and we had nothing better to do.

Alice seemed to feel the same way. I guess any bugger that could kid religion the way Pop could got a little silver star in her books. Bronze, anyway.

Right away the atmosphere got easier. To start with we asked Pop to tell us about this "us" he kept mentioning, and he said it was some dozens (or hundreds—nobody had accurate figures) of killers who'd quit and went nomading around the Deathlands trying to recruit others and help those who wanted to be helped. They had semipermanent meeting places where they tried to get together at prearranged dates, but mostly they kept on the go, by twos and threes or—more rarely—alone. They were all men so far, at least

Pop hadn't heard of any women members, but—he assured Alice earnestly—he would personally guarantee that there would be no objections to a girl joining up. They had recently taken to calling themselves Assassins Anonymous, after some prewar organization Pop didn't know the original purpose of. Quite a few of them had slipped and gone back to murdering again, but some of these had come back after a while, more determined than ever to make a go of it.

"We welcomed 'em, of course," Pop said. "We welcome everybody. Everybody that's a genuine murderer, that is, and says he wants to quit. Guys that aren't blooded yet we draw the line at, no matter how fine they are."

Also, "We have a lot of fun at our meetings," Pop assured us. "You never saw such high times. Nobody's got a right to go glooming around or pull a long face just because he's done a killing or two. Religion or no religion, pride's a sin."

Alice and me ate it all up like we was a couple of kids and Pop was telling us fairy tales. That's what it all was, of course, a fairy tale—a crazy mixed-up fairy tale. Alice and me knew there could be no fellowship of Deathlanders like Pop was describing—it was impossible as blue sky—but it gave us a kick to pretend to ourselves for a while to believe in it.

Pop could talk forever, apparently, about murder and murderers, and he had a bottomless bag of funny stories on the same topic and character vignettes—the murderers who were forever wanting their victims to understand and forgive them, the ones who thought of themselves as little kings with divine rights of dispensing death, the ones who insisted on laying down (chastely) beside their finished victims and playing dead for a couple of hours, the ones who weren't so chaste, the ones who could only do their killings when they were dressed a certain way (and the troubles they had with their murder costumes), the ones who could only kill people with certain traits or of a certain appearance (red-heads, say, or people who read books, or who couldn't carry tunes, or who used bad language), the ones who always mixed sex and murder and the ones who believed that murder was contaminated by the least breath of sex, the sticklers and the Sloppy Joes, the artists and the butchers, the ax- and stiletto-types, the *com*pulsives and the *re*pulsives—honestly, Pop's portraits from life added up to a Dance of Death as good as anything the Middle Ages ever produced, and they ought to have been illustrated like those by some great artist. Pop told us a lot about his own killings too. Alice and me was interested, but neither of us wasn't tempted into making parallel revelations about ourselves. Your private life's your own business, I felt, as close as your guts, and no joke's good enough to justify revealing a knot of it.

Not that we talked about nothing but murder while we were bulleting along toward Atla-Hi. The conversation was free-wheeling and we got onto all sorts of topics. For instance, we got to talking about the plane and how it flew itself—or levitated itself, rather. I said it must generate an antigravity field that was keyed to the body of the plane but nothing else, so that *we* didn't feel lighter, nor any of the objects in the cabin—it just worked on the dull silvery metal—and I proved my point by using Mother to shave a little wisp of metal off the edge of the control board. The curlicue stayed in the air wherever you put it, and when you moved it you could feel the faintest sort of gyroscopic resistance. It was very strange.

Pop pointed out it was a little like magnetism. A germ riding on an iron filing that was traveling toward the pole of a big magnet wouldn't feel the magnetic pull—it wouldn't be operating on him, only on the iron—but just the same the germ'd be carried along with the filing and feel its acceleration and all, provided he could hold on—but for that purpose you could imagine a tiny cabin in the filing. "That's what we are," Pop added. "Three germs, jumbo size."

Alice wanted to know why an antigravity plane should have even the stubbiest wings or a jet for that matter, for we remembered now we'd noticed the tubes, and I said it was maybe just a reserve system in case the antigravity failed, and Pop guessed it might be for extra-fast battle maneuvering or even for operating outside the atmosphere (which hardly made sense, as I proved to him).

"If we're a battle plane, where's our guns?" Alice asked. None of us had an answer.

We remembered the noise the plane had made before we saw it. It must have been using its jets then. "And do you suppose," Pop asked, "that it was something from the antigravity that made electricity flare out of the top of the cracking plant? Like to have scared the pants off me!" No answer to that either.

Now was a logical time, of course, to ask Pop what he knew about the cracking plant and just who had done the scream if not him, but I figured he still wouldn't talk; as long as we were acting friendly there was no point in spoiling it.

We guessed around a little, though, about where the plane came from. Pop said Alamos, I said Atla-Hi, Alice said why not from both, why couldn't Alamos and Atla-Hi have some sort of treaty and the plane be traveling from the one to the other. We agreed it might be. At least it fitted with the Atla-Hi violet and the Alamos blue being brighter than the other colors.

"I just hope we got some sort of anticollision radar," I said. I guessed we had, because twice we'd jogged in our course a little, maybe to clear the Alleghenies. The easterly green star was by now getting pretty close to the violet blot of Atla-Hi. I looked out at the orange soup, which was *one* thing that hadn't changed a bit so far, and I got to wishing like a baby that it wasn't there and to thinking how it blanketed the whole Earth (stars over the Riviera?—don't make me laugh!) and I heard myself asking, "Pop, did you rub out that guy that pushed the buttons for all this?"

"Nope," Pop answered without hesitation, just as if it hadn't been four hours or so since he'd mentioned the point. "Nope, Ray. Fact is I welcomed him into our little fellowship about six months back. This is *his* knife here, this horn-handle in my boot, though he never killed with it. He claimed he'd been tortured for years by the thought of the millions and millions he'd killed with blast and radiation, but now he was finding peace at last because he was where he belonged, with the murderers, and could start to do something about it. Several of the boys didn't want to let him in. They claimed he wasn't a real murderer, doing it by remote control, no matter how many he bumped off."

"I'd have been on their side," Alice said, thinning her lips.

"Yep," Pop continued, "they got real hot about it. *He* got hot too and all excited and offered to go out and kill somebody with his bare hands right off, or try to (he's a skinny little runt), if that's what he had to do to join. We argued it over. I pointed out that we let ex-soldiers count the killings they'd done in service, and that we counted poisonings and booby traps and such too— which are remote-control killings in a way—so eventually we let him in. He's doing good work. We're fortunate to have him."

"Do you think he's really the guy who pushed the buttons?" I asked Pop.

"How should I know?" Pop replied. "He claims to be."

I was going to say something about people who faked confessions to get a little easy glory, as compared to the guys who were really guilty and would sooner be chopped up than talk about it, but at that moment a fourth voice started talking in the plane. It seemed to be coming out of the violet patch on the North America screen. That is, it came from the general direction of the screen at any rate, and my mind instantly tied it to the violet patch at Atla-Hi. It gave us a fright, I can tell you. Alice grabbed my knee with her pliers (she had changed again), harder than she'd intended, I suppose, though I didn't let out a yip—I was too defensively frozen.

The voice was talking a language I didn't understand at all that went up and down the scale like atonal music.

"Sounds like Chinese," Pop whispered, giving me a nudge.

"It *is* Chinese. Mandarin," the screen responded instantly in the purest English—at least that was how I'd describe it. Practically Boston. "Who are you? And where is Grayl? Come in, Grayl."

I knew well enough who Grayl must be—or rather, have been. I looked at Pop and Alice. Pop grinned, maybe a mite feebly this time, I thought, and gave me a look as if to say, "*You* want to handle it?"

I cleared my throat. Then, "We've taken over for Grayl," I said to the screen.

"Oh." The screen hesitated, just barely. Then, "Do any of 'you' speak Mandarin?"

I hardly bothered to look up at Pop and Alice. "No," I said.

"Oh." Again a tiny pause. "Is Grayl aboard the plane?"

"No." I said.

"Oh. Incapacitated in some way, I suppose?"

"Yes," I said, grateful for the screen's tactfulnes, unintentional or not.

"But you have taken over for him?" the screen pressed.

"Yes," I said, swallowing. I didn't know what I was getting us into, things were moving too fast, but it seemed the merest sense to act cooperative.

"I'm very glad of that," the screen said with something in its tone that made me feel funny—I guess it was sincerity. Then it said, "Is the—" and hesitated, and started again with "Are the blocks aboard?"

I thought. Alice pointed at the stuff she dumped out of the other seat. I said. "There's a box with a thousand or so one-inch underweight steel cubes in it. Like a child's blocks, but with buttons in them. Alongside a box with a parachute."

"That's what I mean," the screen said, and somehow, maybe because whoever was talking was trying to hide it, I caught a note of great relief.

"Look," the screen said, more rapidly now, "I don't know how much you know, but we may have to work very fast. You aren't going to be able to deliver the steel cubes to us directly. In fact you aren't going to be able to land in Atlantic Highlands at all. We're sieged in by planes and ground forces of Savannah Fortress. All our aircraft, such as haven't been destroyed, are pinned down. You're going to have to parachute the blocks to a point as near as possible to one of our ground parties that's made a sortie. We'll give you a signal. I hope it will be later—nearer here, that is—but it may be sooner. Do you know how to fight the plane you're in? Operate its armament?"

"No," I said, wetting my lip.

"Then that's the first thing I'd best teach you. Anything you see in the haze from now on will be from Savannah. You must shoot it down."

V

And we are here as on a darkling plain
Swept with confused alarms of struggle and flight,
Where ignorant armies clash by night.

—Dover Beach

BY MATTHEW ARNOLD

I AM not going to try to describe point by point all that
happened the next half hour because there was too much
of it and it involved all three of us, sometimes doing different
things at the same time, and although we were told a
lot of things, we were seldom if ever told the why of them,
and through it all was the constant impression that we were
dealing with human beings (I almost left out the "human,"
and I'm still not absolutely sure whether I shouldn't) of
vastly greater scope—and probably intelligence too—than
ourselves.

And that was just the *basic* confusion, to give it a
name.

To begin with, it was extremely weird to plunge from
a rather leisurely confab about a fairytale fellowship of
nonpracticing murderers into a shooting war between a
violet blob and a dark red puddle on a shadowy fluorescent
map. The voice didn't throw any great shining lights on
this topic, because after the first—and perhaps unguarded—
revelation, we learned little more of the war between Atla-Hi
and Savannah Fortress and nothing of the reasons behind
it. Presumably Savannah was the aggressor, reaching out
north after the conquest of Birmingham, but even that
was just a guess. It is hard to describe how shadowy it
all felt to me; there were some minutes while my mind
kept mixing up the whole thing with what I'd read long
ago about the Civil War: Savannah was Lee, Atla-Hi was
Grant, and we had been dropped spang into the middle
of the Second Battle of the Wilderness.

Apparently the Savannah planes had some sort of needle

ray as part of their armament—at any rate I was warned to watch out for "swinging lines in the haze, like straight strings of pink stars," and later told to aim at the sources of such lines. And naturally I guessed that the steel cubes must be some crucial weapon for Atla-Hi, or ammunition for a weapon, or parts for some essential instrument like a giant computer, but the voice ignored my questions on that point and didn't fall into the couple of crude conversational traps I tried to set. We were to drop the cubes when told, that was all. Pop had the box of them closed again and rigged to the parachute—he took over that job because Alice and me were busy with other things when the instructions on that came through—and he was told how to open the door of the plane for the drop (you just held your hand steadily on a point beside the door), but, as I say, that was all.

Naturally it occurred to me that once we had made the drop, Atla-Hi would have no more use for us and might simply let us be destroyed by Savannah or otherwise—perhaps *want* us to be destroyed—so that it might be wisest for us to refuse to make the drop when the signal came and hang onto those myriad steel cubes as our only bargaining point. Still, I could see no advantage to refusing *before* the signal came. I'd have liked to discuss the point with Alice and maybe Pop too, but apparently everything we said, even whispered, could be overheard by Atla-Hi. (We never did determine, incidentally, whether Atla-Hi could *see* into the cabin of the plane also. I don't believe they could, though they sure had it bugged for sound.)

All in all, we found out almost nothing about Atla-Hi. In fact, three witless germs traveling in a cabin in an iron filing wasn't a bad description of us at all. As I often say of my deductive faculties—think—shmink! But Atla-Hi (always meaning, of course, the personality behind the voice from the screen) found out all it wanted about us—and apparently knew a good deal to start with. For one thing, they must have been tracking our plane for some time, because they guessed it was on automatic and that we could reverse its course but nothing else. Though they seemed under the impression that we could reverse its course to Los Alamos, not the cracking plant. Here obviously I did get a nugget of new data, though it was just about the only one. For a moment the voice from the screen got real unguarded-anxious as it asked, "Do you know if it is true that they have stopped dying at Los Alamos, or are they merely broadcasting that to cheer us up?"

I answered, "Oh yes, they're all fine," to that, but I couldn't have made it very convincing, because the next thing I knew the voice was getting me to admit that we'd only boarded the plane somewhere in the Central Deathlands. I even had to describe the cracking plant and freeway and gas tanks—I couldn't think of a lie that mightn't get us into as much trouble as the truth—and the voice said, "Oh, did Grayl stay there?" and I said, "Yes," and braced myself to do some more admitting, or some heavy lying, as the inspiration took me.

But the voice continued to skirt around the question of what exactly had happened to Grayl. I guess they knew well enough we'd bumped him off, but didn't bring it up because they needed our cooperation—they were handling us like children or savages, you see.

One pretty amazing point—Atla-Hi apparently knew something about Pop's fairy-tale fellowship of nonpracticing murderers, because when he had to speak up, while he was getting instructions on preparing the stuff for the drop, the voice said, "Excuse me, but you sound like one of those A. A. boys."

Assassins Anonymous, Pop had said some of their boys called their unorganized organization.

"Yep, I am," Pop admitted uncomfortably.

"Well, a word of advice then, or perhaps I only mean gossip," the screen said, for once getting on a side track. "Most of our people do not believe you are serious about it, although you may think that you are. Our skeptics (which includes all but a very few of us) split quite evenly between those who think that the A. A. spirit is a terminal psychotic illusion and those who believe it is an elaborate ruse in preparation for some concerted attack on cities by Deathlanders."

"Can't say that I blame the either of them," was Pop's only comment. "I think I'm nuts myself and a murderer forever." Alice glared at him for that admission, but it seemed to do us no damage. Pop really did seem out of his depth though during this part of our adventure, more out of his depth than even Alice and me—I mean, as if he could only really function in the Deathlands with Deathlanders and wanted to get anything else over quickly.

I think one reason Pop was that way was that he was feeling very intensely something I was feeling myself: a sort of sadness and bewilderment that beings as smart as the voice from the screen sounded should still be fighting wars. Murder, as you must know by now, I can understand and sympathize with deeply, but war?—no!

Oh, I can understand cultural queers fighting city squares and even get a kick out of it and whoop 'em on, but these Atla-Hi and Alamos folk seemed a different sort of cat altogether (though I'd only come to that point of view today)—the kind of cat that ought to have outgrown war or thought its way around it. Maybe Savannah Fortress had simply forced the war on them and they had to defend themselves. I hadn't contacted any Savannans—they might be as blood-simple as the Porterites. Still, I don't know that it's always a good excuse that somebody else forced you into war. That sort of justification can keep on until the end of time. But who's a germ to judge?

A minute later I was feeling doubly like a germ and a very lowly one, because the situation had just got more difficult and depressing too.

The voice was just repeating its instructions to Pop on making the drop, when it broke off of a sudden and a second voice came in, a deep voice with a sort of European accent (not Chinese, oddly)—not talking *to* us, I think, but to the first voice and overlooking or not caring that we could hear.

"*Also* tell them," the second voice said, "that we will blow them out of the sky the instant they stop obeying us! If they should hesitate to make the drop or if they should put a finger on the button that reverses their course, then—*pouf!* Such brutes understand only the language of force. *Also* warn them that the blocks are atomic grenades that will blow them out of the sky too if—"

"Dr. Kovalsky, will you permit me to point out—" the first voice interrupted, getting as close to expressing irritation as I imagine it ever allowed itself to do. Then both voices cut off abruptly, and the screen was silent for ten seconds or so. I guess the first voice thought it wasn't nice for us to overhear Atla-Hi bickering with itself, even if the second voice didn't give a damn (any more than a farmer would mind the pigs overhearing him squabble with his hired man; of course this guy seemed to overlook that we were killer-pigs, but there wasn't anything we could do in that line just now except get burned up).

When the screen came on again, it was just the first voice talking once more, but it had something to say that was probably the result of a rapid conference and compromise.

"Attention, everyone! I wish to inform you that the plane in which you are traveling can be exploded—melted in the air, rather—if we activate a certain control at this end. We will *not* do so, now or subsequently, if you make the drop when we give the signal and if you remain on your present course until then. Afterward you will be at liberty to reverse your course and escape as best you may. Let me re-emphasize that when you told me you had taken over for Grayl I accepted that assertion in full faith and still so accept it. Is that all fully understood?"

We all told him "Yes," though I don't imagine we sounded very happy about it, even Pop. However, I did get that funny feeling again that the voice was being really sincere—an illusion, I supposed, but still a comforting one.

Now while all these things were going on, believe it or not, and while the plane continued to bullet through the orange haze—which hadn't shown any foreign objects in it so far, thank God, even vultures, let alone "straight strings of pink stars"—I was receiving a cram course in gunnery! (Do you wonder I don't try to tell this part of my story consecutively?)

It turned out that Alice had been brilliantly right about one thing: if you pushed some of the buttons simultaneously in patterns of five they unlocked and you could play on them like organ keys. Two sets of five keys, played properly, would rig out a sight just in front of the viewport and let you aim and fire the plane's main gun in any forward direction. There was a rearward firing gun too, that you aimed by changing over the world screen to a rear-view TV window, but we didn't get around to mastering that one. In fact, in spite of my special talents, it was all I could do to achieve a beginner's control over the main gun, and I wouldn't have managed even that except that Alice, from the thinking she'd been doing about patterns of five, was quick at understanding from the voice's descriptions which buttons were meant. She couldn't work them herself, of course, what with her stump and burnt hand, but she could point them out for me.

After twenty minutes of drill I was a gunner of sorts, sprawled in the right-hand kneeling seat and intently scanning the onrushing orange haze which at last was beginning to change toward the bronze of evening. If something showed up in it I'd be able to make a stab at getting a shot in. Not that I knew what my gun fired—the voice wasn't giving away any unnecessary data.

Naturally I had asked why didn't the voice teach me to fly the plane so that I could maneuver in case of attack, and naturally the voice had told me it was out of the question—much too difficult and besides they wanted us on a known course so they could plan better for the drop and recovery. (I think maybe the voice would have given me some hints—and maybe even told me more about the steel cubes too and how much danger we were in from them—if it hadn't been for the second voice, which presumably had issued from a being who was keeping watch to make sure among other things that the first voice didn't get soft-hearted.)

So there I was being a front gunner. Actually a part of me was getting a big bang out of it—from antique Banker's Special to needle cannon (or whatever it was)—but at the same time another part of me was disgusted with the idea of acting like I belonged to a live culture (even a smart, unqueer one) and working in a war (even just so as to get out of it fast), while a third part of me—one that I normally keep down—was very simply horrified.

Pop was back by the door with the box and 'chute, ready to make the drop.

Alice had no duties for the moment, but she'd suddenly started gathering up food cans and packing them in one bag—I couldn't figure out at first what she had in mind. Orderly housewife wouldn't be exactly my description of her occupational personality.

Then of course everything had to happen at once.

The voice said, "Make the drop!"

Alice crossed to Pop and thrust out the bag of cans toward him, writhing her lips in silent "talk" to tell him something. She had a knife in her burnt hand too.

But I didn't have time to do any lip-reading, because

just then a glittering pink asterisk showed up in the darkening haze ahead—a whole half-dozen straight lines spreading out from a blank central spot, as if a superfast gigantic spider had laid in the first strands of its web.

Wind whistled as the door of the plane started to open.

I fought to center my sight on the blank central spot, which drifted toward the left.

One of the straight lines grew dazzlingly bright.

I heard Alice whisper fiercely, "Drop *these!*" and the part of my mind that couldn't be applied to gunnery instantly deduced that she'd had some last-minute inspiration about dropping a bunch of cans instead of the steel cubes.

I got the sight centered and held down the firing combo. The thought flashed to me: *it's a city you're firing at, not a plane,* and I flinched.

The dazzlingly pink line dipped down toward me.

Behind me, the sound of a struggle. Alice snarling and Pop giving a grunt.

Then all at once a scream from Alice, a big whoosh of wind, a flash way ahead (where I'd aimed), a spatter of hot metal inside the cabin, a blinding spot in the middle of the world screen, a searing beam inches from my neck, an electric shock that lifted me from my seat and ripped at my consciousness!

When I came to (if I really ever was out—seconds later, at most) there were no more pink lines. The haze was just its disgustingly tawny evening self with black spots that were only after-images. The cabin stunk of ozone, but wind funneling through a hole in the onetime world screen was blowing it out fast enough—Savannah had gotten in one lick, all right. And we were falling, the plane was swinging down like a crippled bird—I could feel it and there was no use kidding myself.

But staring at the control panel wouldn't keep us from crashing if that was in the cards. I looked around and there were Pop and Alice glaring at each other across the closing door. He looked mean. She looked agonized and was pressing her burnt hand into her side with her elbow as if he'd stamped on the hand, maybe. I didn't see any blood though. I didn't see the box and 'chute either, though I did see Alice's bag of groceries. I guessed Pop had made the drop.

Now, it occurred to me, was a bully time for Voice Two to melt the plane—if he hadn't already tried. My first thought had been that the spatter of hot metal had come from the Savannah craft spitting us, but there was no way to be sure.

I looked around at the viewport in time to see rocks and stunted trees jump out of the haze. *Good old Ray,* I thought, *always in at the death.* But just then the plane took a sickening bounce, as if its antigravity had only started to operate within yards of the ground. Another lurching fall and another bounce, less violent. A couple of repetitions of that, each one a little gentler, and, then we were sort of bumping along on an even keel with the rocks and such sliding past fast about a hundred feet below, I judged. We'd been spoiled for altitude work, it seemed, but we could still cripple along in some sort of low-power repulsion field.

I looked at the North America screen and the buttons, wondering if I should start us back west again or leave us set on Atla-Hi and see what the hell happened—at the moment I hardly cared what else Savannah did to us. I needn't of wasted the mental energy. The decision was made for me. As I watched, the Atla-Hi button jumped up by itself and the button for the cracking plant went down and there was some extra bumping as we swung around.

Also, the violet patch of Atla-Hi went real dim, and the button for it no longer had a violet nimbus. The Los Alamos blue went dull too. The cracking-plant dot glowed a brighter green—that was all.

All except for one thing. As the violet dimmed I thought I heard Voice One very faintly (not as if speaking directly but as if the screen had heard and remembered—not a voice but the fluorescent ghost of one): "Thank you and good luck!"

VI

Many a man has dated his ruin from some murder or other that perhaps he thought little of at the time.

BY THOMAS DE QUINCEY

"AND a long merry siege to you, sir, and roast rat for Christmas!" I responded, very out loud and rather to my surprise.

"War! How I hate war!"—that was what Pop exploded with. He didn't exactly dance in senile rage—he was still keeping too sharp a watch on Alice—but his voice sounded that way.

"Damn you, Pop!" Alice contributed. "And you too, Ray! We might have pulled something, but you had to go obedience-happy." Then her anger got the better of her grammar, or maybe Pop and me was corrupting it. "Damn the both of you!" she finished.

It didn't make much sense, any of it. We were just cutting loose, I guess, after being scared to say anything for the last half hour.

I said to Alice, "I don't know what you could have pulled, except the chain on us." To Pop I remarked, "You may hate war, but you sure helped that one along. Those grenades you dropped will probably take care of a few hundred Savannans."

"That's what you always say about me, isn't it?" he snapped back. "But I don't suppose I should expect any kinder interpretation of my motives." To Alice he said, "I'm sorry I had to squeeze your burnt fingers, sister, but you can't say I didn't warn you about my lowdown tactics." Then to me again: "I *do* hate war, Ray. It's just murder on a bigger scale, though some of the boys give me an argument there."

"Then why don't you go preach against war in Atla-Hi and Savannah?" Alice demanded, still very hot but not quite so bitter.

"Yeah, Pop, how about it?" I seconded.

"Maybe I should," he said, thoughtful all at once. "They sure need it." Then he grinned, "Hey, how'd this sound: HEAR THE WORLD-FAMOUS MURDERER POP TRUMBULL TALK AGAINST WAR. WEAR YOUR STEEL THROAT PROTECTORS. Pretty good, hey?"

We all laughed at that, grudgingly at first, then with a touch of wholeheartedness. I think we all recognized that things weren't going to be very cheerful from here on in and we'd better not turn up our noses at the feeblest fun.

"I guess I didn't have anything very bright in mind," Alice admitted to me, while to Pop she said, "All right, I forgive you for the present."

"Don't!" Pop said with a shudder. "I hate to think of what happened to the last bugger made the mistake of forgiving me."

We looked around and took stock of our resources. It was time we did. It was getting dark fast, although we were chasing the sun, and there weren't any cabin lights coming on and we sure didn't know of any way of getting any.

We wadded a couple of satchels into the hole in the world screen without trying to probe it. After a while it got warmer again in the cabin and the air a little less dusty. Presently it started to get too smoky from the cigarettes we were burning, but that came later.

We screwed off the walls the few storage bags we hadn't inspected. They didn't contain nothing of consequence, not even a flashlight.

I had one last go at the buttons, though there weren't any left with nimbuses on them—the darker it got, the clearer that was. Even the Atla-Hi button wouldn't push now that it had lost its violet halo. I tried the gunnery patterns, figuring to put in a little time taking pot shots at any mountains that turned up, but the buttons that had been responding so well a few minutes ago refused to budge. Alice suggested different patterns, but none of them worked. That console was really locked—maybe the shot from Savannah was partly responsible, though Atla-Hi remote-locking things was explanation enough.

"The buggers!" I said. "They didn't have to tie us up *this* tight. Going east we at least had a choice—forward or back. Now we got none."

"Maybe we're just as well off," Pop said. "If Atla-Hi had been able to do anything more for us—that is, if they hadn't been sieged in, I mean—they'd sure as anything have pulled us in. Pulled the plane in, I mean, and picked us out of it—with a big pair of tweezers, likely as not. And contrary to your flattering opinion of my preaching (which by the way none of the religious boys in my outfit share—they call me 'that misguided old atheist'), I don't think none of us would go over big at Atla-Hi."

We had to agree with him there. I couldn't imagine Pop or Alice or even me cutting much of a figure (even if we weren't murder-pariahs) with the pack of geniuses that seemed to make up the Atla-Alamos crowd. The Double-A Republics, to give them a name, might have their small-brain types, but somehow I didn't think so. There must be more than one Edison-Einstein, it seemed to me, back of antigravity and all the wonders in this plane and the other things we'd gotten hints of. Also, Grayl had seemed bred for brains as well as size, even if us small mammals had cooked his goose. And none of the modern "countries" had more than a few thousand population yet, I was pretty sure, and that hardly left room for a dumbbell class. Finally, too, I got hold of a memory I'd been reaching for for the last hour—how when I was a kid I'd read about some scientists who learned to talk Mandarin just for kicks. I told Alice and Pop.

"And if *that's* the average Atla-Alamoser's idea of mental recreation," I said, "well, you can see what I mean."

"I'll grant you they got a monopoly of brains," Pop agreed. "No sense, though," he added doggedly.

"Intellectual snobs," was Alice's comment. "I know the type and I detest it." ("You *are* sort of intellectual, aren't you?" Pop told her, which fortunately didn't start a riot.)

Still, I guess all three of us found it fun to chew over a bit the new slant we'd gotten on two (in a way, three) of the great "countries" of the modern world. (And as long as we thought of it as fun, we didn't have to admit the envy and wistfulness that were behind our wisecracks.)

I said, "We've always figured in a general way that Alamos was the remains of a community of scientists and technicians. Now we know the same's true of the Atla-Hi group. They're the Brookhaven survivors."

"Manhattan Project, don't you mean?" Alice corrected.

"Nope, that was in Colorado Springs," Pop said with finality.

I also pointed out that a community of scientists would educate for technical intelligence, maybe breed for it too. And being a group picked for high I. Q. to begin with, they might make startlingly fast progress. You could easily imagine such folk, unimpeded by the boobs, creating a wonder world in a couple of generations.

"They got their troubles though," Pop reminded me and that led us to speculating about the war we'd dipped into. Savannah Fortress, we knew, was supposed to be based on some big atomic plants on the river down that way, but its culture seemed to have a fiercer ingredient than Atla-Alamos. Before we knew it we were musing almost romantically about the plight of Atla-Hi, besieged by superior and (it was easy to suppose) barbaric forces, and maybe distant Los Alamos in a similar predicament—Alice reminded me how the voice had asked if they were still dying out there. For a moment I found myself fiercely proud that I had been able to strike a blow against evil aggressors. At once, of course, then, the revulsion came.

"This is a hell of a way," I said, "for three so-called realists to be mooning about things."

"Yes, especially when your heroes kicked us out," Alice agreed.

Pop chuckled. "Yep," he said, "they even took Ray's artillery away from him."

"You're wrong there, Pop," I said, sitting up. "I still got one of the grenades—the one the pilot had in his fist." To tell the truth I'd forgotten all about it, and it bothered me a little now to feel it snugged up in my pocket against my hip bone where the skin is thin.

"You believe what that old Dutchman said about the steel cubes being atomic grenades?" Pop asked me.

"I don't know," I said, "He sure didn't sound enthusiastic about telling us the truth about anything. But for that matter he sounded mean enough to tell the truth figuring we'd think it was a lie. Maybe this *is* some sort of baby A-bomb with a fuse timed like a grenade." I got it out and hefted it. "How about I press the button and drop it out the door? Then we'll know." I really felt like doing it—restless, I guess.

"Don't be a fool, Ray," Alice said.

"Don't tense up, I won't," I told her. At the same time I made myself the little promise that if I ever got to feeling restless, that is, restless and *bad*, I'd just go ahead and punch the button and see what happened—sort of leave my future up to the gods of the Deathlands, you might say.

"What makes you so sure it's a weapon?" Pop asked.

"What else would it be," I asked him, "that they'd be so hot on getting them in the middle of a war?"

"I don't know for sure," Pop said. "I've made a guess, but I don't want to tell it now. What I'm getting at, Ray, is that your first thought about anything you find—in the world outside or in your own mind—is that it's a weapon."

"Anything worthwhile in your mind is a weapon!" Alice interjected with surprising intensity.

"You see?" Pop said. "That's what I mean about the both of you. That sort of thinking's been going on a long time. Caveman picks up a rock and right away asks himself, 'Who can I brain with this?' Doesn't occur to him for several hundred thousand years to use it to start building a hospital."

"You know, Pop," I said, carefully tucking the cube back in my pocket, "you *are* sort of preachy at times."

"Guess I am," he said. "How about some grub?"

It was a good idea. Another few minutes and we wouldn't have been able to see to eat, though with the cans shaped to tell their contents I guess we'd have managed. It was a funny circumstance that in this wonder plane we didn't even know how to turn on the light—and a good measure of our general helplessness.

We had our little feed and lit up again and settled ourselves. I judged it would be an overnight trip, at least, to the cracking plant—we weren't making anything like the speed we had been going east. Pop was sitting in back again, and Alice and I lay half-hitched around on the kneeling seats, which allowed us to watch each other. Pretty soon it got so dark we couldn't see anything of each other but the glowing tips of the cigarettes and a bit of face around the mouth when the person took a deep drag. They were a good idea, those cigarettes—kept us from having ideas about the other person starting to creep around with a knife in his hand.

The North America screen still glowed dimly, and we could watch our green dot trying to make progress. The viewport was dead black at first, then there came the faintest sort of bronze blotch that very slowly shifted forward and down. The Old Moon, of course, going west ahead of us.

After a while I realized what it was like—an old Pullman car (I'd traveled in one once as a kid) or especially the smoker of an old Pullman, very late at night. Our crippled antigravity, working on the irregularities of the ground as they came along below, made the ride rhythmically bumpy, you see. I remembered how lonely and strange that old sleeping car had seemed to me as a kid. This felt the same. I kept waiting for a hoot or a whistle. It was the sort of loneliness that settles in your bones and keeps working at you.

"I recall the first man I ever killed—" Pop started to reminisce softly.

"Shut up!" Alice told him. "Don't you ever talk about anything but murder, Pop?"

"Guess not," he said. "After all, it's the only really interesting topic there is. Do you know of another?"

It was silent in the cabin for a long time after that. Then Alice said, "It was the afternoon before my twelfth birthday when they came into the kitchen and killed my father. He'd been wise, in a way, and had us living at a spot where the bombs didn't touch us or the worst fallout. But he hadn't counted on the local werewolf gang. He'd just been slicing some bread—homemade from our own wheat (Dad was great on back to nature and all)—but he laid down the knife.

"Dad couldn't see any object or idea as a weapon, you see—that was his great weakness. Dad couldn't even see weapons as weapons. Dad had a philosophy of cooperation, that was his name for it, that he was going to explain to people. Sometimes I think he was glad of the Last War, because he believed it would give him his chance.

"But the werewolves weren't interested in philosophy, and although their knives weren't as sharp as Dad's, they didn't lay them down. Afterward they had themselves a meal, with me for dessert. I remember one of them used a slice of bread to sop up blood like gravy. And another washed his hands and face in the cold coffee . . ."

She didn't say anything else for a bit. Pop said softly, "That was the afternoon, wasn't it, that the fallen angels . . ." and then just said, "My big mouth."

"You were going to say 'the afternoon they killed God'?" Alice asked him. "You're right, it was. They killed God in the kitchen that afternoon. That's how I know he's dead. Afterward they would have killed me too, eventually, except—"

Again she broke off, this time to say, "Pop, do you suppose I can have been thinking about myself as the Daughter of God all these years? That that's why everything seems so intense?"

"I don't know," Pop said. "The religious boys say we're all children of God. I don't put much stock in it—or else God sure has some lousy children. Go on with your story."

"Well, they would have killed me too, except the leader took a fancy to me and got the idea of training me up for a Weregirl or She-wolf Deb, you could say.

"That was my first experience of ideas as weapons. He got an idea about me and I used it to kill him. I had to wait three months for my opportunity. I got him so lazy he let me shave him. He bled to death the same way as Dad."

"Hum," Pop commented after a bit, "that was a chiller, all right. I got to remember to tell it to Bill—it was somebody killing his mother that got *him* started. Alice, you had about as good a justification for your first murder as any I remember hearing."

"Yet," Alice said after another pause, with just a trace of the old sarcasm creeping back into her voice, "I don't suppose you think I was right to do it?"

"Right? Wrong? Who knows?" Pop said almost blusteringly. "Sure you were justified in a whole pack of ways. Anybody'd sympathize with you. A man often has fine justification for the first murder he commits. But as you must know, it's not that the first murder's always so bad in itself as that it's apt to start you on a killing spree. Your sense of values gets shifted a tiny bit and never shifts back. But you know all that and who am I to tell you anything, anyway? I've killed men because I didn't like the way they spit.

And may very well do it again if I don't keep watching myself and my mind ventilated."

"Well, Pop," Alice said, "I didn't always have such dandy justification for my killings. Last one was a moony old physicist—he fixed me the Geiger counter I carry. A silly old geek—I don't know how he survived so long. Maybe an exile or a runaway. You know, I often attach myself to the elderly do-gooder type like my father was. Or like you, Pop."

Pop nodded. "It's good to know yourself," he said.

There was a third pause, and then, although I hadn't exactly been intending to, I said, "Alice had justification for her first murder, personal justification that an ape would understand. I had no personal justification at all for mine, yet I killed about a million people at a modest estimate. You see, I was the boss of the crew that took care of the hydrogen missile-group ticketed for Moscow and guaranteed to smash through the roof of any shelter city. And when the ticket was finally taken up, I was the one to punch it. My finger on the firing button, I mean."

I went on, "Yeah, Pop, I was one of the button-pushers. There were really quite a few of us, of course—belt *and* suspenders—that's why I get such a laugh out of stories about being or rubbing out the *one* guy who pushed all the buttons."

"That so?" Pop said with only mild-sounding interest. "In that case you ought to know—"

We didn't get to hear right then who I ought to know because I had a fit of coughing and we realized the cigarette smoke was getting just too thick. Pop fixed the door so it was open a crack, and after a while the atmosphere got reasonably okay though we had to put up with a low lonely whistling sound.

"Yeah," I continued, "I was the boss of the missile crew and I wore a very handsome uniform with impressive insignia —not the bully old stripes I got on my chest now—and I was very young and handsome myself. We were all very young in that line of service, though a few of the men under me were a little older. Young and dedicated. I remember feeling a very deep and grim—and *clean*—responsibility. And when I'd go back on leave to my shelter city, I'd feel very big as the sidewalk whipped me along.

"I had a grandfather flew in the war they fought to lick

fascism, bombadier on a Flying Fortress or something, and once when he got drunk he told me how some days it didn't bother him at all to drop the eggs on Germany; the buildings and people down there seemed just like toys that a kid sets up to kick over, and the whole business about as naïve fun as poking an anthill. Sometimes they just got bored—or maybe scared a bit—and dropped their bombs in the North Sea and headed home.

"*I* didn't even have to fly over at seven miles what I was going to be aiming at. Only I remember sometimes getting out a map and looking at a certain large dot on it and smiling a little and softly saying, 'Pow!'—and then giving a little conventional shudder and folding up the map quick.

"Naturally we told ourselves we'd never have to do it, fire the thing, I mean; we joked about how after twenty years or so we'd all be given jobs as museum attendants of this same bomb, deactivated at last. But naturally it didn't work out that way. There came the day when our side of the world got hit, and the orders started cascading down from Defense Coordinator Bigelow—"

"Bigelow?" Pop interrupted. "Not Joe Bigelow?"

"Joseph A., I believe," I told him, a little annoyed.

"Why he's my boy then, the one I was telling you about—the skinny runt had this hornhandle! Can you beat that?" Pop sounded startlingly happy. "Him and you'll have a lot to talk about when you get together."

I wasn't so sure of that myself; in fact my first reaction was that the opposite would be true. To be honest I was for the first moment more than a little annoyed at Pop interrupting my story of my Big Grief—for it was that to me, make no mistake. Here my story had finally been teased out of me, against all expectation, after decades of repression and in spite of dozens of assorted psychological blocks—and here was Pop interrupting it for the sake of a lot of trivial organizational gossip about Joes and Bills and Georges we'd never heard of and what they'd say or think!

But then all of a sudden I realized that I didn't really care, that it didn't feel like a Big Grief any more, that just starting to tell about it after hearing Pop and Alice tell their stories had purged it of that unnecessary weight of feeling that had made it a millstone around my neck.

It seemed to me now that I could look down at Ray Baker from a considerable height (but not an angelic or contemptuously superior height) and ask myself, *not* why he had grieved so much—that was understandable and even desirable —but why he had grieved so *uselessly* in such a stuffy little private hell.

And it *would* be interesting to find out how Joseph A. Bigelow had felt.

"How does it feel, Ray, to kill a million people?"

I realized that Alice had asked me the question several seconds back and it was hanging in the air.

"That's just what I've been trying to tell you," I told her and started to explain it all over again—the words poured out of me now. I won't put them down here—it would take too long—but they were honest words as far as I knew, and they eased me.

I couldn't get over it: here were us three murderers feeling a trust and understanding and sharing a communion that I wouldn't have believed possible between *any* two or three people in the Age of the Deaders—or in *any* age, to tell the truth. It was against everything I knew of Deathland psychology, but it was happening just the same. Oh, our strange isolation had something to do with it, I knew, and that Pullman-car memory hypnotizing my mind, and our reactions to the voices and violence of Atla-Alamos; but in spite of all that I ranked it as a wonder. I felt an inward freedom and easiness that I never would have believed possible. Pop's little disorganized organization had really got hold of something, I couldn't deny it.

Three treacherous killers talking from the bottoms of their hearts and believing each other!—for it never occurred to me to doubt that Pop and Alice were feeling exactly like I was. In fact, we were all so sure of it that we didn't even mention our communion to each other. Perhaps we were a little afraid we would rub off the bloom. We just enjoyed it.

We must have talked about a thousand things that night and smoked a couple of hundred cigarettes. After a while we started taking little catnaps—we'd gotten too much off our chests and come to feel too tranquil for even our excitement to keep us awake. I remember the first time I dozed waking up with a cold start and grabbing for Mother—and then hearing Pop and Alice gabbing in the dark, and remembering what had happened, and relaxing again with a smile.

Of all things, Pop was saying, "Yep, I imagine Ray must be good to make love to, murderers almost always are, they got the fire. It reminds me of what a guy named Fred told me, one of our boys . . ."

Mostly we took turns going to sleep, though I think there were times when all three of us were snoozing. About the fifth time I woke up, after some tighter shuteye, the orange soup was back again outside and Alice was snoring gently in the next seat and Pop was up and had one of his knives out.

He was looking at his reflection in the viewport. His face gleamed. He was rubbing butter into it.

"Another day, another pack of troubles," he said cheerfully.

The tone of his remark jangled my nerves, as that tone generally does early in the morning. I squeezed my eyes. "Where are we?" I asked.

He poked his elbow toward the North America screen. The two green dots were almost one.

"My God, we're practically there," Alice said for me. She'd waked fast, Deathlands style.

"I know," Pop said, concentrating on what he was doing, "but I aim to be shaved before they commence landing maneuvers."

"You think automatic will land us?" Alice asked. "What if we just start circling around?"

"We can figure out what to do when it happens," Pop said, whittling away at his chin. "Until then, I'm not interested. There's still a couple of bottles of coffee in the sack. I've had mine."

I didn't join in this chit-chat because the green dots and Alice's first remark had reminded me of a lot deeper reason for my jangled nerves than Pop's cheerfulness. Night was gone, with its shielding cloak and its feeling of being able to talk forever, and the naked day was here, with its demands for action. It is not so difficult to change your whole view of life when you are flying, or even bumping along above the ground, with friends who understand, but soon, I knew, I'd be down in the dust with something I never wanted to see again.

"Coffee, Ray?"

"Yeah, I guess so." I took the bottle from Alice and wondered whether my face looked as glum as hers.

"They shouldn't salt butter," Pop asserted. "It makes it lousy for shaving."

"It was the *best* butter," Alice said.

"Yeah," I said. "The Dormouse, when they buttered the watch."

It may be true that feeble humor is better than none. I don't know.

"What are you two yakking about?" Pop demanded.

"A book we both read," I told him.

"Either of you writers?" Pop asked with sudden interest. "Some of the boys think we should have a book about us. I say it's too soon, but they say we might all die off or something. Whoa, Jenny! Easy does it. Gently, please!"

That last remark was by way of recognizing that the plane had started an authoritative turn to the left. I got a sick and cold feeling. This was it.

Pop sheathed his knife and gave his face a final rub. Alice belted on her satchel. I reached for my knapsack, but I was staring through the viewport, dead ahead.

The haze lightened faintly, three times. I remembered the St. Elmo's fire that had flamed from the cracking plant.

"Pop," I said—almost whined, to be truthful, "why'd the bugger ever have to land here in the first place? He was rushing stuff they needed bad at Atla-Hi—why'd he have to break his trip?"

"That's easy," Pop said. "He was being a bad boy. At least that's my theory. He was supposed to go straight to Atla-Hi, but there was somebody he wanted to check up on first. He stopped here to see his girlfriend. Yep, his girlfriend. She tried to warn him off—that's my explanation of the juice that flared out of the cracking plant and interfered with his landing, though I'm sure she didn't intend the last. By the way, whatever she turned on to give him the warning must still be turned on. But Grayl came on down in spite of it."

Before I could assimilate that, the seven deformed gas tanks materialized in the haze. We got the freeway in our sights and steadied and slowed and kept slowing. The plane didn't graze the cracking plant this time, though I'd have sworn it was going to hit it head on. When I saw we *weren't* going to hit it, I wanted to shut my eyes, but I couldn't.

The stain was black now and the Pilot's body was thicker than I remembered—bloated. But that wouldn't last long. Three or four vultures were working on it.

VII

Here now is his triumph where all things falter,
Stretched out on the spoils that his own hand spread,
As a god self-slain on his own strange altar,
Death lies dead.

—A Forsaken Garden

BY CHARLES SWINBURNE

POP was first down. Between us we helped Alice. Before joining them I took a last look at the control panel. The cracking plant button was up again, and there was a blue nimbus on another button. For Los Alamos, I supposed. I was tempted to push it and get away solo, but then I thought, *nope, there's nothing for me at the other end, and the loneliness will be worse than what I got to face here.* I climbed out.

I didn't look at the body, although we were practically on top of it. I saw a little patch of silver off to one side and remembered the gun that had melted. The vultures had waddled off but only a few yards.

"We could kill them," Alice said to Pop.

"Why?" he responded. "Didn't some Hindus use them to take care of dead bodies? Not a bad idea, either."

"Parsees," Alice amplified.

"Yep, Parsees, that's what I meant. Give you a nice clean skeleton in a matter of days."

Pop was leading us past the body toward the cracking plant. I heard the flies buzzing loudly. I felt terrible. I wanted to be dead myself. Just walking along after Pop was an awful effort.

"His girl was running a hidden observation tower here," Pop was saying now. "Weather and all that, I suppose. Or maybe setting up a robot station of some kind. I couldn't tell you about her before, because you were both in a mood to try to rub out anybody remotely connected with the Pilot. In fact, I did my best to lead you astray, letting you think I'd been the one to scream and all. Even now, to be honest about it, I don't know if I'm doing the right thing telling and showing you all this, but a man's got to take some risks whatever he does."

"Say Pop," I said dully, "isn't she apt to take a shot at us or something?" Not that I'd have minded on my own account. "Or are you and her that good friends?"

"Nope, Ray," he said, "she doesn't even know me. But I don't think she's in a position to do any shooting. You'll see why. Hey, she hasn't even shut the door. That's bad."

He seemed to be referring to a kind of manhole cover standing on its edge just inside the open-walled first story of the cracking plant. He knelt and looked down the hole the cover was designed to close off.

"Well, at least she didn't collapse at the bottom of the shaft," he said. "Come on, let's see what happened." And he climbed into the shaft.

We followed him like zombies. At least that's how I felt. The shaft was about twenty feet deep. There were foot- and hand-holds. It got stuffy right away, and warmer, in spite of the shaft being open at the top.

At the bottom there was a short horizontal passage. We had to duck to get through it. When we could straighten up we were in a large and luxurious bomb-resistant dugout, to give it a name. And it was stuffier and hotter than ever.

There was a lot of scientific equipment around and several small control panels reminding me of the one in the back of the plane. Some of them, I supposed, connected with instruments, weather and otherwise, hidden up in the skeletal structure of the cracking plant. And there were signs of occupancy, a young woman's occupancy—clothes scattered around in a frivolous way, and some small objects of art, and a slightly more than life-size head in clay that I guessed the occupant must have been sculpting. I didn't give that last more than the most fleeting look, strictly unintentional to begin with, because although it wasn't finished I could tell whose head it was supposed to be—the Pilot's.

The whole place was finished in dull silver like the cabin

of the plane, and likewise it instantly struck me as having a living personality, partly the Pilot's and partly someone else's—the personality of a marriage. Which wasn't a bit nice, because the whole place smelt of death.

But to tell the truth I didn't give the place more than the quickest look-over, because my attention was riveted almost at once on a long wide couch with the covers kicked off it and on the body there.

The woman was about six feet tall and built like a goddess. Her hair was blonde and her skin tanned. She was lying on her stomach and she was naked.

She didn't come anywhere near my libido, though. She looked sick to death. Her face, twisted towards us, was hollow-cheeked and flushed. Her eyes, closed, were sunken and dark-circled. She was breathing shallowly and rapidly through her open mouth, gasping now and then.

I got the crazy impression that all the heat in the place was coming from her body, radiating from her fever.

And the whole place stunk of death. Honestly it seemed to me that this dugout was Death's underground temple, the bed Death's altar, and the woman Death's sacrifice. (Had I unconsciously come to worship Death as a god in the Deathlands? I don't really know. There it gets too deep for me.)

No, she didn't come within a million miles of my libido, but there was another part of me that she was eating at . . .

If guilt's a luxury, then I'm a plutocrat.

. . . eating at until I was an empty shell, until I had no props left, until I wanted to die then and there, until I figured I had to die . . .

There was a faint sharp hiss right at my elbow. I looked and found that, unbeknownst to myself, I'd taken the steel cube out of my pocket and holding it snuggled between my first and second fingers I'd punched the button with my thumb just as I'd promised myself I would if I got to really feeling bad.

It goes to show you that you should never give your mind any kind of instructions even half in fun, unless you're prepared to have them carried out whether you approve later or not.

Pop saw what I'd done and looked at me strangely. "So you had to die after all, Ray," he said softly. "Most of us find out we have to, one way or another."

We waited. Nothing happened. I noticed a very faint milky cloud a few inches across hanging in the air by the cube.

Thinking right away of poison gas, I jerked away a little, dispersing the cloud.

"What's that?" I demanded of no one in particular.

"I'd say," said Pop, "that that's something that squirted out of a tiny hole in the side of the cube opposite the button. A hole so nearly microscopic you wouldn't see it unless you looked for it hard. Ray, I don't think you're going to get your baby A-blast, and what's more I'm afraid you've wasted something that's damn valuable. But don't let it worry you. Before I dropped those cubes for Atla-Hi I snagged one."

And darn if he didn't pull the brother of my cube out of his pocket.

"Alice," he said, "I noticed a half pint of whiskey in your satchel when we got the salve. Would you put some on a rag and hand it to me."

Alice looked at him like he was nuts, but while her eyes were looking her pliers and her gloved hand were doing what he told her.

Pop took the rag and swabbed a spot on the sick woman's nearest buttock and jammed the cube against the spot and pushed the button.

"It's a jet hypodermic, folks," he said.

He took the cube away and there was the welt to substantiate his statement.

"Hope we got to her in time," he said. "The plague is tough. Now I guess there's nothing for us to do but wait, maybe for quite a while."

I felt shaken beyond all recognition.

"Pop, you old caveman detective!" I burst out. "When did you get that idea for a healing hand grenade?" Don't think I was feeling anywhere near that gay. It was reaction, close to hysterical.

Pop was taken aback, but then he grinned. "I had a couple of clues that you and Alice didn't," he said. "I knew there was a very sick woman involved. And I had that bout with Los Alamos fever I told you. They've had a lot of trouble with it, I believe—some say its spores come from outside the world with the cosmic dust—and now it seems to have been carried to Atla-Hi. Let's hope they've found the answer this time. Alice, maybe we'd better start getting some water into this gal."

After a while we sat down and fitted the facts together more orderly. Pop did the fitting mostly. Alamos researchers must have been working for years on the plague as it ravaged intermittently, maybe with mutations and ET tricks to make the job harder. Very recently they'd found a promising treatment (cure, we hoped) and prepared it for rush shipment to Atla-Hi, where the plague was raging too and they were sieged in by Savannah as well. Grayl was picked to fly the serum, or drug or whatever it was. But he knew or guessed that this lone woman observer (because she'd fallen out of radio communication or something) had come down with the plague too, and he decided to land some serum for her, probably without authorization.

"How do we know she's his girlfriend?" I asked.

"Or wife," Pop said tolerantly. "Why, there was that bag of woman's stuff he was carrying, frilly things like a man would bring for a woman. Who else'd he be apt to make a special stop for?

"Another thing," Pop said. "He must have been using jets to hurry his trip. We heard them, you know."

That seemed about as close a reconstruction of events as we could get. Strictly hypothetical, of course. Deathlanders trying to figure out what goes on inside a "country" like Atla-Alamos and *why* are sort of like foxes trying to understand world politics, or wolves the Gothic migrations. Of course we're all human beings, but that doesn't mean as much as it sounds.

Then Pop told us how he'd happened to be on the scene. He'd been doing a "tour of duty," as he called it, when he spotted this woman's observatory and decided to hang around anonymously and watch over her for a few days and maybe help protect her from some dangerous characters that he knew were in the neighborhood.

"Pop, that sounds like a lousy idea to me," I objected. "Risky, I mean. Spying on another person, watching them without their knowing, would be the surest way to stir up in me the idea of murdering them. Safest thing for me to do in that situation would be to turn around and run."

"*You* probably should," he agreed. "For now, anyway. It's all a matter of knowing your own strength and stage of growth. Me, it helps to give myself these little jobs. And the essence of 'em is that the other person shouldn't know I'm helping."

It sounded like knighthood and pilgrimage and the Boy Scouts all over again—for murderers. Well, why not?

Pop had seen this woman come out of the manhole a couple of times and look around and then go back down, and he'd got the impression she was sick and troubled. He'd even guessed she might be coming down with Alamos fever. He'd seen us arrive, of course, and that had bothered him. Then when the plane landed she'd come up again, acting out of her head, but when she'd seen the Pilot and us going for him she'd given that scream and collapsed at the top of the shaft. He'd figured the only thing he could do for her was keep us occupied. Besides, now that he knew for sure we were murderers he'd started to burn with the desire to talk to us and maybe help us quit killing if we seemed to want to. It was only much later, in the middle of our trip, that he began to suspect that the steel cubes were jet hypodermics.

While Pop had been telling us all this, we hadn't been watching the woman so closely. Now Alice called our attention to her. Her skin was covered with fine beads of perspiration, like diamonds.

"That's a good sign," Pop said and Alice started to wipe her off. While she was doing that the woman came to in a groggy sort of way, and Pop fed her some thin soup and in the middle of his doing it she dropped off to sleep.

Alice said, "Any other time I would be wild to kill another woman that beautiful. But she has been so close to death that I would feel I was robbing another murderer. I suppose there is more behind the change in my feelings than that, though."

"Yeah, a little, I suppose," Pop said.

I didn't have anything to say about my own feelings. Certainly not out loud. I knew that they had changed and that they were still changing. It was complicated.

After a while it occurred to me and Alice to worry whether we mightn't catch this woman's sickness. It would serve us right, of course, but plague is plague. But Pop reassured us. "Actually I snagged three cubes," he said. "That should take care of you two. I figure I'm immune."

Time wore on. Pop dragged out the harmonica, as I'd

been afraid he would, but his playing wasn't too bad. "Tenting Tonight," "When Johnnie Comes Marching Home," and such. We had a meal.

The Pilot's woman woke up again, in her full mind this time or something like it. We were clustered around the bed, smiling a little I suppose and looking inquiringly. Being even assistant nurses makes you all concerned about the patient's health and state of mind.

Pop helped her sit up a little. She looked around. She saw me and Alice. Recognition came into her eyes. She drew away from us with a look of loathing. She didn't say a word, but the look stayed.

Pop drew me aside and whispered, "I think it would be a nice gesture if you and Alice took a blanket and went up and sewed him into it. I noticed a big needle and some thread in her satchel." He looked me in the eye and added, "You can't expect this woman to feel any other way toward you, you know. Now or ever."

He was right, of course. I gave Alice the high sign and we got out.

No point in dwelling on the next scene. Alice and me sewed up in a blanket a big guy who'd been dead a day and worked over by vultures. That's all.

About the time we'd finished, Pop came up.

"She chased me out," he explained. "She's getting dressed. When I told her about the plane, she said she was going back to Los Alamos. She's not fit to travel, of course, but she's giving herself injections. It's none of our business. Incidentally, she wants to take the body back with her. I told her how we'd dropped the serum and how you and Alice had helped and she listened."

The Pilot's woman wasn't long after Pop. She must have had trouble getting up the shaft, she had a little trouble even walking straight, but she held her head high. She was wearing a dull silver tunic and sandals and cloak. As she passed me and Alice I could see the look of loathing come back into her eyes, and her chin went a little higher. I thought, why shouldn't she want us dead? Right now she probably wants to be dead herself.

Pop nodded to us and we hoisted up the body and followed her. It was almost too heavy a load even for the three of us.

As she reached the plane a silver ladder telescoped down

to her from below the door. I thought, *the Pilot must have had it keyed to her some way, so it would let down for her but nobody else. A very lovely gesture.*

The ladder went up after her and we managed to lift the body above our heads, our arms straight, and we walked it through the door of the plane that way, she receiving it.

The door closed and we stood back and the plane took off into the orange haze, us watching it until it was swallowed.

Pop said, "Right now, I imagine you two feel pretty good in a screwed-up sort of way. I know I do. But take it from me, it won't last. A day or two and we're going to start feeling another way, the *old* way, if we don't get busy."

I knew he was right. You don't shake old Urge Number One anything like that easy.

"So," said Pop, "I got places I want to show you. Guys I want you to meet. And there's things to do, a lot of them. Let's get moving."

So there's my story. Alice is still with me (Urge Number Two is even harder to shake, supposing you wanted to), and we haven't killed anybody lately. (Not since the Pilot, in fact, but it doesn't do to boast.) We're making a stab (my language!) at doing the sort of work Pop does in the Deathlands. It's tough but interesting. I still carry a knife, but I've given Mother to Pop. He has it strapped to him alongside Alice's screw-in blade.

Atla-Hi and Alamos still seem to be in existence, so I guess the serum worked for them generally as it did for the Pilot's Woman; they haven't sent us any medals, but they haven't sent a hangman's squad after us either—which is more than fair, you'll admit. But Savannah, turned back from Atla-Hi, is still going strong: there's a rumor they have an army at the gates of Ouachita right now. We tell Pop he'd better start preaching fast—it's one of our standard jokes.

There's also a rumor that a certain fellowship of Death-landers is doing surprisingly well, a rumor that there's a new America growing in the Deathlands—an America that never need kill again. But don't put too much stock in it. Not *too* much.

The society that grew out across the Deathlands, as the cobalt lost its poison, achieved stability by a brilliant paradox. Man started on his way to the stars again. Mars shrugged his shoulders.

The elected executives of this new society had a great respect for the League of Sanity, though they often smiled at it. They were devoted humanists, yet they had a few quirks.

There was a man who decided to cure their quirks and achieve the ideal for humanity. No one in human history ever thought as much about sanity as he did. We may call him (and now is the time to guess whether he is Phy or Carrsbury)—

CRAZY WOLF

"COME in, Phy, and make yourself comfortable."

The mellow voice—and the suddenly dilating doorway—caught the general secretary of the World playing with a blob of greenish gasoid, squeezing it in his fist and watching it ooze between his fingers in spatulate tendrils that did not dissipate. Slowly, crookedly, he turned his head. World Manager Carrsbury became aware of a gaze that was at once oafish, sly, vacuous. Abruptly the expression was replaced by a nervous smile. The thin man straightened himself, as much as his habitually drooping shoulders would permit, hastily entered, and sat down on the extreme edge of a pneumatically form-fitting chair.

He embarrassedly fumbled the blob of gasoid, looking around for a convenient disposal vent or a crevice in the upholstery. Finding none, he stuffed it hurriedly into his pocket. Then he repressed his fidgetings by clasping his hands resolutely together, and sat with downcast eyes.

"How are you feeling, old man?" Carrsbury asked in a voice that was warm with a benign friendliness.

The general secretary did not look up.

"Anything bothering you, Phy?" Carrsbury continued solicitously. "Do you feel a bit unhappy, or dissatisfied, about your . . . er . . . transfer, now that the moment has arrived?"

Still the general secretary did not respond. Carrsbury leaned forward across the dully silver, semicircular desk and, in his most winning tones, urged, "Come on, old fellow, tell me all about it."

The general secretary did not lift his head, but he rolled up his strange, distant eyes until they were fixed directly on Carrsbury. He shivered a little, his body seemed to contract, and his bloodless hands tightened their interlocking grip.

"I know," he said in a low, effortful voice. "You think I'm insane."

Carrsbury sat back, forcing his brows to assume a baffled frown under the mane of silvery hair.

"Oh, you needn't pretend to be puzzled," Phy continued, swiftly now that he had broken the ice. "You know what that word means as well as I do. Better—even though we both had to do historical research to find out.

"Insane," he repeated dreamily, his gaze wavering. "Significant departure from the norm. Inability to conform to basic conventions underlying all human conduct."

"Nonsense!" said Carrsbury, rallying and putting on his warmest and most compelling smile. "I haven't the slightest idea of what you're talking about. That you're a little tired, a little strained, a little distraught—that's quite understandable, considering the burden you've been carrying, and a little rest will be just the thing to fix you up, a nice long vacation away from all this. But as for your being . . . why, ridiculous!"

"No," said Phy, his gaze pinning Carrsbury. "You think I'm insane. You think all my colleagues in the World Management Service are insane. That's why you're having us replaced with those men you've been training for ten years in your Institute of Political Leadership—ever since, with my help and connivance, you became World Manager."

Carrsbury retreated before the finality of the statement.

For the first time his smile became a bit uncertain. He started to say something, then hesitated and looked at Phy, as if half hoping he would go on.

But that individual was once again staring rigidly at the floor.

Carrsbury leaned back, thinking. When he spoke it was in a more natural voice, much less consciously soothing and fatherly.

"Well, all right, Phy. But look here, tell me something, honestly. Won't you—and the others—be a lot happier when you've been relieved of all your responsibilities?"

Phy nodded somberly. "Yes," he said, "we will . . . but"—his face became strained—"you see—"

"But—?" Carrsbury prompted.

Phy swallowed hard. He seemed unable to go on. He had gradually slumped toward one side of the chair, and the pressure had caused the green gasoid to ooze from his pocket. His long fingers crept over and kneaded it fretfully.

Carrsbury stood up and came around the desk. His sympathetic frown, from which perplexity had ebbed, was now quite genuine.

"I don't see why I shouldn't tell you all about it now, Phy," he said simply. "In a queer sort of way I owe it all to you. And there isn't any point now in keeping it a secret . . . there isn't any danger—"

"Yes," Phy agreed with a quick bitter smile, "you haven't been in any danger of a *coup d'état* for some years now. If ever we should have revolted, there'd have been"—his gaze shifted to a point in the opposite wall where a faint vertical crease indicated the presence of a doorway—"your secret police."

Carrsbury started. He hadn't thought Phy had known. Disturbingly, there loomed in his mind a phrase: *the cunning of the insane*. But only for a moment. Friendly complacency flooded back. He went behind Phy's chair and rested his hands on the sloping shoulders.

"You know, I've always had a special feeling toward you, Phy," he said, "and not only because your whims made it a lot easier for me to become World Manager. I've always felt that you were different from the others, that there were times when—" He hesitated.

Phy squirmed a little under the friendly hands. "When I had my moments of sanity?" he finished flatly.

"Like now," said Carrsbury softly, after a nod the other could not see. "I've always felt that sometimes, in a kind of twisted, unrealistic way, you *understood*. And that has meant a lot to me. I've been alone, Phy, dreadfully alone, for ten whole years. No companionship anywhere, not even among the men I've been training in the Institute of Political Leadership—for I've had to play a part with them too, keep them in ignorance of certain facts, for fear they would try to seize power over my head before they were sufficiently prepared. No companionship anywhere, except for my hopes—and for occasional moments with you. Now that it's over and a new regime is beginning for us both, I can tell you that. And I'm glad."

There was silence. Then—Phy did not look around, but one lean hand crept up and touched Carrsbury's. Carrsbury cleared his throat. Strange, he thought, that there could be even a momentary rapport like this between the sane and the insane. But it was so.

He disengaged his hands, strode rapidly back to his desk, turned.

"I'm a throwback, Phy," he began in a new, unused, eager voice. "A throwback to a time when human mentality was far sounder. Whether my case was due chiefly to heredity, or to certain unusual accidents of environment, or to both, is unimportant. The point is that a person had been born who was in a position to criticize the present state of mankind in the light of the past, to diagnose its condition, and to begin its cure. For a long time I refused to face the facts, but finally my researches—especially those in the literature of the twentieth century—left me no alternative. The mentality of mankind had become—aberrant. Only certain technological advances, which had resulted in making the business of living infinitely easier and simpler, and the fact that war had been ended with the creation of the present world state, were staving off the inevitable breakdown of civilization. But only staving it off—delaying it. The great masses of mankind had become what would once have been called hopelessly neurotic. Their leaders had become . . . you said it first, Phy . . . insane. Incidentally, this latter phenomenon—the drift of psychological aberrants toward leadership—has been noted in all ages."

He paused. Was he mistaken, or was Phy following his words with indications of a greater mental clarity than he had ever noted before, even in the relatively nonviolent World Secretary? Perhaps—he had often dreamed wistfully of the possibility—there was still a chance of saving Phy. Perhaps, if he just explained to him clearly and calmly—

"In my historical studies," he continued, "I soon came to the conclusion that the crucial period was that of the Final Amnesty, concurrent with the founding of the present world state. We are taught that at that time there were released from confinement millions of political prisoners—and millions of others. Just who were those others? To this question, our present histories gave only vague and platitudinous answers. The semantic difficulties I encountered were exceedingly obstinate. But I kept hammering away. Why, I asked myself, have such words as insanity, lunacy, madness, psychosis, disappeared from our vocabulary—and the concepts behind them from our thought? Why has the subject 'abnormal psychology' disappeared from the curricula of our schools? Of greater significance, why is our modern psychology strikingly similar to the field of abnormal psychology as taught in the twentieth century, and to that field alone? Why are there no longer, as there were in the twentieth century, any institutions for the confinement and care of the psychologically aberrant?"

Phy's head jerked up. He smiled twistedly. "Because," he whispered slyly, "everyone's insane now."

The cunning of the insane. Again that phrase loomed warningly in Carrsbury's mind. But only for a moment. He nodded.

"At first I refused to make that deduction. But gradually I reasoned out the why and wherefore of what had happened. It wasn't only that a highly technological civilization had subjected mankind to a wider and more swiftly tempoed range of stimulations, conflicting suggestions, mental strains, emotional wrenchings. In the literature of twentieth-century psychitary there are observations on a kind of psychosis that results from success. An unbalanced individual keeps going so long as he is fighting something, struggling toward a goal. He reaches his goal—and goes to pieces. His repressed confusions come to the surface, he realizes that he doesn't know what he wants at all, his energies hitherto engaged in combatting something outside himself are turned against himself, he is destroyed. Well, when war was finally outlawed, when the whole world became one unified state, when social inequality was abolished . . . you see what I'm driving at?"

Phy nodded slowly. "That," he said in a curious, distant voice, "is a very interesting deduction."

"Having reluctantly accepted my main premise," Carrsbury went on, "everything became clear. The cyclic six-months' fluctuations in world credit—I realized at once that Morgenstern of Finance must be a manic-depressive with a six-months' phase, or else a dual personality with one aspect a spendthrift, the other a miser. It turned out to be the former. Why was the Department of Cultural Advancement stagnating? Because Manager Hobart was markedly catatonic. Why the boom in Extraterrestrial Research? Because McElvy was a euphoric."

Phy looked at him wonderingly. "But naturally," he said, spreading his lean hands, from one of which the gasoid dropped like a curl of green smoke.

Carrsbury glanced at him sharply. He replied, "Yes, I know that you and several of the others have a certain warped awareness of the differences between your . . . personalities, though none whatsoever of the basic aberration involved in them all. But to get on. As soon as I realized the situation, my course was marked out. As a sane man, capable of entertaining fixed realistic purposes, and surrounded by individuals of whose inconsistencies and delusions it was easy to make use, I was in a position to attain, with time and tact, any goal at which I might aim. I was already in the Managerial Service. In three years I became World Manager. Once there, my range of influence was vastly enhanced. Like the man in Archimedes' epigram, I had a place to stand from which I could move the world. I was able, in various guises and on various pretexts, to promulgate regulations the actual purpose of which was to soothe the great neurotic masses by curtailing upsetting stimulations and introducing a more regimented and orderly program of living. I was able, by humoring my fellow executives and making the fullest use of my greater capacity for work, to keep world affairs staggering along fairly safely—at least stave off the worst. At the same time I was able to begin my Ten Years' Plan—the training, in comparative isolation, first in small numbers, then in larger, as those instructed could in turn become instructors, of a group of prospective leaders carefully selected on the basis of their relative freedom from neurotic tendencies."

"But that—" Phy began rather excitedly, starting up.

"But what?" Carrsbury inquired quickly.

"Nothing," muttered Phy dejectedly, sinking back.

"That about covers it," Carrsbury concluded, his voice suddenly grown a little duller. "Except for one secondary matter. I couldn't afford to let myself go ahead without any protection. Too much depended on me. There was always the risk of being wiped out by some ill-coordinated but none the less effective spasm of violence, momentarily uncontrollable by tact, on the part of my fellow executives. So, only because I could see no alternative, I took a dangerous step. I created"—his glance strayed toward the faint crease in the side wall—"my secret police. There is a type of insanity known as paranoia, an exaggerated suspiciousness involving delusions of persecution. By means of the late-twentieth-century Rand technique of hypnotism, I inculcated a number of these unfortunate individuals with the fixed idea that their lives depended on me and that I was threatened from all sides and must be protected at all costs. A distasteful expedient, even though it served its purpose. I shall be glad, very glad, to see it discontinued. You can understand, can't you, why I had to take that step?"

He looked questioningly at Phy—and became aware with a shock that that individual was grinning at him vacuously and holding up the gasoid between two fingers.

"I cut a hole in my couch and a lot of this stuff came out," Phy explained in a thick naïve voice. "Ropes of it got all over my office. I kept tripping." His fingers patted at it deftly, sculpturing it into the form of a hideous transparent green head, which he proceeded to squeeze out of existence. "Queer stuff," he rambled on, "rarefied liquid. Gas of fixed volume. And all over my office floor, tangled up with the furniture."

Carrsbury leaned back and shut his eyes. His shoulders slumped. He felt suddenly a little weary, a little eager for his day of triumph to be done. He knew he shouldn't be despondent because he had failed with Phy. After all, the main victory was won. Phy was the merest of side issues. He had always known that, except for flashes, Phy was hopeless as the rest. Still—

"You don't need to worry about your office floor, Phy,"

he said with a listless kindliness. "Never any more. Your successor will have to see about cleaning it up. Already, you know, to all intents and purposes, you have been replaced."

"That's just it!" Carrsbury started at Phy's explosive loudness. The World Secretary jumped up and strode toward him, pointing an excited hand. "That's what I came to see you about! That's what I've been trying to tell you! I can't be replaced like that! None of the others can, either! It won't work! You can't do it!"

With a swiftness born of long practice, Carrsbury slipped behind his desk. He forced his features into that expression of calm, smiling benevolence of which he had grown unutterably weary.

"Now, now, Phy," he said brightly, soothingly, "if I can't do it, of course I can't do it. But don't you think you ought to tell me why? Don't you think it would be very nice to sit down and talk it all over and you tell me why?"

Phy halted and hung his head, abashed.

"Yes, I guess it would," he said slowly, abruptly falling back into the low, effortful tones. "I guess I'll have to. I guess there just isn't any other way. I had hoped, though, not to have to tell you everything." The last sentence was half question. He looked up wheedlingly at Carrsbury. The latter shook his head, continuing to smile. Phy went back and sat down.

"Well," he finally began, gloomily kneading the gasoid, "it all began when you first wanted to be World Manager. You weren't the usual type, but I thought it would be kind of fun—yes, and kind of helpful." He looked up at Carrsbury. "You've really done the World a lot of good in quite a lot of ways, always remember that," he assured him. "Of course," he added, again focusing on the tortured gasoid, "they weren't exactly the ways you thought."

"No?" Carrsbury prompted automatically. *Humor him. Humor him.* The wornout refrain droned in his mind.

Phy sadly shook his head. "Take those regulations you promulgated to soothe people—"

"Yes?"

"—they kind of got changed on the way. For instance, your prohibition, regarding reading tapes, of all exciting literature . . . oh, we tried a little of the soothing stuff you suggested at first. Everyone got a great kick out of it. They laughed and laughed. But afterward, well, as I said, it kind of got changed—in this case to a prohibition of all *unexciting* literature."

Carrsbury's smile broadened. For a moment the edge of his mind had toyed with a fear, but Phy's last remark had banished it.

"Every day I coast past several reading stands," Carrsbury said gently. "The fiction tapes offered for sale are always in the most chastely and simply colored containers. None of those wild and lurid pictures that one used to see everywhere."

"But did you ever buy one and listen to it? Or project the visual text?" Phy questioned apologetically.

"For ten years I've been a very busy man," Carrsbury answered.

"Of course I've read the official reports regarding such matters, and at times glanced through sample résumés of taped fiction."

"Oh, sure, that sort of official stuff," agreed Phy, glancing up at the wall of tape files beyond the desk. "What we did, you see, was to keep the monochrome containers but go back to the old kind of contents. The contrast kind of tickled people. Remember, as I said before, a lot of your regulations have done good. Cut out a lot of unnecessary noise and inefficient foolishness, for one thing."

That sort of official stuff. The phrase lingered unpleasantly in Carrsbury's ears. There was a trace of irrepressible suspicion in his quick over-the-shoulder glance at the tiered tape files.

"Oh, yes," Phy went on, "and that prohibition against yielding to unusual or indecent impulses, with a long listing of specific categories. It went into effect all right, but with a little rider attached: 'unless you really want to.' That seemed absolutely necessary, you know." His fingers worked furiously with the gasoid. "As for the prohibition of various stimulating beverages—well, in this locality they're still served under other names, and an interesting custom has grown up of behaving very soberly while imbibing them. Now when we come to that matter of the eight-hour working day—"

Almost involuntarily, Carrsbury had got up and walked over to the outer wall. With a flip of his hand through an invisible U-shaped beam, he switched on the window. It was as if the outer wall had disappeared. Through its near-perfect transparency, he peered down with fierce curiosity past the sleekly gleaming façades to the terraces and parkways below.

The modest throngs seemed quiet and orderly enough. But then there was a scurry of confusion—a band of people, at this angle all tiny heads with arms and legs, came out from a shop far below and began to pelt another group with what looked like foodstuffs. While, on a side parkway, two small ovoid vehicles, seamless drops of silver because their vision panels were invisible from the outside, butted each other playfully. Someone started to run.

Carrsbury hurriedly switched off the window and turned around. Those were just off-chance occurrences, he told himself angrily. Of no real statistical significance whatever. For ten years mankind had steadily been trending toward sanity despite occasional relapses. He'd seen it with his own eyes, seen the day-by-day progress—at least enough to know. He'd been a fool to let Phy's ramblings affect him—only tired nerves had made that possible.

He glanced at his timepiece.

"Excuse me," he said curtly, striding past Phy's chair, "I'd like to continue this conversation, but I have to get along to the first meeting of the new Central Managerial Staff."

"Oh but you can't!" Instantly Phy was up and dragging at his arm. "You just can't do it, you know! It's impossible!"

The pleading voice rose toward a scream. Impatiently Carrsbury tried to shake loose. The seam in the side wall widened, became a doorway. Instantly both of them stopped struggling.

In the doorway stood a cadaverous giant of a man with a stubby dark weapon in his hand. Straggly black beard shaded into gaunt cheeks. His face was a cruel blend of suspicion and fanatical devotion, the first directed along with the weapon at Phy, the second—and the somnambulistic eyes—at Carrsbury.

"He was threatening you?" the bearded man asked in a harsh voice, moving the weapon suggestively.

For a moment an angry, vindictive light glinted in Carrsbury's eyes. Then it flicked out. What could he have been thinking, he asked himself. This poor lunatic World Secretary was no one to hate.

"Not at all, Hartman," he remarked calmly. "We were

discussing something and we became excited and allowed our voices to rise. Everything is quite all right."

"Very well," said the bearded man doubtfully, after a pause. Reluctantly he returned his weapon to its holster, but he kept his hand on it and remained standing in the doorway.

"And now," said Carrsbury, disengaging himself, "I must go."

He had stepped onto the corridor slidewalk and had coasted halfway to the elevator before he realized that Phy had followed him and was plucking timidly at his sleeve.

"You can't go off like this," Phy pleaded urgently, with an apprehensive backward glance. Carrsbury noted that Hartman had also followed—an ominous pylon two paces to the rear. "You must give me a chance to explain, to tell you why, just like you asked me."

Humor him. Carrsbury's mind was deadly tired of the drone, but mere weariness prompted him to dance to it a little longer. "You can talk to me in the elevator," he conceded, stepping off the slidewalk. His finger flipped through a U-beam and a serpentine movement of light across the wall traced the elevator's obedient rise.

"You see, it wasn't just that matter of prohibitory regulations," Phy launched out hurriedly. "There were lots of other things that never did work out like your official reports indicated. Departmental budgets for instance. The reports showed, I know, that appropriations for Extraterrestrial Research were being regularly slashed. Actually, in your ten years of office, they increased tenfold. Of course, there was no way for you to know that. You couldn't be all over the world at once and see each separate launching of suprastratospheric rockets."

The moving light became stationary. A seam dilated. Carrsbury stepped into the elevator. He debated sending Hartman back. Poor babbling Phy was no menace. Still—*the cunning of the insane.* He decided against it, reached out and flipped the control beam at the sector which would bring them to the hundredth and top floor. The door snipped softly shut. The cage became a surging darkness in which floor numerals winked softly. Twenty-one. Twenty-two. Twenty-three.

"And then there was the Military Service. You had it sharply curtailed."

"Of course I did." Sheer weariness stung Carrsbury into

talk. "There's only one country in the world. Obviously, the only military requirement is an adequate police force. To say nothing of the risks involved in putting weapons into the hands of the present world population."

"I know," Phy's answer came guiltily from the darkness. "Still, what's happened is that, unknown to you, the Military Service has been increased in size, and recently four rocket squadrons have been added."

Fifty-seven. Fifty-eight. *Humor him.* "Why?"

"Well, you see we've found out that Earth is being reconnoitered. Maybe from Andromeda. Maybe hostile. Have to be prepared. We didn't tell you . . . well, because we were afraid it might excite you."

The voice trailed off. Carrsbury shut his eyes. How long, he asked himself, how long? He realized with dull surprise that in the last hour people like Phy, endured for ten years, had become unutterably wearisome to him. For the moment even the thought of the conference over which he would soon be presiding, the conference that was to usher in a sane world, failed to stir him. Reaction to success? To the end of a ten years' tension?

"Do you know how many floors there are in this building?"

Carrsbury was not immediately conscious of the new note in Phy's voice, but he reacted to it.

"One hundred," he replied promptly.

"Then," asked Phy, "just where are we?"

Carr opened his eyes to the darkness. One hundred twenty-seven, blinked the floor numeral. One hundred twenty-eight. One hundred twenty-nine.

Something cold dragged at Carrsbury's stomach, pulled at his brain. He felt as if his mind were being slowly and irresistibly twisted. He thought of hidden dimensions, of unsuspected holes in space. Something remembered from elementary physics danced through his thoughts: If it were possible for an elevator to keep moving upward with uniform acceleration, no one inside an elevator could determine whether the effects they were experiencing were due to acceleration or to gravity—whether the elevator were standing motionless on some planet or shooting up at ever-increasing velocity through free space.

One hundred forty-one. One hundred forty-two.

"Or as if you were rising through consciousness into

an unsuspected realm of mentality lying above," suggested Phy in his new voice, with its hint of gentle laughter.

One hundred forty-six. One hundred forty-seven. It was slowing now. One hundred forty-nine. One hundred fifty. It had stopped.

This was some trick. The thought was like cold water in Carrsbury's face. Some cunning childish trick of Phy's. An easy thing to hocus the numerals. Carrsbury groped irascibly about in the darkness, encountered the slick surface of a holster, Hartman's gaunt frame.

"Get ready for a surprise," Phy warned from close at his elbow.

As Carrsbury turned and grabbed, bright sunlight drenched him, followed by a gripping, heart-stopping spasm of vertigo.

He, Hartman, and Phy, along with a few insubstantial bits of furnishings and controls, were standing in the air fifty stories above the hundred-story summit of World Managerial Center.

For a moment he grabbed frantically at nothing. Then he realized they were not falling and his eyes began to trace the hint of walls and ceiling and floor and, immediately below them, the ghost of a shaft.

Phy nodded. "That's all there is to it," he assured Carrsbury casually. "Just another of those charmingly odd modern notions against which you have legislated so persistently—like our incomplete staircases and roads to nowhere and those charming garden paths which ended in drops, not stairs, and the British called 'ha-has.' The Buildings and Grounds Committee decided to extend the range of the elevator for sightseeing purposes. The shaft was made air-transparent to avoid spoiling the form of the original building and to improve the view. This was achieved so satisfactorily that an electronic warning system had to be installed for the safety of passing airjets and other craft. Treating the surfaces of the cage like windows was an obvious detail."

He paused and looked quizzically at Carrsbury. "All very simple," he observed, "but don't you find a kind of symbolism in it? For ten years now you've been spending most of your life in that building below. Every day you've used this elevator. But not once have you dreamed of these fifty extra stories. Don't you think that something of the same sort may be true of your observations of other aspects of contemporary social life?"

Carrsbury gaped at him stupidly.

Phy turned to watch the growing speck of an approaching aircraft. "You might look at it too," he remarked to Carrsbury, "for it's going to transport you to a far happier, more restful life."

Carrsbury parted his lips, wet them. "But—" he said, unsteadily. "But—"

Phy smiled. "That's right, I didn't finish my explanation. Well, you might have gone on being World Manager all your life, in the isolation of your office and your miles of taped official reports and your occasional confabs with me and the others. Except for your Institute of Political Leadership and your Ten-Years' Plan. That upset things. Of course, we were as much interested in it as we were in you. It had definite possibilities. We hoped it would work out. We would have been glad to retire from office if it had. But, most fortunately, it didn't. And that sort of ended the whole experiment."

He caught the downward direction of Carrsbury's gaze.

"No," he said, "I'm afraid your pupils aren't waiting for you in the conference chamber on the hundredth story. I'm afraid they're still in the Institute." His voice became gently sympathetic. "And I'm afraid that it's become . . . well . . . a somewhat different sort of institute."

Carrsbury stood very still, swaying a little. Gradually his thoughts and his will power were emerging from the waking nightmare that had paralyzed them. *The cunning of the insane*—he had neglected that trenchant warning. In the very moment of victory—

No! He had forgotten Hartman! This was the very emergency for which that counterstroke had been prepared.

He glanced sideways at the chief member of his secret police. The black giant, unconcerned by their strange position, was glaring fixedly at Phy as if at some evil magician from whom any malign impossibility could be expected.

Now Hartman became aware of Carrsbury's gaze. He divined his thought.

He drew his dark weapon from its holster, pointed it unwaveringly at Phy.

His black-bearded lips curled. From them came a hissing sound. Then, in a loud voice, he cried, "You're dead, Phy! I disintegrated you."

Phy reached over and took the weapon from his hand.

"That's another respect in which you completely miscalculated the modern temperament," he remarked to Carrsbury, a shade argumentatively. "All of us have certain subjects on which we're a trifle unrealistic. That's only human nature. Hartman's was his suspiciousness—a weakness for ideas involving plots and persecutions. You gave him the worst sort of job—one that catered to and encouraged his weaknesses. In a very short time he became hopelessly unrealistic. Why for years he's never realized that he's been carrying a dummy pistol."

"But," he added, "give him the proper job and he'd function well enough—say something in creation or exploration or social service. Fitting the man to the job is an art with infinite possibilities. That's why we had Morgenstern in Finance—to keep credit fluctuating in a safe, predictable rhythm. That's why a euphoric is made manager of Extraterrestrial Research—to keep it booming. Why a catatonic is given Cultural Advancement—to keep it from tripping on its face in its haste to get ahead."

He turned away. Dully, Carrsbury observed that the aircraft was hovering close to the cage and sidling slowly in.

"But in that case why—" he began stupidly.

"Why were you made World Manager?" Phy finished easily. "Isn't that fairly obvious? Haven't I told you several times that you did a lot of good, indirectly? You interested us, don't you see? In fact, you were practically unique. As you know, it's our cardinal principle to let every individual express himself as he wants to. In your case, that involved letting you become World Manager. Taken all in all it worked out very well. Everyone had a good time, a number of constructive regulations were promulgated, we learned a lot— oh, we didn't get everything we hoped for, but one never does. Unfortunately, in the end, we were forced to discontinue the experiment."

The aircraft had made contact.

"You understand, of course, why that was necessary?" Phy continued hurriedly, as he urged Carrsbury toward the opening port. "I'm sure you must. It all comes down to a question of sanity. What is sanity—now, in the twentieth century, any time? Adherence to a norm. Conformity to certain basic conventions underlying all human conduct. In our age, departure from the norm has become the norm.

Inability to conform has become the standard of conformity. That's quite clear, isn't it? And it enables you to understand, doesn't it, your own case and that of your protégés? Over a long period of years you persisted in adhering to a norm, in conforming to certain basic conventions. You were completely unable to adapt yourself to the society around you. You could only pretend—and your protégés wouldn't have been able to do even that. Despite your many engaging personal characteristics, there was obviously only one course of action open to us."

In the port Carrsbury turned. He had found his voice at last. It was hoarse, ragged. "You mean that all these years you've just been *humoring* me?"

The port was closing. Phy called, "There was an Oglala Sioux Indian named Crazy Horse. He licked Crook and he licked Custer. Don't think I'm underestimating your strength, Carrsbury."

As the aircraft edged out, he waved farewell with the blob of green gasoid.

"It'll be very pleasant where you're going," he shouted encouragingly. "Comfortable quarters, adequate facilities for exercise, and a complete library of twentieth-century literature to while away your time."

He watched Carrsbury's rigid face, staring whitely from the vision port, until the aircraft had diminished to a speck.

Then he turned away, looked at his hands, noticed the gasoid, tossed it out the open door of the cage, studied its flight for a few moments, then flicked the downbeam.

"I'm glad to see the last of that fellow," he muttered, more to himself than to Hartman, as they plummeted toward the roof. "He was beginning to have a very disturbing influence on me. In fact, I was beginning to fear for my"—his expression became suddenly vacuous—"insanity."

THE men who tamed Crazy Wolf lost their superb balance. Their successors reintroduced man's basic insanity—for humane reasons, they thought, and in the most humane way. Once more, Mars roared.

Yet by this time the League of Sanity was organized, though on a carefree basis. Mars, laughing like a maniac, was worried.

We may call the leaders of the League of Sanity—

THE WOLF PACK

I

JUST INSIDE the weatherdome Normsi stripped off his flying togs and hung them on the family rack. He noticed Allisoun's and her brother Willisoun's, his father's and mother's, and his own walking togs.

Outside it was chilly winter with a low red sun, but under the intangible hemisphere of the weatherdome the atoms were domesticated. Here were light, heat, life-giving radiation. The warm, moist air moved in gentle currents—a little kept leaking from the lee side of the dome, to condense into white vapor and whirl away.

Flowers bloomed, buds opened, grass pushed up. Here was perpetual spring.

Norm's world was like the weatherdome. He was a healthy, well-educated, uninjured young man, had an attractive job as a teletaction technician, looked forward to an early marriage with the girl he loved.

A world economy of abundance supplied him with conveniences, luxuries, and recreations almost beyond the dreams of earlier ages. There were even charming female psychiatrists to teach him sexual behavior.

A single government had ruled the world for two centuries. There had been no civil war for more than a hundred years.

The exploration of the nearer planets had brought to light no intelligent or dangerous nonintelligent enemies of mankind. Indeed, the opening up of Mars and Venus had proved rather anticlimactic, since their harsh environments prevented easy colonization and Earth's synthetics-based self-sufficiency took the urgency from the search for new sources of mineral and organic wealth. The new planets would serve chiefly as stations for cosmological research, until gradual scientific exploration of their life-patterns opened yet unseen vistas.

Nor was Norm's body the uneasy prey of disease germs and degenerative processes. He had far better than a 99 percent chance of escaping such dangers as long as he lived.

Yet, standing there in the garden beside the togsrack, Norm did not look like that fortunate man. If his eyes had been closed, his face would have registered as young, fresh, healthy. But with them open, the fear of death infected every feature.

He delayed near the togsrack, running his hand through his close-cropped hair, smoothing his pajama neckband, where a line of red, white, and blue recalled the necktie of ancient times.

With a sudden headshake, he started up the path toward the house. Halfway there his eye strayed to the grass. He pushed at a weed with the toe of his moccasin, remained staring at the tiny green world at his feet.

Even the vastest weatherdome has its outside, its region of storms and darkness and the unknown.

An ant struggled up one of the grassblades. Without thinking he set his foot on it, then drew back, wincing as though he had glimpsed something particularly unpleasant, and hurried on to the house. As the door opened, he readied his lips for a grin of relief.

But the grin never came. He stopped, and surveyed his family circle.

His mother, plumped down on the pneumatic blob of couch, had what he called her hurt look.

His father, sitting beside her, stared straight ahead. His

mouth was pursed in a way that might have seemed grim in a bigger man.

Allisoun, sprawled on the resilient floor where it tilted up to merge with the wall at the other end of the room, looked doped. Her face was white, her eyelids red.

Willisoun, near her, studied Norm queerly. His fingers played with a cut flower, rolling and unrolling the petals, occasionally tugging one out.

Norm went over to the teletaction panel and plucked from the slot the newly engraved golden card bearing his death notice.

He studied the neat print. "You, Normsi," (there followed his citizenship number) "have been singled out by lot for a service of the highest honor that a citizen can render this world. You will . . ."

He heard an inane voice say, "Oh well, somebody has to get them," and realized that it was his own.

At that his mother reacted. She was on her feet and talking in a hoarsely agonized way, as if she'd been going on for half an hour, "You don't know what you're saying, Norm! It's horrible! Horrible! Don't you realize that you'll be . . ."

". . . solely for the good of humanity, of course, and to avert far worse destruction . . . ." his father put in hurriedly, apologetically.

". . . Destroyed! Destroyed!" It was Allisoun who sobbed out the words, throwing her arms around him.

He looked at them warily—his mother gripping his arm, demanding attention, his father peering over her shoulder, Allisoun's soft hair pushing against his cheek, Willisoun keeping his distance.

He heard the inane voice say, "Oh well, that's war for you. Can't be helped."

"Don't say it!" his mother implored. "Oh, Norm, I can't bear to think of them taking you away. Why should it have to happen to us?"

His father was staring at the far wall, working his lips. ". . . And when he's so young, just starting life. . . ." He muttered the words, as if accusing someone invisible.

"Don't let them, Norm," Allisoun sobbed into his neck.

"There's nothing you can do about it," the inane voice observed. He was beginning to hate its very sound.

His mother stood back. There were tears running down her cheeks.

"I won't let them take you," she said.

For a moment the others just looked at her. Then they caught fire from her spark.

"We'll fight them!" chimed his father, clenching his little fists and grinning spasmodically as he always did when he said anything in the least violent.

"Can't be done—" But the inane voice was swallowed up in a confused chorus of "We'll find ways," "You're ours, and we don't care what they do to us," and "Yes, by Man, we'll fight them!"

Allisoun said nothing, but she kept nodding her head against his chin and clung to him like death.

Willisoun dropped the half-stripped flower and shuffled up. "I've got influence," he said uneasily. "I'll see you get out. I won't let you down."

Suddenly the voices all stopped. In the silence Norm looked around. It occurred to him that they were waiting for him to say something. He looked around again. The faces wavered a little, but the look of anxious expectation stayed in the eyes. There was something embarrassing about that look.

"All right," he said quietly. "The worst they can do is kill me in disgrace instead of honor. I won't let them take me."

For a moment the significance of the dropped jaws, the raised eyebrows, didn't dawn on him. Even when Allisoun recoiled from him, lifting her tear-smeared disconcerted face.

Then it hit him.

His jaw tightened.

It was almost amusing to see the hasty, aggrieved way they began to backtrack, once he had called their bluff. His father began it.

"Now, Norm, I wouldn't do anything rash. We're all for you, my boy, of course, but there are so many things that have to be considered. It's terrible, I know, but the government has reasons for doing this thing—reasons which it's hard for a single individual to understand."

"Reasons for killing me?"

"Oh, it's ghastly when you put it that way, of course. But—did you hear Director M'Caslrai this afternoon?"

"No."

"You should have. He stressed that they were taking this

step only with the greatest reluctance, after exploring every conceivable alternative. He emphasized that this time we'd managed to avoid war for a period of thirty-five years, longer than ever before—in itself a notable accomplishment. But he pointed out that we dared not frustrate the mounting death-wish of mankind any longer. That death-wish is the realest thing in the world, Norm. It's the same guilt-urge that led thousands to confess to hideous crimes they never committed in the ancient witchcraft trials and political purges. It's the same hate-urge that piled pyramids of skulls before conquered cities and hills of human ashes before conquered countries. It's the thing that caused all past two-sided wars, with their messiness and inefficiency and their horrible unpredictability—their tendency to leap all bounds and engulf everyone. That inexorable death-wish, clearly indicated by the rocketing suicide and murder rates and a thousand other statistics, would inevitably break out in revolution or collective bestiality and probably, considering our degree of technical advancement, destroy all mankind—unless (as we have done successfully before—that's the big point!) *unless we declare war.*"

"And he mentioned the religious side," his mother broke in, using what Norm called her hushed voice. "He said—" She choked a little but continued bravely, "—that Man the Hero must sacrifice himself to Man the Devil in order that Man the God may be able to go on."

"Oh that rot!"

She stepped back. Norm's father put his arm around her.

"I know what you're feeling, Norm," he said. "I was through it all myself, last time, and—"

"Were you picked?" Norm's voice was like a thrown rock.

"No, of course not—"

"Then you don't understand anything." He whirled on Willisoun. "I suppose they missed you too. Yes, of course they would. Bureaucracy's darling." As Willisoun bristled, Norm turned back to his parents.

"Let's get this straight now. Do you mean to tell me that you're willing to see my life snuffed out by war? Yes, Mother, I realize it's an intensely painful subject, but what I want to know is this: Do you think it's all right to kill fifty million people in order to save five billion from some possible greater injury? Don't look at me that way, Mother!

I know I'm being crude and unkind, but it's the way I feel."

She lifted her head. Her lips trembled, but her voice was almost imploringly sweet as she said, "I know that no son of mine will do anything that will bring disgrace on himself and his family."

Her husband's arm tightened around her protectively, and the little man said, "Don't you see, Norm, you wouldn't be asked to do this unless it were absolutely necessary? Do you imagine I'd stand by without protesting if I thought it were? But the collective death-wish is a terrible thing and, as M'Caslrai kept hammering home, we've got to be realistic about it. We can only hold it in check by great sacrifices. For two hundred years we've been making those sacrifices. When absolutely necessary, we've declared war. But if we ever stopped . . ."

Norm snorted. "Do you believe everything M'Caslrai shoves down your throat? Can't you see that war is an inhuman device, a confession of failure, a throwback to the dirtiest superstitions? Men have been sacrificed before now to jealous gods and bloodhungry demons. Ever since history began, scapegoats have been selected and stoned. I wouldn't mind war against a tangible enemy—"

"What!" his mother interrupted. "Why, that would be horrible. To go out with hate in your heart and *kill* other people . . ."

"I can think of some cases in which it would be eminently worthwhile," said Norm harshly. "At least I'd get a run for my money. But this business of donating my body as a safety valve for man's destructive impulses—"

"But only to prevent worse destruction," his father cut in, his face contorted monkeywise in his eagerness to assuage. "It's only because any alternative would be far worse, that you're being called upon. It's to save people like your mother and Allisoun from indescribable horrors. I'm sure, Norm, that if you could see it in that light, you'd be only too willing—"

"To die? In order to preserve the present unholy setup that fattens on these sacrifices? To keep fossils like M'Caslrai in their present position? For that's all it really comes down to—a conspiracy against the young men so they won't upset the old men's applecart."

"Now you're talking like you used to when you went with

that radical crowd." His mother looked aggrieved. Then, shrewdly, "You talk that way about M'Caslrai because deep in your heart you look up to him. He's a great man. You wouldn't listen to him this afternoon because you were afraid he'd persuade you. And now you say anything nasty about him that comes into your head."

Her husband patted her arm. "We all said some foolish things in the peace days, Gret," he reminded her. "We weren't realistic. Lord, I wish we could still afford illusions. I'm sure you'd feel very differently, Norm, if only you'd seen the sincerity and suffering in M'Caslrai's face this afternoon." The little man's voice was placating, almost cheerful. His nervous smile had come back. Norm understood plainly: His father, always hating rows, figured that this one was over and the "smoothing out" time (his specialty) had arrived.

Norm watched him scamper spryly to the teletaction panel, heard him say, "Tell you what, they're reteletacting M'Caslrai's address. You'll listen to it—eh, Norm?"

Feeling sick at his stomach, he hurried out of the room.

When he reached his bedroom he uncovered his ears, and was relieved to hear only an unintelligible sibilance of whispered conversation coming from the living room—none of those detestable, friendly, understanding, solemn mouthings of M'Caslrai.

It wasn't true, what his mother had said, he assured himself angrily. The World Director had no emotional hold on him. It was just that the man was such a boring, sanctimonious old hypocrite!

He repeated this to himself more than once as he stared at the blank bedroom wall.

The resilient floor was noiseless. He only became aware of Allisoun's presence a moment before her hand touched his shoulder. He let it stay there.

The room was dark except for a fan of dim light coming through the door and the ghostly glow outlining the furniture. The voices conferring out in the living room were muted to an unintelligible drone. It felt warm and stuffy and nauseous with flower-odors, like a funeral—the sweet stink of the weatherdome.

"Norm," said Allisoun softly, "you know how it is with those who go to war—"

"Yes?"

"They let them have whatever they want. Give them any pleasure they desire."

"Well?"

"I was thinking that . . . well, you and I could be together, and sooner than we thought. We could do things and enjoy things that wouldn't be possible under other circumstances. We could have the sort of fun we had in our sex-introductory lessons—"

He turned around. The soft silhouetting light made her hair a bronze aureole around the darkness of her face. Her shoulders stood out whitely above her black slip.

"You'd like that, eh?" he asked.

Her "Yes" was almost inaudible.

"You'd really like it?"

She nodded. "And afterward . . . there'd be your son."

He surveyed her for a long moment. Then he reached for the white shoulders.

He pushed her back, held her at arm's length.

"So you'd like to be a hero's wife, eh?" he said loudly. "You'd get a thrill out of making love to a dead man? You'd like to be in on the orgies? You'd like to be one of the flower-decked concubines of the petted one who next year will have his heart torn out on a primeval God's stone altar? You'd like to count the remaining moments gloatingly? You'd like to bear a dead man's son for the next general bloodletting? Well, *I wouldn't* like it."

Willisoun stumbled into the room. "Look here," he blatted, snatching at Norm, "you can't talk to my sister that way."

"Oh yes I can." He shoved Willisoun against the bed and walked back into the living room. By the time Willisoun had followed him out, he was standing with his back to the outer door. He stopped Willisoun with a gesture and looked around—at his father with upraised hands fluttering the air, his mother slumped on the couch like a sick cow, Allisoun in the shadow of the opposite doorway, her brother a little ahead of her, face flushed and hands clenched.

"I'll say my say and then get out," Norm told them.

"Maybe I'm doing the wrong thing. Maybe I'm just showing myself up as selfish and ignorant. I know that there are times when the few must perish for the sake of the many—when we must have a 'finest hour' and a goriest, most glorious day. I know there are a lot of things we don't understand, especially about human nature. Maybe I ought to let myself be destroyed gladly. Maybe war is the greatest social invention since Brotherly Love. Maybe it's magnificent long-range thinking and M'Caslrai's a benign genius. Maybe in view of the ugliness of human nature, it's the only alternative to universal chaos.

"But if that's the way human nature works, I don't want any part of it. Oh, I know I should have thought of all this before, and that it looks as if I were squealing just because I happened to be the one who drew the unlucky number. But better late than never! I decline to perform the service requested of me. I'll use any means to avoid performing it. And I'll urge others to do the same. Good-by, folks, I'm cutting loose."

Willisoun walked toward him stiff-legged. "You won't get far, you cowardly . . ."

Norm's right to the jaw connected. Willisoun hit the tilted floor-section, bounced, came to rest. His fogged eyes, glaring crookedly at Norm, were half-moons of sick hate. Groping for support, his hands happened to close on the flower he had dropped earlier. Fingers and thumb squeezed the remaining petals to mush.

Norm turned and walked out.

At the togsrack he jerked on his walking clothes, automatically transferring his death notice from hand to hand. A blast of chill air cut his face as he left the weatherdome, but he did not pull down his veil.

A red sunset struck golden glints from the fantastic, cloud-piercing spires of the New City, made a golden pillar to heaven of Supracenter, whence M'Caslrai might even now be looking paternalistically down. Norm turned his back on that fancied gaze and headed for the Old City's ragged, low skyline, blackly silhouetted by the angry rays.

A half-hour's furious walking carried him out of the interurban green belt with its bizarre mingling of weatherdomes and winter. The tree-lined avenues gave way to steep-walled canyons, through which the wind dipped and tore. Resilient plastic pavement of a relatively recent date blotted out the distinction between sidewalk and street, as no vehicular traffic was permitted in these narrow ways. Occasional roofs, however, had been adapted as landing stages for riding sticks and copters.

There were people abroad. All over the world, old city populations were dropping, and there was talk of clearing them out altogether. But individuals clung to these outmoded, time-hallowed warrens, the more tenaciously as it became possible to live a more isolated life in them. Not everyone relished the highly paced and socialized existence of the new city skylons.

Unconsciously Norm increased his alertness. One thing M'Caslrai was supposed to have said this afternoon was quite true: the murder rate had soared fantastically—and the Old City was a Mecca for deviants and discontents.

Every night brought its quota of killings and assaults, most of them purposeless outbursts of cruelty and lust, as if all the Jack-the-Rippers of the past had been reincarnated a hundredfold. Everyone was suspect. The gray-garbed police Norm passed were too ostentatious in their disregard of him, and once or twice he got the impression he was being followed.

He paid no particular attention. His mind kept chewing on the scene that had occurred back home, rehearsing it again and again—sometimes in its rightful setting, sometimes against a background of darkness, sometimes against a magnified ghostly version of M'Caslrai's gaunt, homely, reproachful face—until the lesser faces of his family circle became the painful, too vivid distortions of an olden time surrealist painter, with personalities to match. Gret, his mother, sunk most of the time in a kind of heavy brooding that almost cut her off from the world; hungrily affectionate yet completely unsympathetic, taking all emotion for her province and no one else's. Jon, his father, whittled by timidity down to the tiniest shred of a man, driven frantic by the slightest friction, living in a painstakingly fabricated dream-world where his decisions amounted to something. Allisoun, constantly veering between a hysterical romance-fed primness and an equally hysterical love-thirst. Willisoun, superficially more adjusted than the rest, with his important, quietly mysterious government job, but alternating his hail-fellow-well-met manner with a surliness that might hide anything—Norm couldn't forget the diseased hate that had been in his eyes at the last and the way his hand had closed on the flower.

A panorama from which past centuries peered out more and more often, slipped by half-noticed as he pushed deeper and deeper into the Old City. Walls of brick and stone, patched here and there with panels of glastic indicating still-inhabited dwelling units. Rusted vents that might be the remains of pre-electronic air-conditioning systems. Boxes over-head that had housed microwave traffic control systems. Once he went down an alleyway paved with a worn stone-substitute, and occasionally the fringe of his attention strayed to dusty windows that looked suspiciously like ancient glass.

As he turned out of the alleyway into a scarcely wider street, he met a small hurrying figure in green walking togs. He brushed past her, but she turned and stared at him closely after a quick glance at his gloved left hand. For a moment impulse and prudence fought in her narrowly elfin face. Then she turned and followed him.

She was not Norm's only follower. Another, taller and more darkly clad, melted back into the alleyway at her appearance, then after a moment continued his hungrily striding pursuit, avoiding the broad luminescent bands on pavement and walls. Except for the ghostly light cast by those stripes, it was becoming rapidly darker.

Gradually and silently, the two pursuers closed in. The one farther back took something thin and bright from his pouch, held it so that it was masked by his forearm.

Suddenly, at the mouth of another and darker alleyway, Norm stopped. He had come to a decision about the four faces leering in his mind.

"They're insane," he said aloud, lifting his clenched hands, "The whole pack of them."

A golden gleam caught his attention. He realized that he had been clutching his death notice all this time. He held it up to the phosphorescent wall-band.

It was his passport back to respectability. By means of it he could still be reconciled with his family and associates, still die with honor. It symbolized the fact that it was not too late to turn back.

He took it between his fingers and prepared to rip it across.

Someone touched his arm. He jerked around. He vaguely remembered having passed this girl in green a few corners back, but now for the first time he saw her slim face, her oddly animated eyes. Something tugged at his memory.

"You said you think they're all insane?" she asked softly.

He nodded doubtfully. He didn't understand how she could know to whom he was referring.

An unusual look, an evil joyful look, came into her eyes,

which never left his face. She smiled slyly and leaned forward. After a considerable pause she whispered.

"You're right. They *are* all insane. You and I too. The whole world is crazy. The only difference is that you and I *know*."

For an extraordinary moment the only things Norm could see clearly were her strange fey eyes. Everything else was darkly rocking. The floor of his mind had tilted and the ideas were slipping, sliding.

"You believe that?" she whispered.

Norm realized that he was nodding his head.

She laughed. "Then you'd better not tear up your death notice," she said. "You may find a better use for it."

It is hard to say what made Norm whirl around again at that moment. Hardly a noise, for the attack, though swift, was horribly soundless. Perhaps he got his cue from a movement of the air, or a doubly reflected gleam from the blade gripped in the second follower's hand.

But whirl he did, and simultaneously duck, and the blade, abruptly glowing as if white-hot, drove just over his shoulder, inches from his face.

Hardly losing a moment in recovering, the dark attacker ripped sidewise at the girl.

But Norm was swift too, as if his subconscious had long been preparing for this. He caught hold of a fold of dark fabric and jerked. The glowing blade sliced air in front of the green girl's throat.

Riding with the jerk, the attacker swung around with a serpentine swiftness, like a murderer in a nightmare, and stabbed out at his victim.

But Norm caught the knife hand and drove blow after blow at the black-swathed jaw, unmindful of the fingers that tried to pry his loose and of the electron-edged blade that twitched at his undersleeve, slicing the tough fabric to ribbons.

He felt the figure weaken. He set his feet and drove home a solider blow.

Sparking as it hit, the knife dropped to the pavement. The figure slumped, sprawled full length across one of the phosphorescent bands.

Norm bent over it. Faintly in his ears, a police-screech echoed. The girl tugged at his sleeve, saying, "Why did he . . . ? Do you know who he is?"

Yet when Norm pulled aside the black veil, it was the girl who whispered, "Willisoun!"

The police-screech sounded clearer. A search-beam probed up and down.

The girl said, "They mustn't find us."

Norm was fumbling around on his hands and knees.

"Come on!" The girl caught hold of his sleeve.

The search-beam found them. The screech came three times, rapidly.

"Please!" The girl was trying to drag him toward the alleyway. "If you're what I think you are, and if you're willing to trust me at all—"

But it was because Norm did trust her—and remembered what she had said—that he delayed. Scooping up the fallen gold death notice, he jumped to his feet. Together they hurried down the dark alleyway.

II

THERE WAS little sleep as that night went around the world. In scattered offices weary-eyed actuaries fed information tapes into machines for a last check on their figures. It was not only the number of war deaths that must be accurately calculated, (and if they calculated one too many, they were morally guilty of murder), but also the exact amounts of material slated for destruction. There were thousands of factors that must never be lost sight of. Some were real, such as prices, availability, production and transportation costs, statistics on total expenditures from the last wars. Some were arbitrary, such as the equating of so many wounded casualties to one death, or the substitution of raw for processed materials. While some were frank extrapolations, such as the regrettable necessity for allowing for the greater destruction made possible by modern technology. Although this factor must of course be shaved as much as possible, it would never do to overlook it completely.

Elsewhere, electronic wheels were set in motion that would result in sharply upped transmutation, synthesizing, processing, and agricultural production. Auxiliary power plants were opened. Amazingly dispersed munitions factories began to take form. The first of the great triphibian transports started down the production line.

Teletaction made it possible for major and minor executives all over the world to hold thousands of conferences as efficiently and comfortably as if each conferring group were together in the same room—and, indeed, it gave just that effect. Arrangements for a quarter-billion job transfers were smoothly concluded. Priorities on critical materials were argued out. Psychologists put the finishing touches on courses of orientation for death. Deadlines were determined for putting into effect a complete system of civilian rationing, for a period of belt-tightening was a profoundly necessary part of the war.

Various entertainment-chains and vice-rings, openly encouraged or at least winked at by police authorities, prepared for expanded activities.

Religion, which had turned its back on God and devoted itself to the worship of man and man's destiny, likewise laid plans.

In a billion homes the lights stayed on. In one out of twenty there was numbing shock, hopeless horror, agonized grief, unanswerable questionings, spasms of rebellion. In the other nineteen there was a feeling of relief so intense as to preclude sleep, mingled with stern self-questionings and an uneasy sense of guilt.

Everywhere was mounting nervous tension, which would hold for months, until the thing was over. Despite this, scattered experts scanning the hourly statistics gave vent to long-anticipated sighs of relief, as they saw the suicide rate drop almost to zero and the murder and assault rates swoop almost as low. Mankind had something bigger to worry about than personal miseries and ecstasies and compulsions.

If there was any single emotion that came close to being universal, that touched both the high and the low, those on the spot and those off it, it was fear—an irrational, nerve-tightening dread. More than a century had passed since the last true conflict, but the sense of an enemy lingered subconsciously, to be revived when the war-patterns were reestablished. Odd noises and odors brought quickening heartbeats. Men who walked or flew abroad looked over their hunched shoulders, as if expecting the plunge of the robot bomb or the blue stab of the ray or the silent snowfall of radioactive death. Men on shipboard scanned the empty waters, as if expecting them to be broken, stealthily or with a convulsive splash, by the emerging of a murder-bent triphibian. Men inside were troubled by an uneasiness about the lights, as if all those bright windows on the night side of Earth formed too conspicuous a beacon for some unknown foe lurking in the depths of space.

III

IN WORLD Director M'Caslrai's office atop Supracenter there was a total absence of bustle and noise, as was perhaps appropriate at the focal point of all this activity. No lights blinked, no secretary-machines hummed, no color-changing maps and graphs troubled the cool gray of the walls, no distant subordinates appeared in teletactive counterpart seeking okays or advice. M'Caslrai was alone.

His tall, tired, gangling frame was relaxed. Superficially his face was tranquil. It was a big brooding face, seamed with significant wrinkles. As capable of stern decision as of drollery, but somehow always genial. A face on which history was clearly written. The face of a man who knew men, and how to handle them.

In the whole room, only one thing moved: M'Caslrai's gnarled forefinger. Back and forth it scratched an inch of chair-arm. Back and forth. Back and forth.

He looked like a great leader who, after a momentous decision, permits himself the painful luxury of weighing his actions for a last time, of asking himself whether he could possibly have taken any other course, of toting up the suffering his decision would cause against the suffering it had averted.

And yet, beneath the surface, there was something shockingly wrong in the picture M'Caslrai presented. A certain uncouthness of posture may have had something to do with it, a hint of stiffness in the dark garments. Yet those were only details. You couldn't put your finger on the main cause. But whatever that was, there was a sense of monstrous hidden abnormality about the man, the persistent suggestion that

M'Caslrai was profoundly out of place—either in space, or time.

He did not look up as J'Wilobe entered unannounced. The slim, lean-jawed Secretary of Dangers had an expression that would have seemed fretful, had it not been so intense. Again there was that instant impression of abnormality, but with J'Wilobe its cause was not obscure. You felt you were looking at the human counterpart of a highly intelligent hybrid of lemur and ferret—a super-Goebbels.

His gaze roved suspiciously to either side as he came through the door. He paced back and forth for a few moments biting his lip, then let fall, "I found another of those damned chess sets."

M'Caslrai stirred, slowly rubbed his dark-guttered eyelids.

"Makes three in a week," J'Wilobe continued in staccato bursts. "I destroyed it, of course, but it shook me up. Obviously, someone knows I could have been the greatest chess-player in the world." He threw back his head. "Knows I gave up the game to devote myself wholly to government— couldn't serve two masters. Knows what a vice chess is. Knows how I'm still tempted. Leaves the sets around to upset me. Knows what the sight of one does to me."

He continued to pace.

M'Caslrai raised his tangled eyebrows.

"Mister J'Wilobe . . ." he began, waggling a forefinger at the Secretary of Dangers.

J'Wilobe stared intently at the extended digit. His lean arms tightened against his sides. His face paled a trifle.

M'Caslrai made a fist of his hand. "Your pardon, sir," he said, smiling humbly. "I had forgotten your . . . idiosyncrasy. But to continue. You're getting at something bigger than the chessmen?"

J'Wilobe faced him. "Right! The chessmen are only a single minor instance. I can put my finger on . . . I mean, point out . . . I mean, designate, a hundred comparable cases. Could have told you weeks ago, except I wanted to be absolutely sure. It's so unlikely, you see. But unlikely or not, the evidence is overwhelming. We are up against an organized underground opposition, the methods and like of which . . ."

M'Caslrai raised his hand. "One moment, Mister J'Wilobe. I believe that this matter you are about to expound is of the highest significance. I think it best, therefore, that we call in the others."

J'Wilobe pressed his lips together, shook his head.

"Inscra and Heshifer at a minimum," M'Caslrai pressed.

J'Wilobe shrugged an unwilling consent. While M'Caslrai used the teletactor, he stepped outside and signaled to a bruised-jawed young man who was fingering a cut flower.

"You're in shape for a job tonight, Willisoun?" he asked.

Willisoun nodded.

"Any word as yet on the thugs who assaulted you in the Old City?"

Willisoun shook his head.

"I dislike men who run into danger," said J'Wilobe. "Be more cautious in the future. Regarding your present assignment, a secret conference is about to be held in M'Caslrai's office. When it breaks up, hold yourself in readiness to follow anyone whom I designate. Remember, it may be anyone—even M'Caslrai. And be sure to make yourself invisible. You too frequently neglect that precaution. I dislike careless men."

When he returned, M'Caslrai was busying himself taking a box out of a cabinet, setting it on his desk. The World Director went out of his way to pull forward a chair, so that there were four arranged at comfortable distances around the desk. His movements were tired and slow, but suggested reservoirs of inward strength.

Inscra arrived first by a matter of moments. The General Secretary was an expressionless, ponderous individual, who always seemed to be moving through a denser medium than air. Only his eyes looked alive, and even there one could not be sure that the animating force was life.

Secretary of Minds Heshifer was almost the exact opposite. A small man, ridiculously spry for one so aged, with bald head and a bushy white beard. Fussy, pedantic, quick-witted, expression always ashift.

M'Caslrai welcomed them with a friendly gesture. Then he opened the box and lifted out a bottle.

The movement dislodged a tiny grey something which scuttled across the desk. No one else reacted, but Inscra jerked back with a convulsive gasp.

Heshifer captured the something with a flick of his hand, as though it were an insect. "A scrap of memo tape," he remarked, looking. No one said anything, though it was with difficulty that Inscra tore his gaze away from Heshifer's half-closed hand.

M'Caslrai carefully tilted the bottle. From the seemingly sealed neck an amber liquid poured.

"Afterward you can serve yourself, gentlemen," he said, indicating the four glasses with courtly awkwardness. "Mister J'Wilobe has something to tell us."

Hand shaking a little, Inscra tossed his drink. Heshifer sipped appreciatively. J'Wilobe lifted his to his lips, sniffed it, looked around suspiciously, hesitated, set it down.

"You all know that there are forces working against us," he began abruptly. "Though some of you don't like to admit it." He glared at Heshifer, who shrugged blithely. "Secret, underground forces, bent on upsetting the social order, on destroying the present government, and especially on sabotaging the war. There is evidence that similar forces were active to some degree during past wars. They could have been brought into the open long before this, if there had not been so much objection in some quarters to the unlimited questioning of suspects which I urged—the employment of emotional urging and similar methods of persuasion."

"You know I do not like to see people treated that way," said M'Caslrai gently. "Though, of course, if the safety of the world and the glory of Man are at stake . . . and if there is a threat to the young men who are giving up their lives . . ."

"Naturally any opposition must be liquidated," said Inscra sharply, "*if* it exists."

J'Wilobe smiled. "The opposition exists. It is only the strangeness of its methods—the puzzling quality of its strategems—that keeps most individuals from becoming aware of it." He looked around with a veiled contemptuousness, then said suddenly, "Who would suspect—gifts? I mean, if the gifts were perfectly okay and each happened to be the thing its recipient most wanted. Yet gifts can be deadly. You don't give drink to a drunkard just before the day's work. Especially you don't give it to a reformed drunkard. Nevertheless, within the past two weeks dozens of such 'gifts' have been made, always anonymously, to some of our highest executives and most trusted subordinates. There is, in my own case, a matter of chess sets."

Heshifer muttered something that ended with ". . . as impossible as telepathy," then snorted, "If that's all you have to tell us—"

"It's only a beginning. Next among these nuisance tactics

of the opposition, comes—voices. Voices in the dark or over dark teletactors, voices dubbed into reading tapes, unplaceable voices heard for a moment in crowds—all reminding the individual of unpleasant incidents that happened in his childhood, incidents he wants to forget, or incidents that never happened but that the voice is trying to convince him did.

"Yet another secret weapon—monotony. Lights that begin to blink, sounds that begin to drone, taped words and sentences that repeat themselves over and over.

"Think how such 'harmless' means can be used to distract men, to upset them, to ruin their efficiency!

"Finally, something you all know about—this epidemic of what we've called convulsive accidents. Cases of mild poisoning and electric shock, with the victim suffering muscular spasms and going into a hazy and unrealistic mental state that sometimes lasts for days. There have been altogether too many of those 'accidents.' It's as if there were a silent wolf pack around us—dozens of the red-eyed beasts—"

He broke off to look at Inscra. The General Secretary had just given an abrupt nod, and his eyes looked more than ever alive—or whatever it was. His voice was like them.

"I think I see what you're getting at, J'Wilobe. I've come across similar cases myself, and I believe now that you are right in considering them significant. What is more, I can add another type of occurrence. Several workers in one of my subdepartments have been troubled by what we called overtiredness. They gradually become slow in their movements, their eyes seem to glaze, they go into what you could describe as a mild trance. In that trance they give utterance to irresponsible, foolish ideas. For brief hazy periods, they doubt things which should not be ever doubted—even war. I have paid no attention—these days, a certain amount of mental fatigue is taken for granted. In one case, though, I remember that an analysis of the blood happened to be made, and traces of a primitive chemical noted—lysergic acid. I thought nothing of it at the time, but now . . ."

He broke off and restlessly reached for the bottle—just at the moment Heshifer happened to do likewise. The smaller man was ahead of him, so Inscra set his glass on the table. As Heshifer picked up the bottle, the small gray thing fluttered from his hand to the floor. Instantly Inscra shrank back, repeating his former erratic behavior. There was a moment of confusion. Heshifer set his foot on the thing, muttered a quick "I'm sorry," stooped, picked it up, shoved it in his pouch. Then he poured the drinks, handing Inscra his.

As they settled back, M'Caslrai spoke. He had been sprawling back in his armchair, listening carefully, making no comment.

"Mister J'Wilobe, that's a mighty interesting matter you've been narrating to us, and one we've got to act on right quick, but I don't think you've quite got the hang of it. You see what's happening—and you're right in thinking that it's hostile. Yes, you can bet you are—but you don't yet see the *why*."

With almost a twinkle in his eye, he turned to Heshifer. "I'd have thought you'd have spotted it. After all, you're Secretary of Minds. But no, it would be unfair to expect any of you to get it. I never would myself, except I like to poke around in the byways of history. And that's where you have to poke this time, boys—way back in the twentieth century, old reckoning. Mighty interesting times . . . though not as much as the nineteenth. . . ."

His voice was both droll and dead serious as he continued, "In those days they didn't treat deviants and eccentrics as we do now. They had a lot of queer methods, some barbaric, some rather fanciful. I happened to read up on them. They had a thing called hypnotism, a little like our mental persuasion. A way of opening someone's mind to suggestion, chiefly through the skillful use of monotony.

"Then there was psychoanalysis—a prying into the depths of the victim's mind; a searching for his earliest experiences, to be used as levers to change his attitudes.

"Occupational therapy was another. Like the other methods, they used it on the people they called insane. It was a matter of getting the person to do something he liked to do, something that would occupy his mind—you presented him with a well-chosen 'gift.'

"Mustn't forget shock treatment, of course. That was a prime favorite of theirs for the insane, and pretty barbaric. Electric or chemical shock, to dredge up forgotten thoughts and emotions.

"Or what they called truth serums. Chemicals designed to let down inhibitions, to make the victim speak out his hidden thoughts.

"Reckon you get it, gentlemen?"

The silence lasted. Inscra looked stupified. Heshifer half-befuddled, half-incredulous. While J'Wilobe's reaction was closer to anger.

"Do you mean to tell me that the opposition thinks we are 'insane'?" J'Wilobe pronounced the archaic word distastefully.

M'Caslrai nodded. "That's the way I figure it."

"And they're treating us as such? Trying to 'cure' us?"

"That's about the size of it, Mister J'Wilobe," said M'Caslrai mildly.

"But . . . but . . ." The thick, mumbly quality of Inscra's words focused attention on him. He looked more than stupified now. He looked drugged.

"What I want to know . . ." He stumbled again.

"His eyes!" breathed J'Wilobe. "The truth serum!"

Over them, a few minutes ago so unpleasantly alive, there had fallen a veil.

He managed to finish:

". . . is, are we really? I mean, are we really insane? Tell me, someone, are we?"

IV

THE entry-indicator blinked as Heshifer bustled into the limited elevator.

"Anyone in your family get a death notice?" he asked conversationally.

The fat operator shook his head. "But I got a nephew who did."

Heshifer clucked sympathetically.

"He's a crazy kid," the operator volunteered. "Be the making of him, except . . ."

"Yes, of course," said Heshifer gently and leaped into abstraction.

Plummeting from the eyrie atop Supracenter toward the deepest basement, the elevator accelerated, then achieved such a smooth and steady speed that it seemed to stop.

The Secretary of Minds looked the perfect pedant. Judging

from his vague eyes, pursed lips, and jutting beard, he might have been thinking of something highly obscure or of nothing at all—in no case anything practical.

He swung around. Save for himself and the operator, the cage was empty. Restlessly he walked to the stair, popped up far enough to survey the second floor of the elevator.

With a shrug he resumed his meditations. But one might have noticed the faintest of frowns troubling his tufty white eyebrows.

The elevator stopped. Again the indicator blinked as, with an amiable but abstracted nod, Heshifer stepped out and turned sharply to the left.

The operator craned his neck curiously and took a step sideways—then recoiled, clutching his shoulder.

There had been no second passenger, the indicator had not blinked, but his eyes, watching the resilient flooring a few paces behind Heshifer, filled with horror. In a panic of haste he shut the door and started back up.

Like a self-important little mole returning to his lair, Heshifer hurried along the lonely corridor until he reached the insulated precincts of the Deep Mental Lab. As he scuttled through the file room, he blinked familiarly at the clerks, who were busy getting taped transcripts of brainwave records for mental dossiers of deviants and troublemakers. A large number of such dossiers were being requested by psychologists at war-reception centers.

Inside his private office, Heshifer's manner changed. The blink and bustle dropped away, leaving a soft-footed, enigmatic watchfulness. After a few minutes efficiently spent in teletacting requests and instructions, he slipped through an inner door.

He had gone fifty feet down a narrow gray corridor when, without warning, he swung around. This time he did not bother to mask the suspicious frown. For ten seconds he stood motionless, his eyes roving over the empty corridor behind him, his ears drinking in the faintest sounds. Arriving at a decision, he returned to his office and searched it thoroughly. Then he set auxiliary electronic locks on the outer and inner doors and, with a shrug, started once more down the narrow corridor.

He did not notice the faint imprints that appeared and disappeared in the flooring a dozen feet behind him.

After a short walk he paused and traced with his forefinger

a design on the blank wall. He ducked through the doorway that suddenly yawned.

The secondary corridor descended at a gentle angle. Some hundred feet from the entrance a barely audible clink brought him to a stop. A section of wall beside him became transparent, revealing a young, vigilant face.

"The tunnel's clear?" asked Heshifer.

The watcher nodded.

"All electronic barriers set? No visitants for the Old City ahead of me? No indications of spy-beams?"

More nods answered him.

"Thanks, doc," said Heshifer.

The transparency became a blank wall. Heshifer hurried on.

The imprints followed him. There was no clink as they passed the critical point.

Heshifer emerged on a small platform in a chamber of moderate size. Beyond the platform were two gleaming metallic troughs, which led off side by side, into the mouths of twin tunnels. In the troughs were cradled a number of small cylindrical vehicles.

Heshifer opened the port of the nearest and climbed in. Almost silently, with swift smooth acceleration, the vehicle glided into the tunnel and whisked out of sight.

Nothing happened for perhaps a dozen seconds. Then—no one appeared, but the port of the second vehicle opened and, after a brief pause, closed. Softly the vehicle started forward.

V

NORM LOOKED up doubtfully at the girl in green. He was still uncertain whether to take her idly-tossed revelations as confetti or grenades. Coming here had been a confusion of screeching alleys, ruinous basements, ambiguous passageways, a careening ride inside a metal mole, until he had stumbled out into the final surprise of soft silent corridors lined with flowers. His mind still fluoresced with it.

Nevertheless he was sure of one thing: that he felt more

at home in this strange little subterranean room than he ever had in his own dwelling.

The girl in green swung her legs from a table near the archway. It was obvious that she was aware of their trimness. She looked at him innocently, like an elf on the witness stand.

"You mean," he fumbled, "that you consider yourselves attendants in one huge insane asylum?"

She grinned approvingly. "Except that the lunatics hold the balance of power. And so we have to walk very softly. Or else—it really doesn't matter—we're the insane ones, bent on warping the minds of the majority. We're monomaniacs on the topic, I warn you of that. And with all the dangerousness of monomaniacs." She suddenly looked at him like a short-haired cat. "What's the matter anyway? Beginning to doubt that a world which devised war could be anything but insane?"

"Of course not, but in spite of what you started to say about your organization's long historical background, it all seems so . . ."

"Hit or miss? We don't live up to your idea of a powerful secret society?"

"I guess that's what I mean."

She smiled.

"But look at the casual way you picked me up and started to tell me things," he protested. "How do you know I won't betray you?"

"You'd prefer a lot of mumbojumbo—oaths, tests, initiations?" she inquired solicitously. "It wouldn't occur to you, I suppose, that we might have been watching you for a long time? Or that any organization is strong only insofar as it *can* act on the spur of the moment?"

"Yes, but . . ."

"And, as for betraying us, where are we now?"

"Under the Old City."

"But where?"

"I don't know. It was dark, and there were those crazy tunnels."

"Exactly. And who am I?"

"You said to call you J'Quilvens."

"Yes, but who am I? Where would you find me?"

"I don't know."

"You see. You wouldn't make such a valuable traitor

after all." She smoothed her green slip. "Besides we have reason to trust you. You passed a test when we first met."

He shook his head. He was beginning to like her very much. "You're wrong there. I was just fighting in self-defense. And Willisoun wasn't after you."

She smiled. "You've a lot to learn about your precious potential brother-in-law. You didn't even know that he worked for J'Wilobe.

"He's quite a problem child, Willisoun," she added dreamily. Then, after a moment, "You're in love with his sister?"

"Look," said Norm quickly, "you were going to tell me about the background of your movement."

J'Quilvens smiled, lit two smolder-sticks, tossed him one, leaned back, sniffing the aromatic smoke, and casually began. Very much like a small girl uttering whatever fancies came into her head—the muse of history's brat tattling.

"It started in the twentieth century, old reckoning. There was still some insight then into the psychological state of the world. It was before the big propaganda engines went wild—and a person still had some idea of what was coming into his mind and from where. They realized that certain nations were for all practical purposes insane—paranoid, regressive, schizoid.

"But the larger truth was ignored. Only a few men realized that abnormal psychology was far more fruitful than the normal variety for the simple reason that it was truer. That from the beginning man had behaved abnormally, believing fiercely in things that didn't exist, positing all sorts of weird forces for which there wasn't a grain of evidence, exalting his prejudices and eccentricities, his little private experiences, into vast, cosmic fabrics of morality. That to a large extent all civilization was just one gigantic case history.

"Of those few doubtful men, a handful happened to contact each other. They shared their insights and grew a little more certain of their ground. They said, 'We're not like ordinary psychiatrists, who seek only to make sound maniacs out of sick maniacs. We presume to view man against the cosmic background, his littleness and misery and hunger, his boastings and cringings, his tricks and pretenses, his terrors and hallucinations, his kickings and squirmings, his shrieks and snarls. We want to teach him to laugh at himself. And someday, in spite of himself, we'll drive him sane!'"

For a moment Norm felt that she was looking through him.

Then, leaning forward, lightly resting elbows on knees, she continued quietly, "Whenever they had the time and opportunity—for all of them were tied to irksome routines—they investigated. Some of them studied the modern symptoms of the world's madness, probed the symbolic mass-dreams hidden in art, propaganda, and advertising. Others concentrated on the traumas that had occurred while mankind was groping from barbarism to civilization—the wars, enslavements, and superstitious delusions that had warped civilization's childhood. Still others tried to determine the prognosis of the ailment.

"The prognosis was negative. Society took several wrong turns. Under the pressure of a ruthless new puritanism, the promising spirit of scientific skepticism was mummified into learned specialities. Basic questions were dodged so often that a general inferiority complex came into existence. Pretense took the place of progress. Fear was enthroned.

"At times the tiny enlightened minority met to exchange their augmented information. Differences of opinion rose. Some boldly attempted to set up the psychiatry of history as a new branch of knowledge. This resulted in a split. Those who resisted realized that their knowledge would merely be assimilated into the general insanity and become a worthless pedantry. As indeed happened—you can still find traces in the present philosophy that a certain degree of irrational eccentricity, within strict social limits, is desirable."

Norm nodded. She continued lightly, almost humorously, as if too much seriousness were dangerous. "Times changed. There came the first and second world leagues, the first and second world federations, the all-out Nuclear War that reduced Earth's population to a fraction of one percent, the reclaiming of the Deathlands, the rule of the Benevolent Lunatics—we aren't the only crazy ones, Norm—the re-pioneering of the planets.

"The main group kept working in secret. At intervals, after the carefullest consideration, new members were admitted.

"The organization shifted with the times, responsive to winds of influence. Sometimes it was almost open; sometimes, when suspicious tyranny was enthroned, it was secret—though there were times, I imagine, when it survived solely because no policeman or politician would take it seriously—it inclined to such long-range views that it seldom became involved in practical action. And that," she added bitterly, "is not entirely a past matter.

"Sometimes the members considered it little more than a nonsensical hobby. Sometimes they were almost dead serious. Sometimes there were bursts of activity—meetings, discussions, plans. Sometimes they were a wolf pack, nipping at man's heels and almost forgetting not to snap at the jugular vein—a lot of them weren't humanity-lovers, believe me! Sometimes members lost touch with each other for decades, almost for lifetimes.

"They never had a real name. Sometimes they called themselves the Company of the Sane, or the League of Psychiatrists. They got into the habit of addressing each other as 'doctor' or 'geodoc' because the world was their patient.

"Times continued to change. The world state was born and the worship of man. War as we know it today came into existence—not, like you've been taught to believe, as the result of logical analysis, but because a civil-war army, sworn to suicide in case of failure, thought they'd been trapped before the war began and jumped the gun on self-destruction.

"The final, fixed phase in the psychosis of history had set in. The docs half woke from their centuries of dabbling and realized that they could no longer evade the problem facing them. Though their organization was almost at its lowest ebb, the time had come to act.

"In the face of a socialization, regimentation, and surveillance more intense than any they had faced before, they went back to the practices of their secretest days—and improved on them. If they had gone underground before, this time they really burrowed. Elaborate precautions were taken to prevent infiltration by spies. A cell-system was set up, to avoid too much mutual acquaintance of members.

"Cautiously they began to experiment at influencing the world. Sometimes they worked on individuals, sometimes on groups. They tried out all the psychological and secret propaganda techniques that had been developed through the ages, discarding, reviving, improving, inventing. They perfected their methods, gathered data, distributed their members in the most effective pattern for action.

"Wars, being the most tragic of mankind's symptoms, were their chief target. Each war they opposed with every weapon they dared use. Each time they planned and put into effect elaborate psychological counterprograms.

"And yet each time they failed. Wars marched on relentlessly. The counterprograms always dissolved into futile nuisance tactics. Each generation produced its quota of sacrificial deaths. Until now . . ."

A silvery tone sounded from beyond the archway. J'Quilvens reacted to it, but did not break off. Her eyes burned, there were spots of color in her cheeks, her lips were tight lines. For a moment the elf was a fury.

"And now . . . we know that we dare not let this war succeed. If we fail, it's the finish. We've studied our own symptoms as well as those of the world. If we fail, we'll merely become an integral part of the universal madness—a futile countersymptom. We've been too careful, been too much afraid for our own skins, perhaps we've secretly gloried in our position as the only sane persons in an insane world. We've got to take chances, try *every* method, fight!"

"Did I hear someone mention that irrational word?" a cool voice inquired.

A tall shaven-headed man in amber pajamas was standing in the archway. He was handsome, after the fashion of an ancient Eastern god—aloof, faintly amused, coldly compassionate.

J'Quilvens turned slowly. "I did, F'Sibr."

"He has arrived," he informed her. He looked at Norm, who began to feel uncomfortable.

"I'm coming." J'Quilvens dropped from the table. "Wait here," she told Norm.

The shaven-headed man gave Norm another unrevealing look and followed her out.

VI

"THEY'RE on to us," Heshifer affirmed, his white beard wagging. "This time J'Wilobe's paranoid delusions coincide with reality. And M'Caslrai actually spotted our aims and the sources of our methods."

"And yet you're sure you weren't followed." F'Sibr inquired unperturbedly.

"Impossible! As impossible as telepathy!" Heshifer grinned. "Oh, I'll admit my suspicions were roused for a moment, but it wasn't anything. The electronic barriers were all in order."

"You have a weakness for running risks," said F'Sibr mildly. "That business of the chess sets was injudicious. And putting the truth drug into Inscra's drink was impudently foolhardy."

"But don't you see, we've got to be foolhardy!" J'Quilvens broke in eagerly.

"And it did shake them up so beautifully," Heshifer added, smiling reminiscently.

They were conferring in a low, large, comfortably furnished room from which several corridors radiated. There were softly glowing three-dimensional pictures, bits of sculpture, bunches of flowers, as if a conscious effort had been made to suppress any feeling of underground grimness or of wide-webbed, long-tentacled efficiency.

F'Sibr sat, arms folded. Heshifer paced, sometimes almost skipping, as if trying to keep up with the sudden twists and turns of his thoughts. J'Quilvens perched, playing with a smolder-stick.

"I see no reason to put our general plan in jeopardy," said F'Sibr. "The masked trend toward sanity is increasing as calculated. The propaganda of doubt and distrust, foolproof and insanityproof by test, is successfully invading every phase of the war. The master propaganda—"

Heshifer picked up a fragile jar of reddish powder and tossed it in his hand. "What's this?"

"A dyed sample of the new antidissociation drug. To resume, the master propaganda, designed to convince every last individual that the war is crookedly administered, is set to go. Everywhere our agents stand ready to usurp key positions as soon as present civilian executives and war officers gain sufficient insight into the irrationality of their motives as to become incapable of carrying on. You, like the others, have that job to do when, but only when, M'Caslrai and the others—"

"You know, it's a funny thing about M'Caslrai," said Heshifer, stopping dead. "He always reminds me of someone, but I can't think who."

"A living person?" F'Sibr asked patiently.

"No, I don't think so. I almost get it—and then it's gone. You know, we've never really understood M'Caslrai. We've never gotten a convincing line on his phobias or the general form of his delusions. We cannot even classify his psychosis with any confidence. Compared to the others, his mind's a dark book."

"True. To continue, you'll have your job, and a very important one, when M'Caslrai and J'Wilobe and the others lose their grip. Just as I'll have my job, and J'Quilvens hers. There is no justification for endangering the total plan by psychological guerrilla tactics and unnecessary risk-running. J'Quilvens, I disapprove of your bringing that boy here." He nodded toward an archway flanked by bowls of flowers.

"There was no other place."

"That is hardly accurate."

"But he did us a service. Besides, he's gotten his death notice, and we'll need every agent we can get in the war forces. He's obvious officer material—and a teletaction expert. You'll need an aide you can trust, and he might fill the bill."

"Conceivably. Nevertheless, I disapprove of the risk you ran in bringing him here."

"Look, F'Sibr," said Heshifer, his eyes twinkling. "Are you getting a leadership complex?"

"Of course I am. Doubtless if I were a glorified mental sniper, I too could maintain a charming irresponsibility." And F'Sibr grinned, every whit as delightedly as Heshifer. But only for a moment. "To conclude, reports indicate that our plan is proceeding according to schedule. Premature assaults, however appealing, might wreck it."

Heshifer sighed. "It's such a good plan," he said wistfully.

"Well?"

"I was thinking of all the past wars and our counterplans. They were such good plans too."

"On the contrary, they failed because they contained major flaws. Our present plan is well-calculated."

"The others seemed well-calculated too," said Heshifer softly. "I don't mean to be pessimistic, but I'm the sort of person who doesn't really begin to worry about anything until it threatens his friends—I'd hate to see you two snuffed out along with the rest of the war forces, just because we had such a good plan." Abruptly he grinned. "Look, F'Sibr, I'm worried. Let's get ready—merely get ready—the Chaos Plan, in case."

"The Chaos Plan is worse than no plan at all." F'Sibr's voice had grown gentler than ever, but his face was that of a carven god.

"I don't think so."

"It and the present plan are incompatible. The one would ruin the other."

Heshifer's beard bobbed. "Agreed. But I'm not asking that we put the Chaos Plan into effect—only that we transmit the necessary knowledge to all agents, so they'll be able to use it if the necessity should arise. I have the information in my dossiers on key personnel here and at the Deep Mental Lab."

"The information alone would be too much of a temptation. It could only be imparted with the strict injunction that it never be used except on order from above, and even then we couldn't be sure. I am against it."

"But I'm worried. Ever since that conference with M'Caslrai and J'Wilobe, I've had the feeling . . ." Heshifer paused and glanced around uneasily.

For once F'Sibr's voice was sharp. "Are you *sure* that you weren't followed?"

Heshifer didn't reply.

VII

NORM WAS getting uneasy. Alone in this gray little room it was all too easy to wonder whether this wasn't insanity, rather than what he'd left. The outside world was getting in its licks.

It was hard to keep M'Caslrai's face out of his mind. Like the mask of a guilty conscience, that gaunt solemn visage kept trying to peer over his shoulder, sorrow rather than anger in the dark-circled eyes.

When he thought of his father and mother, of Allisoun, even of Willisoun, the sense of nauseous abnormality, recently so keen, was blunted. He pictured them doing the familiar, inconsequential things that make up the round of daily life.

They were his people. They were home.

Whereas these strangers—

If he'd listened to M'Caslrai—

Perhaps he'd make a big mistake—

He didn't exactly ask himself these questions, but it was becoming hard not to.

He wished J'Quilvens would return. He walked over to the archway, simultaneously becoming aware of a flowery odor that registered unpleasantly—why, he couldn't for the moment remember.

It occurred to him that her "Wait here" hardly constituted an order. Almost before he realized it, he was tiptoeing down the curving corridor.

With every step the odor of flowers became more pronounced.

A little later he saw the source—a room thick as a garden with blooms, each one pouring into the air its sickening stench.

He took a couple more silent steps. He made out among the flowers the amber sleeve of the cryptic fellow who had summoned J'Quilvens. He became aware of a mumble of talk and thought he recognized her voice.

He began to feel embarrassed. He couldn't hear what they were saying, but he knew his actions would be interpreted as those of an eavesdropper—and a silly eavesdropper at that.

Yet to tiptoe back would be sillier still.

Nevertheless, he had about decided to, when something caught his eye.

It was a blue flower in the bowl to the righthand side of the archway ahead.

One of its petals was rolling and unrolling, like a tiny scroll.

The horror of this tiny action was not diminished by his dreamlike conviction that it was familiar—something he had witnessed a hundred times.

Unwillingly, helplessly, as in a dream, one hand outstretched, he stole forward.

Like trivial detail at the edge of an absorbing picture, the amber-coated man came into view, and beyond him J'Quilvens and a small gnomish person with a white beard.

The petal jerked from the flower, fluttered down, came to rest beside an odd irregularity in the flooring—a double depression like that made by a pair of moccasins.

Another petal began to roll and unroll.

The mumble of talk stopped.

He reached for the flower and his hand encountered in the air a cold, flexible, metallic surface.

There was a whirl of movement. Something slammed into his shoulder. The block in his mind lifted. He remembered who always fingered flowers.

Half reflex, half calculation—his hands grabbed at the air and closed on a metal-sleeved forearm. There was a jerk and he rocked forward. From where the forearm's hand would be, a dazzling blue beam hissed past his face, scorching his cheek. Twisting away, he shifted his grip, one hand sliding toward the wrist, the other twining, getting leverage.

There was a spatter of molten drops as the blue beam traveled along the ceiling into the room ahead, and down. He was dimly aware of figures diving to either side.

There was a smothered grunt of pain. The blue beam was extinguished and something hit the floor with a tiny thud. The pinioned arm writhed free of his grip. Two bowls of flowers crashed to the floor a dozen feet ahead.

Then everything froze. As if they were parts of a scene revealed by a lightning flash, Norm noted the smouldering path of the beam, the scattered flowers, J'Quilvens crouched beyond them, the gnomelike old man peering over an upset table, the amber-coated man on hands and knees but starting up, like a leopard about to spring. In the whole room, nothing moved, save the eyes of those three.

Where the tiny thud had come from, Norm noted a faint depression in the flooring, as if a lightweight object rested there.

Something crushed one of the scattered flowers.

The old man popped up, arm raised and threw. A small jar shattered in the air a few feet from Norm, loosing a splash of red dust.

A partial man of red dust darted toward Norm. He recoiled.

The amber-coated man sprang.

Red dust and amber coat tangled, slammed down near the faint depression.

The blue beam flared again, charred a crazy design on

the ceiling, came down, shortened to inches, splashed molten sparks from fading red dust, seared something else.

There was a muffled scream of agony. The beam continued to flare for several more seconds.

Then Norm realized the amber-coated man was getting to his feet, that the old man was fumbling near a smoking hole in the dust-freighted air eight inches off the floor, that J'Quilvens was watching.

The amber-coated man was looking at him coolly, and he heard him say, "I think you were right about the boy, J'Quilvens."

He heard the old man remark pedantically, "Now that's an interesting reflection on scientific progress. Here we have a complete electronic warning system, and this invisible fellow slips right through because every radiant impulse is neatly routed around him. Whereas any primitive alarm system set off by the weight of a passing person would have shown him up instantly. Though that too would have failed if he had combined levitation with invisibility. But if we had a sure, simple way of detecting air displacement . . ."

He pulled something away, and after a brief scrutiny rolled it back. Willisoun's dead face was not pleasant.

"Useful, this fabric," he commented. "Though fortunately not strong enough to reroute a burn blast. J'Wilobe must have some research projects we don't know about. Bad. We'll want to analyze this stuff carefully."

"Yes," said the amber-coated man sharply. "But not now, and not here." J'Quilvens and the old man looked around.

"We have only minutes," he told them. "Maybe they didn't have a spy-beam tracing Willisoun—or another invisible man! —but you can bet their instruments picked up that burn blast. And how long does it usually take J'Wilobe's men to draw a cordon in the Old City? Come on!"

The amber-clad man looked exactly like a wolf then, and Heshifer like an old wolf, well exercised, and J'Quilvens like a pliant wolf girl.

VIII

Like a dark star traveling toward collision with Earth, hurtling or barely crawling across the interstellar void according to which time-scale nervous minds chose, the war entered its fifth month.

From thousands of noiseless, nerve-wrackingly unreal factories weapons and equipment poured forth. Silently triphibian-sections swung together, interwove, were flawlessly joined. In an unending slow-paced stream the completed transports slid stealthily into the air, bound on test runs outside the atmosphere and in the depths of the ocean on whose restless surface their final destiny would be worked out.

From robot farm and mine, streams of grain and metal flowed to dumps near ports of embarkation. There too went the barges that would carry the materials on the last leg of their journey. People gazed in awe at these gargantuan stockpiles. An ancient war would eat them steadily, day by day, but this war must take them at one gulp.

Civilians went about with surface casualness, working longer, eating skimpier, playing less. The fear that had troubled them on the first night had retreated deep into their nerves, where it did not lack for companions.

Amusement areas were closed, except to those who could show a death notice. Inside them, unlimited pleasure was provided, since a softening as well as a hardening of fiber was part of the plan for the chosen.

Religion, such as it was, thrived. The ministers of the man-worshipping cult did boom-town business. Monster mass-meetings were held daily, with believers either telepresent or in the flesh. At them, emotions were purged almost as effectively as, though less painfully than, by the machines in the dungeons of J'Wilobe's secret police. Afterward a few hysterical women would offer themselves for the volunteer service. Among the gray-clad female officers who swore them in was one whose elfin features and smile contrasted sharply with the acid-lipped masculine visage of the average.

Crime was no longer in the spotlight. Except for unpublicized hunts for deserters and even more hushed proceedings against violators of the morale-code, police activities were nil.

High-ranking officers of the war-forces, already so worried as to how the men under them would behave that they hardly thought of their own approaching fate, met more frequently to work out exercises in logistics. At one such meeting—fair sample of the rest—a dozen men gathered around a transparent globe on which colored dots and dashes represented triphibian squadrons, barge assemblies, divisions. The ranking officer rose. "Today's problem presupposes a rendezvous in the South Atlantic at the point indicated. How would you handle it, F'Sibr?" An odd note entered his voice as he mentioned the name. Both he and the others showed a peculiar mingling of uneasiness, attraction, and respect as they listened to the big, remote-eyed man explain how the war forces might best make their final five-day voyage.

At thousands of training centers and in the field, men were oriented for death. They met it in every form and guise. They became inured to the hot windy whine of burn-blast and stab-ray, no matter how near were the misses. They learned to face the robot projectile with their number on it and to trap it in a web of close-range fire no matter with what sentient cleverness it ducked and dodged. In transparent armor they crawled on hands and knees through phosphorescent miles of deadly radioactive dust. They were marooned in bathyspheres on the ocean floor and in space suits beyond the moon, only to be rescued at the last moment. At the word of command they stepped unequipped onto the clouds and were caught a few dozen yards above the ground by diving fliers. In conclaves suggesting those of ancient secret societies they drank down cups of wine, every thousandth one of which was supposedly poisoned. An illusion of invulnerability was built up, along with the habit of absolute obedience. A crammed routine of hardship, pain, pleasure, peril, and glory erased private thoughts almost before they occurred and fostered the feeling that each individual was only a cell in the hand that was fingering the gun, would soon raise it to the temple.

IX

NORM WAS home on furlough. He sat paying lazy attention to a color tune turned on so low that it was only a shifting of shadowy hues around the teletactor. Allisoun leaned her head on his shoulder. His father and mother sat side by side and gazed proudly at the sleek gray uniform with its insignia of rank.

"Who'd ever have thought four months ago," his father philosophized, "that you'd become an officer."

"Not just an officer," his mother corrected. "An aide."

"That's right, Mother. Say, what do you think of this F'Sibr fellow, Norm?"

"Oh—he's rather quiet."

"Now that's very interesting," observed his father, leaning forward brightly. "Tell me all about your work, Norm. I know it's teletaction, but what exactly do you do?"

"He's tired of talking about that. He wants to enjoy himself. Don't bother him."

"I guess you're right, Mother." But he still regarded Norm hopefully.

Allisoun squeezed Norm's hand gently.

Norm smiled. He was remembering J'Quilvens. Last week they had been alone together, just after he had received a routine hypnotic treatment from F'Sibr to strengthen his mind against government propaganda. He had made love to her. She had threatened to have F'Sibr implant a posthypnotic dislike for her in his mind. And then she had started him talking about his original ideas for communications sabotage.

J'Quilvens was an oddly attractive girl, oddly enticing . . . and oddly remote.

He returned the pressure of Allisoun's hand and put his arm around her.

He didn't admire himself for it, but he had to admit that he enjoyed Allisoun's submissiveness and the way she crawled for favors.

Just as he took a cruel pleasure in playing up to his

parents' admiration of his uniform and egging them on to say ridiculous things—despite his new understanding of them.

It made him feel uneasy and rather disgusted, but he was unable to resist, basking ironically in his pseudoglory.

His father couldn't keep quiet. "It certainly is amazing the way Norm's come along. I'll frankly admit—because I was wrong—that I didn't think he'd make a good soldier. And you'll agree that Norm's behavior, when he first got the news, wasn't encouraging. We were even afraid he'd desert! But now it appears that a military career is the very thing for him. Just goes to show how little we know about people—even our own." He stood up, directing his genial lecture at his wife and Allisoun. "Look how he's succeeded. An officer—an aide, Mother!—in four months! Why there's no telling to what heights he may rise, no limit to the positions he may attain—except, of course, that . . ."

He realized his blunder. The silence became painful. He hurried over to the teletactor and began to fiddle with the controls. Faint colors and sounds came and went.

"Any news of Willisoun?" Norm asked lazily.

His mother answered for Allisoun. "Not a word! He must be off on some very important mission, because Allisoun has inquired again and again at his office, but they won't tell her anything."

"I can't understand why he doesn't 'tact' me," Allisoun murmured.

"It must be a very secret mission, dear," Norm's mother said.

Norm nodded.

"I'm sorry," said Allisoun hesitatingly, "that you and he had that . . . disagreement before he went away."

Norm nodded and smiled.

A tall ghostly figure materialized in front of the teletactor, became solider as his father adjusted the controls. It stood with its feet sunk in the floor because the teletactor was a little off level.

The gaunt suffering face was M'Caslrai's. Norm sat up straighter. His jaw set. Allisoun looked around at him curiously.

". . . because it has always been my practice to talk frankly to critics and detractors," came the tired, plodding voice. "The so-called neohumanitarians have made their plea against certain aspects of the war. This is my answer: It is because we do not want to see humanity tortured and degraded by conflict that we do this thing. The conscientious objectors have advanced their claims. But I say to them: Be thankful. You are not asked to kill, only to give your lives. The advocates of a 'token' sacrifice have made their suggestions. But I tell them: You can't fool reality with 'token' payments. You can't appease the death-wish with any such shallow trick. Would that we could, folks! Would that we could!"

Norm clenched his fists and twisted a little, like a small boy being upbraided by his parent. It was insanity that M'Caslrai was mouthing, he reminded himself fiercely. Stark lunacy. And yet . . .

"To all of you I say this: He who casts doubt upon our dreadful sacrifice, he who seeks in the slightest degree to sabotage our war, is a traitor to all . . ."

Norm was on his feet. The others were staring at him astonished.

"Shut if off, will you! Shut it off!"

X

HESHIFER let his thoughts ramble. There were so many ways of playing the present situation—of taking advantage of the cumulative death-wish of mankind—that he wished he lived in a dozen worlds so he could try them all. For instance, they could seek to direct the death-wish at an outside enemy, by faking an invasion—not from Mars or Venus any more, but from one of Jupiter's moons or just the interstellar unknown. But that had been tried seventy-five years ago and it hadn't worked. Or desperate diseases justifying desperate remedies, they might attempt to divide the war forces into two groups that would fight each other. Or, better yet, get them to turn around and to conquer the rest of the world. But that, as bitter experience had shown, was as impossible as telepathy. Of course, he thought wistfully, there was always the Chaos Plan. Dangerous admittedly, and unpredictable, perhaps even ungovernable. But then, what wasn't? Government was ungovernable! He wished they were at least prepared to employ the Chaos Plan. Fortunately, it was beginning to look as if that necessity might never arise. The Sanity Scheme and the F'Sibr propaganda seemed to be working out. Still, plans were treacherous things. One never knew. F'Sibr trusted so completely in the idea that only society was crazy, that individuals were mainly sane and would recognize their insanity if properly propagandized. An attractive paradox, and possibly true. Well—F'Sibr and Sanity must have their day, but if they failed, then Heshifer and Chaos!

"I often wonder," mused M'Caslrai, looking across the desk, "what you're thinking about, Mister Heshifer, when you get that expression on your face."

As Heshifer took a moment to consider his reply, he wondered for the hundredth time of whom the World Director reminded him.

J'Wilobe was lonely. Sometimes he felt horrible sure that of all men, he and he only had the slightest inkling of the myriad murderous conspiracies that were drawing their webs tighter and tighter around the world and him. A circle of malignant intellects, human and alien, surrounded the world and him, sending out tentacles. Their hostile thoughts exerted a tangible pressure. Everywhere you looked, there was evidence. Were the others blind fools, that they could not see? Whom could he really trust? Not even Inscra. Not even M'Caslrai. Of course, those two seemed to have some superficial understanding of the threat to the war, ever since he had demonstrated it so conclusively. M'Caslrai especially. But not even M'Caslrai would permit him to take such obvious steps as arresting Heshifer on suspicion. When it was plain to see, since Willisoun had disappeared while trailing Heshifer, that Heshifer must be in the plot. But M'Caslrai refused to see it, and Heshifer went about his business unchecked. Well, let him! Let the others be blind! He, never more rightfully the Secretary of Dangers than now, had eyes enough for them all. And at least there were no longer any hindrances to his questionings of minor prisoners. When the emotion machines had done with them, when they had laughed and cried and feared and hated until they could no more, then they would talk. Then J'Wilobe would . . .

"I think I know what you're afraid of, Mister J'Wilobe," M'Caslrai said to him, smiling faintly. "But I also think I know how we're going to get around it when the time comes." He waggled his finger, desisting when he saw the expression in J'Wilobe's eyes.

XI

BENEATH the surface, things were not going well with the war.

There were whispers. No one could say who started them, hardly even who repeated them. They were like the muttering voices the mind hears when it is drunk with fatigue. But they traveled. They did things.

A riot in an amusement area. A work-stoppage that left uncompleted triphibians roosting helplessly. At a training center, a veiledly mutinous refusal to undergo further death-tests, with the officers mainly intent on concealing the evidence of their own inefficiency. At a government center, open criticism of officials, mass protests, shocking accusations.

The burden of the whispers was always the same: That the war was being crookedly administered. That it had only been decided upon because M'Caslrai's government was tottering. That death notices had gone only to those individuals whose independence and honesty made them a threat to the M'Caslrai regime. That no actual friend of the M'Caslrai regime had been chosen.

Facts and figures were provided to prove this. Individuals were named. Everyone was supplied with a ready-made personal grievance.

There grew a spirit of negativism, of smoldering resentment, of cynical disbelief in the whole fabric of society. There were sly sneers, spasms of sudden rage, guarded questionings of things held most sacred, deadly accusing glances.

Rehabilitation centers for deviants filled, overflowed. The same thing happened to the temporary detention centers and the unpublicized dungeons. Closely guarded orders went out: "Except for ringleaders, no more arrests. . . ."

Along with the whispering, half-masked by it, there went a more individualized form of psychological sabotage. It was as if, in the midst of a general barrage, a hidden sniper were picking preferred targets with a cold deliberation and slamming into their brains bullets of a far higher speed and greater destructiveness—mental bullets.

Here a morale expert fell foaming with convulsions in the midst of an address, later opened dazed eyes that doubted everything. There a communications specialist began surreptitiously to play with the tape-spools of his trade—pile them up in toy skylons. Elsewhere an actuary was found working out statistically detailed plans for the complete destruction of human life throughout the solar system and the erasing of all signs of its presence.

An empty-eyed officer at a training center recorded for teletaction an announcement beginning: "A token plan has been adopted. Death candidates desiring discharge will report to. . . ." Before the announcement was killed, it was seen by dozens. When questioned, the horror-stricken officer could only recall that, just before going to sleep the previous evening, he had seen rhythmically bobbing lights, heard a drowsy insistent voice.

A police official woke in the night and listened in terror and relief to a voice which told him that his crushing sense of guilt was merely due to a submerged memory of the many times he had imagined the death of his father.

A minor executive looked up with drug-filled eyes and asked: "Are we saviors . . . or murderers? Are we . . . sane?"

A billion throats threatened to take up that most dreaded question, until it became a scream heard around the world.

Gradually the forces opposing the war drew even with those furthering it, until they teetered in precarious balance.

At Supracenter M'Caslrai rose and surveyed his secretaries. His head was bowed, as if the skull, molding the tired flesh in its image, were made of lead.

"Gentlemen," he said, "a greater strength than ours is needed. We must ask guidance of omniscient, omnipotent Man." There was a murmur of agreement. "Dark teleconclaves for that purpose must immediately be called throughout the world. We here, as well as the rest, must join in supplication, ourselves to ourselves."

Across the round table, Heshifer smiled inwardly. This was a moment he had been waiting for.

At the appointed conclave time, the smile appeared openly on Heshifer's face. Sitting alone in his office in the Deep Mental Lab, he made certain trifling adjustments to a small instrument on his desk. Then he slipped on his telemask.

He erased the smile as the black velvet mouths of the mask settled snugly over his eyes, nose, and lips, swung back and covered his ears. Leisurely he pulled on his telegloves. Thus equipped, he could exercise his senses and manipulate objects through electronic counterpart-hands at any place in the world, or off it, where a teletactive unit existed. He could consult tapes in any library, savor a beverage in Africa, sign his name to a document on the moon, or strangle a man on Mars.

He could function in any properly equipped assembly chamber anywhere.

Or, as would happen now, he could functionally assemble with a hundred others in a chamber no bigger than an egg. In such a dark teleconclave, which in some ways resembled an ancient multiway telephone call, the electronic microcounterparts of each participant would be brought together at a central point, according to any chosen assembly pattern, and the resultant images faithfully transmitted back to each participant.

Plunged in soothing darkness, though still perfectly aware that he was sitting at his desk, Heshifer waited. Then, like white masks, other faces floated into view. Gradually the assembly pattern became clear—a sphere of closely packed inward-turned faces.

He recognized J'Wilobe, Inscra, and other high executives and supervisors. Automatically his mind ticked off: paranoia, catatonia, melancholia, cosmic shock, dictatoria, ethical monomania, omniscientia, newsman's psychosis, creative paralysis, hypertrophic realism, commissaria, permanent escapism, Manism, negatimania, the Venusioid delusion, and dementia praecox.

Then he saw M'Caslrai, and his mind ticked off a question mark.

The conclave was complete.

Counterpart-hand grasped neighboring counterpart-hand, linking the elements of the sphere.

There was a feeling of primal pulsation, as if they were

the inward-peering walls of a life-cell swimming in dark immensity.

Then, like the nucleus of such a cell, something pale and pinkish-sallow began to materialize at the central point toward which all eyes were directed.

A reverently mellow voice spoke, "Oh Man, Manipulator of Destiny, from our trouble we appeal to you." And they all repeated, "Oh Man, hear our voice."

The central mistiness grew denser, became the forms of a man and woman of matchless beauty, an eternal Adam and Eve.

Heshifer, like everyone else, knew that these forms were teletactive projections from taped recordings. Religious doctrine, however, hinted that the forms were influenced by the worshippers' ideals.

"Oh Man, Shaper of Earth and Scaler toward Heaven, give us of your inexhaustible wisdom and strength."

The central couple, heads proudly upheld, smiled faintly and distantly, like gods riding on the clouds. Their flesh glowed with an inward radiance, lighting the faces around them.

"Oh Man, grant our desires."

There was to Heshifer something inexpressibly distasteful about this self-worship, this adulation of the species, this slobbering over the image in the mirror. When the voices chorused, it was like fish mouths opening and shutting around a central bait. He took advantage of the flurry of religious fervor to withdraw one of his hands from the web, maneuvering the hand that gripped it to grip instead two free fingers of his other hand.

"We have wandered in darkness, because we did not keep your image in our hearts.

"We erred because we forgot you."

A feeling of cozy and ego-inflating security began to enfold the worship cell. Heshifer withdrew his free hand from its teleglove and touched the instrument on his desk.

"You grant us leadership, and we are in danger.

"You gave us the helm and now storms threaten."

But something had begun to happen to the central figures—though the change was so slight that anyone but Heshifer might have thought it merely a trick of the mind. The glorious forms seemed to stoop a little, there was the barest suggestion of a slouch. The faces shortened and bulked out a trifle. Something sullied infinitesimally the radiance of the flesh. Heshifer smiled gently and continued the adjustments.

"Oh Man, Perfectest of All Things, Apex of Evolution's Pyramid, without whom the universe would be only death and dead matter . . ."

Imperceptibly the change was progressing. The two hairlines were creeping downward and a certain sporadic dark downiness had become apparent. The slouch was definite, the hands reached for the knees. The features were pouting together, thrusting forward a little with a petulant air.

"You who are the Breath of all Beauty, Sensitive and Delicate beyond compare . . ."

And now there was a slight change in the leading voice too. It was still mellow and profound, impeccably so, but one fancied irony rather than reverence. Though that too might merely have been a matter of mood.

Moving only his eyes, Heshifer surveyed the inward wall of faces. Some of them looked definitely worried—and trying to conceal it. That was good.

"You who are the Crown of Life, the Priceless Ornament of Existence, matchless in grace . . ."

And now the trend of the change in the two central figures was obvious. The slouch had become a stoop-shouldered slump. Legs had shortened and bowed. Hands had reached knees and seemed inclined to go beyond. The sporadic downiness had become ever thickening hairy patches. More and more obviously it was becoming an ape-man and his bride squatting in darkness, squinting surlily.

Practically every one of the inward-peering faces seemed to be trying to hide worry now. More than worry—disgust and fear. So far as Heshifer could judge, each thought that only he could see the imperfection of the vision—and feared that the imperfection was a mirroring of his own secret and unclean thoughts—and so tried not to show it.

He felt one electronic grasp on his counterpart-hand tighten conclusively, then guiltily slacken.

"Being without Flaw, Paragon of Gentleness and Humility . . ."

The male figure gave its consort a shove, then smirked and thumped its chest. The color of the light had changed. It was becoming reddish, murky, flickering—a wood fire's glow. The surrounding darkness was that of a soot-blackened cave.

"You who have transcended the animals and are above all gross things . . ."

Both figures were now peering downward with great interest, and scratching.

"You whose thoughts trend always heavenward, whose eyes are fixed on the stars . . ."

The male caught something, inspected it minutely, then snapped it between horny fingernails. The female craned her neck curiously.

Heshifer rejoiced. The inward-peering faces looked sick and sweating as they strove to maintain the pretense. Obviously their value-scales were shaking at the foundation. It was working out better than he ever had hoped. He'd never dreamed he'd be able to let it go this far.

But, he noted suddenly, there was an exception. All the faces showed smothered disgust and horror and shame—except one.

M'Caslrai's dark-ringed eyes were gazing tranquilly at the two ape-creatures with an expression that could only be interpreted as compassion and tenderness. It was as if the spirit behind the gaunt homely face reached out and embraced even these lowly beings, or as if he understood that this too was the nature of man.

The sense of a resemblance to some other and well-known personality was so strong that Heshifer swore that in a moment he'd remember who. But he didn't.

Never had the secret of M'Caslrai's personality seemed so close—or so far.

Heshifer's mood changed abruptly, from one of exulting confidence to gnawing doubt. Somehow, what he saw in M'Caslrai's face took away all his certainty of success.

Abruptly he came to a decision on a matter to which he had not given a thought all day.

F'Sibr or no, he would prepare the Chaos Plan.

XII

It was Embarkation Day. In a score of great harbors around the world, the fleet rode at anchor. The tiny Martian and

Venusian contingents had arrived; their opalescently space-weathered hulls stood out from the rest. The robot barges bearing the vast stores were already at sea, waiting.

In each hull, robot- or man-carrying, even in the smallest auxiliary launches and fliers, was a disintegrative core keyed to a master detonator aboard the fleet flag-triphibian *Finality*.

All was ready, and on the surface all was well. But below the surface . . .

There was mutiny aboard a quarter of the triphibians. It was being temporized with. Elsewhere, mutiny was close to the surface.

Extraordinary rumors were surging about. Perhaps the chief one was that a "token" war plan involving no human deaths was being forced through Supracenter by M'Caslrai himself. Another was that the war forces would be called upon to wipe out rebellious civilians, destroy all the old cities.

Chaplains hurried about, nervously invoking man to remain true to his divine self, calling on him to meet without flinching the supreme enemy Death.

Scattered companies of women's volunteers made hysterical attempts to desert and were forcibly confined to their quarters.

All over the world there was open demand for the dissolution of the M'Caslrai government, the abandonment of the war, and the immediate return home of death noticees.

A powerful civilians' committee, organized overnight, had presented Supracenter with an ultimatum.

And Supracenter did not act. It made no move to crush the mounting rebelliousness. It stayed behind locked doors. No one knew what was going on behind those doors, but from the cracks around them a miasma of weakness welled.

Everywhere there was an extraordinary atmosphere of nervous tension. People cringed, as if fearful that each increase of pressure would set off a universal scream. There was a wild, glorious joyfulness at the idea of stopping the war and saving fifty million lives. At the same time there were waves of guilt at the thought of the reckless daring of the course that was being taken, the blasphemous flaunting of a century's profoundest rituals. And there were recurrent gusts of the early irrational fear of an unknown enemy who would swoop down suddenly out of space.

These opposed feelings beat against each other, drove each other higher and higher, toward an inevitable climax.

And still Supracenter did not act.

Spruce in his pearly dress uniform, Norm stood on the dress bridge of the fleet flagphib *Finality* and looked across the harbor toward the city. Norm had the unnerving feeling that his mind was a sounding board for the confused emotions of humanity—each breath of hope, each blast of guilt. So he tried to keep his mind empty, occupied—not with rehearsing the part he must play in the Fleet Teletaction Room when the crisis came, for he knew that by heart—but with trivial things.

Nature had done her best here to make it a gala Departure Day. One hardly noticed the dark cloudbank to the west. Sunlight glittered on the blue wavelets, shimmered on the silvery hulls of the massed triphibians.

They crowded the harbor, their sleek shapes making them seem like a school of giant silver whales—or the gods of whales.

Tiny, gleamingly uniformed figures thronged the dress bridges, structures which could be retracted for aerial, submarine, or extraterrestrial operations.

Fliers and copters darted about.

Beyond the great silverbacks, the ugly walls of the Old City loomed. But beyond those, dwarfing them, lost in the blue haze, shot up the fairy pinnacles of the New City—midmost the golden shaft of Supracenter, drawing the gaze toward the blinding sky and so back to the bridge in a track paralleling the palisade of storm clouds to the west.

Behind him Norm glimpsed a group hurrying into the Fleet Command Room—Fleet Commander Z'Kafir, Flagphib Commander Sline, and Fleet Communications Officer F'Sibr among them. They exuded an air of portentous secrecy.

He saw J'Quilvens slipping past them in the opposite direction, trim in her Liaison Officer's uniform. He tried to catch her imps' candles of eyes, but failed. He felt a sharp irrational pang of uneasiness and guilt.

Looking toward Supracenter, he noted a silver sliver projecting from its peak; also an increase in the number of clustering fliers. Then his glance wavered as lightning flickered from the approaching storm wall to the west. But his mind did not analyze these impressions.

J'Quilvens had made him think of Allisoun. He pictured her as he'd seen her yesterday—in tears at his departure. Poor kid, he'd treated her rottenly, strutting before her, taking advantage of her hysterical affection, while all the time he didn't care a stick for her.

She had not gloated over their relationship, as he had cynically predicted, gloried in being a doomed man's lover. She hadn't wanted him to die; she'd clung to him.

Of course, there was his feeling toward J'Quilvens, but that only made his behavior toward Allisoun worse.

A fine way for a world-savior to act toward a girl who was only trying to make him happy!

The silver sliver had lengthened a trifle, and the fliers had clustered thicker yet—or else there were other tinier shapes among them. Again lightning flickered, and there came a growl of thunder.

At the very least, he shouldn't have taken such cruel pleasure in her grief, especially when he knew that if all went well he was not going to die. Of course, he couldn't very well have revealed any plans to her, but at least he could have let drop a hint, given her a ray of hope.

And he'd killed her brother, or helped kill him, and then gotten a kick out of her innocent worries over his absence. Willisoun had been a spy and murderer, had deserved to die, but still that didn't justify his own nasty hypocrisy.

The silver sliver was obviously much longer than it had seemed at first. The fact that it was directed toward the harbor had foreshortened it. And still it lengthened. The tinier shapes seemed to be gathered in tiers around it, and there was a suggestion of movement on the roofs of the Old City. This time the thunder was accompanied by some other solemn rumbling.

It was the same with his parents. They weren't the selfish Philistines he had pictured them; they were just a little scared man and woman trying to do their best in a jumbled world. They hadn't deserved his bitter contempt, to be treated as ridiculous buffoons. He remembered his father's handclasp and choked voice, his mother's sobs.

Whatever the silver sliver was, it was directed like a serpent's neck or the arm of a giant crane, from Supracenter's summit out over the agitated roofs of the Old City. The perplexing aerial tiers seemed to be lengthening with it, flanking it on either side. The rumble had become a steady roll, in which the intermittent western thunder joined. There was a suggestion that the flashes of lightning from the encroaching storm were somehow being answered from the city. There was a hint of martial music, a sudden flurry of movement on the bridges of the farther triphibians.

How could he ever have been so rotten to treat them that way? All of a sudden Norm had the horrible feeling that he was no longer a man cleaving to a dangerous course but a boy caught misbehaving, a juvenile delinquent. He had sneered at his elders, disobeyed, broken the rules, joined a forbidden gang, would be punished. Against all logic, this disgustingly childish fear persisted. He remembered old scenes—times he had rebelled, been "talked to," been forced to recant his boyhood heresies.

A sudden swell in the martial music exploded this dark train of reverie. Like a man waking from a dream, he took his hands from the rail, moved backward a step, looked up.

He knew that something was happening around him, something critical involving the fleet, the city, the world. And yet, like a man still half in a dream, he couldn't comprehend what it was.

The sense of fear crystallized to an icy lump.

The silver something arching out from Supracenter was a delicate aerial pontoon bridge, supported by flying components, as it extended itself questingly over the farther triphibians, swaying gently from side to side like a silver serpent's head. There were human figures on it, and the tiers flanking it in the air were made up of human figures too, though how they were supported he couldn't understand. The uniformed mites on the more distant dress bridges were drawing themselves up in ranks. And from the same direction there began to come a steady, frantic cheering, keeping up through the music and the thunderous drumming, building toward a titanic shout.

Z'Kafir, Sline, and the rest of the staff poured suddenly from the Fleet Command Room. He half-expected F'Sibr to address him. But he was brushed by.

There was a running to and fro, a barking of orders. He found himself lining up with the others. He looked around stupidly, realized he was in the first rank.

He saw the women's volunteers lining up, J'Quilvens among them. He heard the flagphib's orchestra join in the general heart-quickening din.

He saw the aerial bridge reaching downward toward the *Finality.*

And then, at last, he became aware of the whispered word running up and down the ranks. His numbed mind patched together the phrases into the single hope-shattering story.

M'Caslrai and his entire secretariat were joining the fleet. They would share in its destruction. This was their answer to the civilians' ultimatum.

Dully he looked at the approaching bridge. Already he thought he could identify some of the figures.

The flanking tiers, he saw now, were teletacted images of people from all over the world, come to witness and applaud Supracenter's sacrifice.

Music, drumroll, and thunder and cheering had now become ear-splitting. Great, unopposable waves of emotion were rolling down from Supracenter across the harbor.

The black storm wall, grown mountain high, had reached the western shore. Lightning flashes played from it and were answered by the electric guns of the fleet, salvoing salutes. But the aerial bridge was still in bright sunlight, backgrounded by blue.

Norm felt the presence of a giant ghostly figure—Man the God, standing behind the storm wall and peering down over it in divine approval.

A telescoped silver gangplank shot upward from the *Finality,* linked with the aerial bridge. Slowly the group of figures started down, acknowledging the homage of the world's massed teletacted ranks.

But for Norm the scene drew in. As they came closer, he failed to note that some of M'Caslrai's companions did not share their leader's sad, tranquil satisfaction—that some faces even showed stunned amazement and dry-lipped horror. He had eyes only for one man.

It was as if he and M'Caslrai were alone at the ends of a long but shortening corridor.

This was the man he could not face, the living symbol of paternalistic loving authority down the ages.

His sense of guilt grew beyond all sane proportion. He told himself that M'Caslrai had come to reprimand him, that M'Caslrai would halt before him and with fatherly sternness denounce him as a traitor, that he would be forced to go down on his knees and beg the world's forgiveness.

It was unfair, he protested to himself. M'Caslrai was only a teletacted speechmaker, a signature on world directives, a thought atop Supracenter. He had no right to come down and face you in the flesh.

M'Caslrai stepped onto the bridge. The tumult reached its climax. It seemed to Norm that the big, gaunt man was walking straight toward him. He wanted to run, to plunge through the deck, to be snatched into the sky, to hurl himself at M'Caslrai and strangle him.

He only stood there licking his lips, trembling.

M'Caslrai looked at him once, closely, then passed by.

At the first possible moment, while the salutes were still thundering the triphibians out of harbor, Heshifer told F'Sibr how the whole maneuver had been engineered by M'Caslrai alone, had come as a complete surprise to practically everyone of the secretariat, himself included.

"And now, the Chaos Plan," he finished.

F'Sibr hesitated, shook his head. "We still have almost a week. Perhaps, all appearances to the contrary, they have played into our hands. Very likely M'Caslrai is contemplating a last-minute escape. But whether he is or not does not matter. We shall see that he escapes—with publicity enough to brand him as a cheat forever. We have the *Unseen*. It will kidnap M'Caslrai and the other higher-ups, including yourself. It will be handled in such a way as to look like deliberate flight—you will help see to that."

Heshifer frowned.

F'Sibr threw up his hands. "Then, if that fails, you can have your way. The Chaos Plan is ready. It would take only a word."

Heshifer thought. "How many besides the officers of the *Unseen* will have to be in on the plot?" he asked.

"My aide Norm. Perhaps one or two more."

Heshifer looked up. "You're sure you can depend on him?"

"Absolutely."

After a pause Heshifer nodded unwillingly.

"We have five days," said F'Sibr.

XIII

FOR THREE days the fleet had driven across calm seas, slowly, at not a tithe of its real speed, a parade of silver hearses. For three days the death tension had mounted.

The time had come when men began to see visions, hear faint whisperings in the air, feel the touch of currents from beyond life.

Alone on the dress bridge, Norm stared at the sunset. The sun was an arched furnace door on the horizon, the sea a metallic expanse. Astern curved the triphibian battle line, a succession of diminishing silver teardrops, until they were lost in the dusky western blue. Ahead some of the scouts could be seen, fanned out expectantly, as if death might make a premature attack. No sound, save the slightest hiss of displaced waters.

It seemed to Norm that his mind quested over all the sea's brazen plain, without finding a place to rest. There was only the feeling of the grandeur of the fleet, the sense of a proudly onrushing destiny, the suggestion of super-natural wings hovering overhead—and those were the last things he wanted to feel.

He remembered the plan for tonight, but his mind veered quickly.

Perhaps if he sent his mind still farther . . . to the rim . . . beyond . . .

M'Caslrai stood beside him, black elbows on the rail.

Norm's heart jumped, thumped, quieted.

For a while they leaned side by side, watching the sea.

"Maybe a man can find peace out there," said M'Caslrai. "Leastways he can look for it."

A pause. "We're all looking for peace, Mister Norm."

Another pause. Then softly, "You've a girl back there, you told me. What did you say she was called?"

He repeated "Allisoun" thoughtfully after Norm. "And there'll be a child? He will bear your name, I suppose, if a boy. Well, Man willing, he will not have to suffer what you suffer. We may hope that your sacrifice will bear fruit, that in the future the world will take the course of wisdom."

He turned his sorrowful tranquil eyes on Norm. "I feel very small and very troubled," he said. "It is not easy to bow to necessity, to see the few doomed for the sake of the many."

Norm started to speak, mumbled an unintelligible word.

"I'm glad I'm going with you," said M'Caslrai.

The moment passed, was lost with the last blinding sliver of sun. Gloom raced across the sea.

"Tell me, Mister Norm," M'Caslrai asked, "are you troubled?"

Norm hesitated, shook his head.

M'Caslrai nodded, smiled, moved away.

For a moment Norm's mind was numb. Then loneliness rushed in, as if he and M'Caslrai were the only two beings in the world and had parted forever.

He felt giddy, as if the sea were suddenly tilting, as if all his intentions and beliefs were swinging on the bob of a gigantic pendulum.

He looked along the rail to where, unapproachable now, the World Director still stared over the sea.

It's true, he thought. I've always run away from him. All my attitudes have been shaped by fear that, if I ever listened to him, he would persuade me.

It's unfair, something childish inside him reiterated bitterly. He has no right to come down from his pedestal and meet you face to face like an ordinary man. If only he wouldn't, it would be so easy to be true to the others.

But he has come down, the adult reminded. And now there are certain thoughts that you must think, even though each one sears your ego like a red-hot iron.

He is great and wise and compassionate. You can see it in his face, hear it in every word he utters.

He thinks only of mankind, and of what must be, if mankind is to go on.

Whereas you and the others, even F'Sibr and Heshifer, are selfish and petty, thinking only of criticism and trouble-making and cynical jibing. You seek to sabotage the great current of history which he guides.

You are crackpot dreamers, one more lunatic fringe trying to pretend that what is, is not. He is a realist. He is right and what he does is right.

The world has always been a horrible place and has exacted horrible sacrifices of humanity. Sanity consists in recognizing the necessity of those sacrifices. *He* is the sane one.

Faces floated before Norm in the gleaming dusk. Faces he knew. Only now F'Sibr looked like a cruel Eastern god, a paranoid who thought he could change the course of history by his personal fiat; Heshifer, a senile mischief-maker, mouth and mind atwitch with fantastic schemes or brutal jests; J'Quilvens, a hysteric trembling on the verge of laughter or screams. Behind them, a pale-faced horde of deviants and discontents. For a moment they all leered at him, snickered. Then they wavered, faded, and were blotted out by the visage of M'Caslrai—profound-eyed, understanding, earthy but rising above it, gaunt and homely, infinitely kind.

All Norm's confused and often-denied religious impulses urged, "He is the One. He is Man!"

He felt the mighty presence of the fleet, the comradeship of the millions marked and trained for death. Through the silver hulls and the dusk and the faint hiss of the waves, that comradeship tugged at and captured his heart.

Feeling that his whole life had only been a preparation for this moment, he turned and followed the rail.

"Sir," he began.

M'Caslrai's "Yes?" was the friendliest of whispers.

"There is a grave threat to the safety of the fleet and the success of the whole expedition."

M'Caslrai nodded wearily, as if he had known all along. His gaze did not leave the sea.

Norm swallowed. He said, "Before I go on, I want your promise that those I betray will not be killed or hurt, only held where they can do no harm until it's all over. Also, I do not want my part in this to become known."

M'Caslrai looked at him. "You have my promise, Mister Norm," he said.

Later that night all the searchbeams of the *Finality* flared out suddenly. For a quarter mile around the flagphib it was bright as day. For yards below the water was milky green.

At first nothing was seen except the towering blunt muzzle of the triphibian next in line.

Then a fine white cloud shot out from the flagphib. It vanished swiftly, but left in its wake a small, bone-white ship grappled to the dress bridge, with a number of similarly white figures swarming aboard the *Finality*.

An order was shouted. The figures hesitated. Some of them turned back.

A blue flicker of small-arms fire cut them down. The ports of the ghost ship were slammed, and in a rainstorm of blue rays it dove like a frightened fish.

Light and explosions pursued it, sending the emerald water in great chunks.

Rocket-tubes blasting, it shot up suddenly into the air, frantically twisting and turning.

The big beams of the *Finality* caught it. The hull glowed red . . . white. . . .

Spinning out of control, it fell like a meteor. There was a great hiss as the *Unseen* plunged for a last time into the sea.

XIV

LATE THE next night Norm stood for a third time on the dress bridge. No lights betrayed the hissing triphibians. They went stealthily as murderers. And yet he sensed the mighty hulls, the millions of sleepless souls cramming them, the incalculably numerous robot barges, all converging on the dawn rendezvous.

But they no longer awakened thoughts of a proud destiny. He could only think of the cylindrical cores and of the disintegratives that packed them.

The sharp sense of reality and duty that had inspired him last night was gone. The sense of guilt that had lifted after his confessions had returned intensified. He remembered the white-hot plunge of the *Unseen*, the hiss of steam. His emotions were frozen, but not numbed. The night might have been black ice encasing him.

That afternoon a sailor had jumped overboard. A watchful dinghy had recovered him, although he had done his best to drown. Later he had pleaded to be killed at once and spared the waiting for tomorrow.

Now Norm kept seeing his frantic, babbling face.

He wondered if he should not have insisted on being imprisoned with F'Sibr and the rest, without revealing that he was the informer.

But he knew he could not have kept the secret in their presence, or endured their reproaches when he confessed.

Well, at any rate, M'Caslrai had kept faith. There was something incredibly honest and noble about the man, something that still bound Norm to him by cords of awe, although in all other respects he had come to regret his action so bitterly that he dared not think about it.

If only he could go back. . . . But it was too late now to do anything. The kidnap ship was destroyed.

Of course, he could make some wild effort. There were still the subordinate agents on the other ships. He could . . .

But a complete paralysis of will power held him helpless. He knew, for example, that in the War Room behind him was the master switch which would disintegrate the fleet at dawn. But if it had been just at his elbow, and if a child had been pressing it down, he could have done nothing to stop it.

Like some guilt-tortured prophet of olden times, he stared into the darkness, looking for a sign.

XV

IN THE utter blackness of the brig, though in the gibberish of code-speech, F'Sibr said calmly, "No, I am the one to blame, if we have to talk about blame. I stubbornly persisted when it was obvious that our whole counterprogram had failed. I clutched at the straw of the kidnap plot. And I trusted Normsi."

"That's not your fault," interjected J'Quilvens, "I was the one who introduced Normsi in the first place."

"Irrelevant. The point is . . ."

"Two thirty," came the toneless voice of an agent named Wavel, who possessed the best sense of time among them.

"The point is," F'Sibr continued, "that I trusted Normsi, even when Heshifer had doubts. It was an unforgiveable executive error."

"But when it comes to that, we aren't absolutely sure that it was Normsi who betrayed us," J'Quilvens urged doubtfully.

"The probabilities all lie in that direction."

"For that matter, we cannot even be sure that the kidnap plot has failed."

F'Sibr did not trouble to answer. They could hear the coded whispers of the two agents conversing at the other end of the brig.

"There must be something we can do," said J'Quilvens.

"Yes," said F'Sibr. "We could have adopted the Chaos Plan four days ago. Unfortunately, my opinion carried too much weight." He paused, as if expecting a comment from Heshifer. When none came, he continued, "True, the plan is fully prepared, but all agents are under the strictest orders to wait for word from above."

"But don't you think some of them will go ahead with it, against orders, at the last minute. Unless they've all been unmasked too?"

"That is unlikely. Normsi was acquainted only with those of us who are here—a fact which incidentally constitutes further evidence against him."

"It's odd, in that case," mused J'Quilvens, "that we haven't been asked to reveal the identity of the agents on the other ships—given a taste of J'Wilobe's persuasion. They must know there are more than us."

"It is odd," agreed F'Sibr. "There was something peculiar about the whole business of our being caught—I mean, the way it was done. I sense M'Caslrai's touch, rather than J'Wilobe's, although it's outside M'Caslrai's line."

"Right!" Heshifer's unexpected comment sounded as if he were following a very different line of thought, which the conversation had only chanced to intersect.

When he said nothing more, J'Quilvens pressed, "But granting the others are free, mayn't they go ahead with the Chaos Plan?"

"Yes, but it won't do any good. The fleet explosives are all keyed to the master switch aboard the *Finality*. Every smallest unit of the fleet, down to the dinghies, is cored with explosives which it would take hours, in some case days, to remove or unkey. At the time of detonation, the water itself will be deadly for leagues around. Everything hinged on our seizing control of the *Finality* and preventing the master switch from being thrown. Without that, minor successes are futile."

"Then there's nothing we can do?"

"Well . . . I am trying to think of something, as we all are."

"Of course. But you don't think much of our chances?"

Again F'Sibr did not reply.

When J'Quilvens next spoke, she seemed to be trying to push back the darkness. "Then, to keep up our spirits, we have only the hope that when the next war comes, our survivors will be wiser, will forge a sounder counterprogram?"

"No!" said F'Sibr. For once his voice was sharp, though still even and well modulated. "We do not have that hope. It would be childish to assume so. It has become clear that the world's insanity has reached its crisis. If we had adopted the Chaos Plan, we might have been able to make use of that crisis—the crisis a gun, the Chaos Plan a trigger. But we failed. The moment will not come again. After the crisis, the slow mental degeneration sets in. When the next war comes, our weakened organization will adopt an even more futile and unrealistic program. The war will be greater, as the often-indulged death-wish intensifies. It is to such a future that we must calmly look ahead, if we are to behave as realistic adults. Any other future is as impossible as . . ." He chuckled icily as he invoked Heshifer's favorite comparison, " . . . as telepathy."

A shiver seemed to go through the darkness. It infected J'Quilvens' voice. "And yet, you continue to speak in code? Why do you do that, if you know that everything's hopeless?"

"There is such a thing as honoring a lost cause."

This time there was no doubting the shiver. Then cutting across it, came Heshifer's excited words.

"We must contact Normsi!"

The anticlimax provided by this ridiculous statement was so great that J'Quilvens had to choke back hysterical laughter.

"We know the boy," Heshifer sped on. "We know he's no planted traitor. He must have been subjected to extraordinary psychological pressure—and through M'Caslrai. He's a cyclic type. By now, surely, he's regretting it . . . wavering . . . waiting for a push."

F'Sibr's reply was ominously gentle, almost soothing. "I'll grant you there is a chance that Norm's behavior has followed some such course. Though in that case the probability is that he is under as close guard as ourselves and in no position to do anything even if he does have a change of heart. But . . ." His voice became doubly cautious ". . . you spoke of contacting him? I don't quite see . . ."

"Right!" replied Heshifer, so eagerly, so enthusiastically even, that you couldn't help visualizing his grinning, grimacing face, his darting eyes. "Like you, I have been thinking—about how to contact Normsi. I have eliminated all reasonable possibilities, except one—the most unlikely. Something that we have no evidence for, although we have looked for it for decades. But since, no matter how unlikely, it is the only reasonable possibility, we *must,* if we are logical, employ it. Telepathy."

There was a pause. "Are you forgetting, 'as impossible as telepathy'?" said F'Sibr. "We might as well try black magic."

"Call it the least impossible of the impossibilities, then! Remember, telepathy may depend on the electrical potential of the nervous system. Think of how great the potential must be at a moment like this. Suppose that our receiver, Normsi, is wavering . . . his mind a blank. Call it anything you like! Call it my last foolish tribute to a lost cause! I, at any rate, shall try."

"And I," said F'Sibr softly after a moment. He was echoed.

Suddenly Heshifer laughed—a rich unlikely laugh.

"Excuse me," he said. "But I just happened to realize of whom M'Caslrai reminds me. It is astounding I never thought of it before. It explains the nature of M'Caslrai's insanity, too. It's not who he is, but who he *thinks* he is. If I'd only realized it before! What I couldn't have done with the man! I've been blind as a bat. . . ."

"Two forty-five," said Wavel.

XVI

J'WILOBE sat alone before the executive panel in the Flagship Security Room next to the brig. His face was more pinched than ever. His jewel-bright eyes kept looking from side to side. An hour ago he had dismissed all the guards and multiply locked the door behind them, and the doors of the two vestibules as well. He had become suspicious. True, he had always trusted the guards before, but now the universe had become a shadow world populated by slinking plotters, and he the lone sentry on the wall.

Of course, as he logically recognized, such a situation couldn't go on indefinitely. But he only had to hold out until dawn, and then he would be relieved forever from his crushing burdens. Unless there were another life . . . But that would be too horrible.

He frowned at the massive circular door of the brig, and decided once and for all that he no longer trusted M'Caslrai. Why had M'Caslrai refused to let him eliminate these danger-mongers, at least question them? Why had he refused to tell him the reasons for their arrest when it was obviously a matter for the Secretariat of Dangers? Even the warning about a possible attack by an invisible ship hadn't come until a few minutes before the occurrence.

Of course he had advised M'Caslrai to arrest Heshifer months ago, had warned him against F'Sibr. But that couldn't be the reason, because M'Caslrai had ignored his proposals.

No, the World Director must have some private source of information. Either he had organized an inner spy-system, or had suborned some of J'Wilobe's own men, or was protecting an informer.

Well, at all events, no one but J'Wilobe knew the present combination to the door of the brig, and he could destroy all life inside it at the touch of a finger. Whatever risky or even traitorous course M'Caslrai might be taking, those in the brig were out of the picture.

At the thought J'Wilobe felt a rush of self-confidence, so exhilarating and intense that he sat there trembling. He suddenly *knew* that whatever threat arose tonight he would be equal to it. It was as if a cloak of invulnerability had been dropped around his shoulders, masking even his one great hidden weakness—the one he dared not even think about, let alone give an outsider a chance of guessing.

There would be threats tonight, yes—he was curiously sure of that—but he would master them.

He looked around the Security Room. It was as neat and metallic as his mind.

He was immune to assault. No one could even telecontact

the room or the inner vestibule, except from the fortified outer vestibule.

The panel before him would inform him of any movements in the restricted areas of the *Finality*. But J'Wilobe had the illusion of a strange clairvoyant extension of his senses that made the panel seem ridiculously crude by comparison. He felt he could sense at once the slightest hostile movement anywhere aboard the ship, throughout the world—even respond to the faintest inimical scratching on the skin of the space-time cosmos.

A light glowed violet, indicating that someone had entered the outer vestibule.

To J'Wilobe it was as if a long-awaited chess-game had begun. Someone had moved pawn to king's fourth.

He instantly whipped on his telemask and was functionally present in the outer vestibule. His hand-counterparts closed on sidearms conveniently present there.

At first glance there seemed to be no one. Suspecting an invisible man, he prepared to crisscross the walls with fire.

Then he saw a hand on the table.

Someone had made an impossible move with a knight.

Just a gloved hand.

Or was it merely a glove, retaining the shape of the hand that had dropped it?

No, it moved. The fingers drummed—or was the hand starting to walk?

It made a fist. Then the forefinger pointed—first away, then swinging it toward him.

Conscious of a greater pang of terror than he had ever known in his life, J'Wilobe found himself back in the Security Room. It spoke well for his courage that moments later, just as the blue light glowed, he was projecting himself into the inner vestibule.

The hand was there. Without hesitating, he directed a needle beam at it. The hand writhed at the touch of the fiery ray, seemed to crumple, then jerked aside—and pointed at him.

Someone had sacrificed a knight.

By a supreme effort of will, he managed for a moment to continue his fire. The hand recoiled, but kept pointing.

Back in the Security Room, he found the hand ahead of him. He tried to pick up a sidearm, but his fingers could not grasp. He lunged toward the control that would flick death through the brig.

But the pointing hand waggled a little, as if to say "No."

The hand looked hurt. Three fingers dangled. They seemed to be crushed.

Perhaps the waggling was only a wounded shaking. But it continued.

J'Wilobe dropped back from the death control.

Someone had played, "Queen takes pawn. Check."

The hand pointed commandingly toward the door of the brig.

J'Wilobe was not conscious of the sting of the sweat running down into his eyes—only that the blur it produced was insufficient to dissolve the hand.

He took a step toward the door.

A part of his mind had analyzed what had happened. The hand was a tele-counterpart, projected by someone who knew his hidden weakness. From the outer vestibule it had reprojected itself to the inner, and so to the Security Room. Now it was only the projection of a projection of a projection. Yet he had badly maimed the original—the impact of the ray had been transmitted.

But that part of his mind had not power over his actions. It was getting farther and farther away from his consciousness, like something fading toward the most distant star.

There was only enough room in his mind for the hand and the combination to the brig, and the former was pushing out the latter.

As he moved step by step toward the door, the moving finger seemed to press on his skull. Now it was a hand of steel, now of marble, now of fleshless bone, now of boneless flesh, now a man's, now a woman's, now M'Caslrai's, now Inscra's, now Heshifer's, now the fingers were serpents' heads with flickering tongues, now they were the red tongues themselves, now the forefinger was a crooked gun pointed at him, now a crushed but inching caterpillar, now a comet zigzagging toward him through blackness . . . eventually all these faded and it became his father's hand, approaching to tickle him, apparently loving, actually cruel. Mind-destroying laughter twitched at his lips.

Checkmate!

The door opened, the finger poked through his skull,

the laughter exploded. . . .and then the whole world blacked out, and J'Wilobe realized that he had fallen millions of miles and landed in a cozy, velvet-lined cell where he could eternally play a thousand simultaneous blindfold chess games and win them all. With a calm happiness that he had never known before, he made his thousand first moves.

XVII

FROM THE stratospheric heights in which his flier idled, Airscout Mardel overlooked the entire curved area of sea constituting the rendezvous. Rank after rank of triphibian and barge, spaced with geometrical precision except for the few lines of late arrivers. Albino soldier ants on a dark field.

Airscout Mardel's features were the set, hopeless ones of a man who must meet an unvanquishable foe. Even if he had been the sort to consider desertion in battle, he knew that it was doubtful whether there was time enough left for the fastest flight to carry him beyond range of the general blast. And granting he escaped the general blast, there was the disintegrative charge buried in his flier—a relatively small one, but ample for its purpose. Moreover, there would be the other fliers to reckon with. And then there was that omnipresent feeling of an unseen, unknown enemy who would surely engulf any man who straggled far.

The sky had been lightening for some time. Now a blinding chunk of sun shoved above the horizon. It occurred to Airscout Mardel that this was a sunrise which those below would not be privileged to watch.

He looked down again and frowned. He fancied there was a slight jumbling of the ships, a disorder in the ranks, the barest suggestion of a scattering. As if an invisible giant had thrust a stick toward the silver ants.

The commander of the *Enterprise* looked around the Command Room. He was a florid, portly man. A glance at the panel showed him that everyone was at battle stations, ready for the event. The communications officer gave him a message. The commander read it twice. He began to laugh, softly at first, then in more and more joyful peals. The others edged away. He dropped the message and began to strip off his clothes. The navigation officer picked up the message and read, "The time has come for you to reveal yourself. The sign has appeared—the bloody star. Drop the mask. Speak!" He looked up uncomprehendingly. Naked, the captain strode out onto the dress bridge, crying, "I am Man! I am Man!" A bit of red glowed beside the doorway—it looked like a star-shaped jewel. Perhaps the communications officer had dropped it—he had come in that way. And now the communications officer was giving orders in a crisp voice.

Aboard the *Decision* order was given to gather in the mess room for religious service. Almost immediately it was followed by an order to return to battle stations. Then the first order was repeated. Then the second. Again the first. Again the second. When the scrambling was at its most frantic, the executive officer turned up suddenly with a glowing knife and ran through the ship, slashing right and left.

Throughout the fleet, key men screamed at shadows, pawed at phantoms, smirked at the invisible. They listened to nonsensical messages whispered over teletactors and their limbs grew hysterically rigid. They glanced at a foolish picture and went blind. They were shown meaningless bric-a-brac and fell into convulsions. They closeted themselves briefly with teletactive messengers and came out unharmed—in body.

Panic was awakened in subordinates. Each man was a fuse exploding those below him. The thing was contagious, though here and there an oddly cool-headed few sought to stem the confusion—but only after it reached a peak.

The crew of the *Mortality* abandoned ship. Hundreds of men simply dropped overboard and swam away. Of the four officers who stayed in the control room, one was laughing, another cried, the third crouched horrified in a corner, the fourth was sunk in apathy. They were looking at something that dangled from the control panel.

There was fighting aboard the *Remote*. Just small arms, until someone ordered the big guns backfired to clear out the corridors. There was a giant flash and a shock wave that smashed a valley in the water. Then there were only the *Remote's* neighbors heaving on a giant swell caked with silver dust.

The *Ultimate* turned her guns on the *Infinity*, disintegrated her, then committed suicide.

The commander of the *Immortality* saw something through the forward telescopes. What it was he would tell no one, but he ordered the forward guns fired into the western darkness and the ship itself sent full-speed ahead in pursuit. No one understood, but he was obeyed. He manifested extraordinary excitement as they blasted first into the air and then into outer space. Perhaps it was Death itself he thought he was attacking, for he muttered such things as, "That hurt him, boys! Look, he runs! But we'll track him down even if he lairs on Uranus! Watch out!—he's raised his sting!" He clung to the telescopes. The *Immortality* blasted away from the sun, toward the outer planets.

There was wild music aboard the *Farewell*. Red-daubed women and green-smeared men were dancing. Food was strewn, liquors sloshed. The drug lockers had been broken open. Someone had dragged out an emotion machine and was experimenting fantastically.

Aboard the *Nightfall* they prayed.

It was an hour when minds were jerked open like long-locked drawers and their dark contents blindly strewn. Secret ideas fumed like smoke, obscuring the face of reality. It was not the actual sky and sea, but a delirium of water and air. The paling stars were a paranoid's dream of grandeur. Only insanity was real.

In the Fleet Command Room of the *Finality*, Commander Sline had collapsed, but Fleet Commander Z'Kafir had the situation well in hand. His mind was clear and cool. He realized what had happened and saw exactly what must be done. But he was speaking at ten times his normal rate, and when he tried to indicate by gestures what must be done, his hands moved too fast to follow. This purely mechanical defect in his ability to communicate rendered all his brilliant ideas useless.

General Secretary Inscra took over smoothly, although he was bothered by the disappearance of M'Caslrai. Phlegmatically he began to give the orders that were locked inside Z'Kafir, when Communications Officer F'Sibr entered the room. Inscra observed that it was only a teletactive counterpart, but he deduced that F'Sibr was operating from the Fleet Communications Room, and he knew how that room could be destroyed. He made a movement, but F'Sibr opened his hand and extended it toward Inscra.

Inscra's eyes—the eyes which had always seemed the only live things in a dummy figure—now died too.

On the outstretched palm was a large gray spider.

Somewhere the word started and went from ship to ship, first a whisper, then a shout growing toward a cheer. "The war's over!" And then a strange comment was added. "We've won! We've won!"

Cold sweat trickled down Airscout Mardel's forehead. An incredulous joy twisted his tight features. The sun was above the horizon. It drenched the whole sea with gold. It glittered from every last vessel. The moment of disintegration had come and gone—a half-hour ago.

The giant's stick had poked. The silver ants were scattering. Two collided as he watched. Silvery splotches marked the grave of the *Remote*, the *Infinity*, and the *Ultimate*. There was no order or intelligence left.

Airscout Mardel grinned, snarled, "I'm alive!" and sent his flier rocketing crazily toward outer space.

Heshifer darted from the Fleet Communications Room. Never had he seemed quite so old, or quite so active. He was followed by J'Quilvens and Norm, the latter with his right hand cased in transparent plastic where J'Wilobe's needle ray had mangled it.

"We sealed off the War Room at the start," Heshifer explained. "Now we'll draw the fangs of the whole setup."

Perhaps in automatic response to the word echoing through the fleet, Norm murmured to J'Quilvens as they hurried along after, "We've won."

J'Quilvens giggled. "Not by a long sight. We've only driven the fleet crazy. And we'll drive the whole world crazy before we're through. From now on, we're attendants in the violent ward. But it's a beginning—a chance!"

The guards before the War Room stepped aside. Heshifer opened the door—and instantly stopped dead. He motioned everyone to stay where they were. "Above all," he whispered, "don't make a move with your weapons."

Over Heshifer's shoulder, framed by the square of the doorway, Norm could see M'Caslrai. He was standing behind a table that resembled an altar. In it a black rod was vertically set. M'Caslrai looked sad and resolute. The way he stared at them was reminiscent of a sleepwalker. Slowly he began to bear down on the lever.

"Mister President," Heshifer called softly.

M'Caslrai paused. "How did you know the name of my real office?" he asked. "I've been careful to keep that a secret from everyone."

"Mr. President," Heshifer said, "the British ambassador wants an audience. There is an important memorandum from General Scott. And Secretary Seward's here to see you. It's very urgent."

"I know," said M'Caslrai. "I'll be right there. But there's something I must do first." Again he bore down on the lever.

"But there's no time, Mister President," Heshifer interjected. "It's come at last. They've fired on Fort Sumter!"

M'Caslrai's hand fell away from the lever. "So," he murmured softly. "Well, what must be must be." He came around the table and started toward the door. He smiled, almost sheepishly, at Heshifer. "It's a funny thing, Mister Nicolay," he said, "but I was having the darnedest dream—it seemed to last a lifetime. I dreamed they'd made me boss in another world, and there was another war, and there was something I had to do. I wonder . . ."

Then he looked ahead, and his face grew grave and prophetic, as if he were thinking of the brave, bitter times ahead, and the part he must play in them. As he shuffled past, Heshifer heard him mutter as if he were rehearsing that part, ". . . that these dead shall not have died in vain—that this nation, under God, shall have a new birth of freedom—and that government of the people, by the people, for the people, shall not perish from the earth."

A Selection of Science Fiction titles from Sphere

MACROSCOPE	Piers Anthony	50p
TRIPLE DETENTE	Piers Anthony	50p
PEBBLE IN THE SKY	Isaac Asimov	35p
THE FALL OF THE TOWERS	Samuel R. Delany	50p
DEATHWORLD 1	Harry Harrison	30p
DEATHWORLD 2	Harry Harrison	30p
DEATHWORLD 3	Harry Harrison	30p
THE STAINLESS STEEL RAT	Harry Harrison	30p
THE STAINLESS STEEL RAT SAVES THE WORLD	Harry Harrison	45p
TACTICS OF MISTAKE	Gordon R. Dickson	60p
SOLDIER, ASK NOT	Gordon R. Dickson	60p
DORSAI!	Gordon R. Dickson	50p
THE OUTPOSTER	Gordon R. Dickson	60p
THE ICE SCHOONER	Michael Moorcock	35p
INCONSTANT MOON	Larry Niven	40p
UP THE LINE	Robert Silverberg	50p
NIGHTWINGS	Robert Silverberg	40p
STAR-BEGOTTEN	H. G. Wells	40p

A Selection of Classic Short Stories from Sphere

THE BEST OF ISAAC ASIMOV	55p
THE BEST OF JOHN WYNDHAM	55p
THE BEST OF ROBERT HEINLEIN	55p
THE BEST OF CLIFFORD SIMAK	60p
THE BEST OF FRITZ LEIBER	60p
THE BEST OF ARTHUR C. CLARKE	65p
THE BEST OF A. E. VAN VOGT	60p
THE BEST OF FRANK HERBERT (1952–64)	55p
THE BEST OF FRANK HERBERT (1965–70)	55p

All the above books are edited by Angus Wells